Lizzie's
Little Mouse

THE HEART *of* THE AMISH

Lizzie's Little Mouse

ANNE BLACKBURNE

BARBOUR
PUBLISHING

Lizzie's Little Mouse ©2025 by Anne Blackburne

Print ISBN 979-8-89151-068-5
Adobe Digital Edition (.epub) 979-8-89151-069-2

This book is a work of fiction. Names, characters, places, and incidents are either products of the author's imagination or used fictitiously. Any similarity to actual people, organizations, and/or events is purely coincidental.

Cover Design: Kirk DouPonce, DogEared Design

Published by Barbour Publishing, Inc., 1810 Barbour Drive, Uhrichsville, Ohio 44683, www.barbourbooks.com

Our mission is to inspire the world with the life-changing message of the Bible.

Member of the
Evangelical Christian
Publishers Association

Printed in the United States of America.

DEDICATION:

As always, to my family who support me without question.

To my fellow authors who have shared their knowledge and time.
You know who you are!

To my wonderful literary agent Tamela Hancock Murray,
who believed in me first.

And to my daughter Kelsey Elizabeth,
lost to me here on Earth, but I know someday I'll
again see your precious face. Sleep in peace, my baby.

CHAPTER ONE

Elizabeth Miller grinned so hard her cheeks hurt as she carefully maneuvered a pair of giant scissors into position to cut the bright green ribbon stretched across the front of her new business in downtown Willow Creek, Ohio. She opened the scissors wide, then closed them with a decisive swish, sending the cut ends of the ribbon fluttering away to each side.

A cheer rose up from those gathered for the grand opening and ribbon cutting of The Plain Beignet, and Elizabeth—Lizzie to her friends and family—looked around in wonder as the people dearest in the world to her celebrated the realization of her dream.

"Congratulations, Elizabeth! Willow Creek is fortunate to have such a unique business opening here!" Anita Frederickson, executive director of Willow Creek Main Street, smiled as she took the enormous scissors from Lizzie.

A photographer stepped forward, camera and notebook in hand. "Hi, I'm Mike Young from *The Budget*. I just want to be sure I have everyone's names spelled correctly." Lizzie spoke with him for a few minutes, answering questions about how an Amish woman from Ohio happened to be opening a combination Amish/French bakery, before he saluted her and hurried off to file his story.

As he moved off toward his car—illegally parked by a fire hydrant, Lizzie noticed—several people hurried forward and surrounded her. Her mother reached out and drew her into a strong hug.

"Lizzie, I'm so proud of you! You always said you'd do it, and you did!" Agnes Miller stood back and held her daughter by the shoulders, her joyful grin mirroring Lizzie's.

Her father stood back a bit, hands shoved into the pockets of his black jacket, smiling fondly at his wife of thirty-five years. "There now, Agnes, let me have a turn."

Agnes laughed, released her daughter, and stepped aside. "*Ach*, sorry, Henry! I'm just so pleased I could burst!"

Henry chuckled as he stepped into the spot vacated by his wife and hugged his daughter. "You did it! You said you would, and I never doubted for a moment that you'd find a way to pull it off. And here you are, a business owner, with a fancy ribbon cutting and pictures for the newspaper."

Lizzie's smile dimmed a bit. "Do you think it's too fancy, *Dat*? I know it's unusual to have our photos taken, but it wasn't really for me, it was for the business."

"Child, don't fret, I was teasing. Bishop Troyer approved it, ain't so?"

"*Ja*, he did," Lizzie said, her smile returning.

"Did I hear my name?" a gruff voice asked as the bishop of their Amish church district made his way through the throng milling around outside Lizzie's newly opened bakery.

"Bishop Troyer!" Lizzie exclaimed. "You came to my ribbon cutting!"

Bushy white eyebrows above kindly blue eyes climbed toward a traditional straw hat. "Of course I did. This is a big deal, ja?"

"It surely is!" a voice piped up from behind Bishop Troyer, who stepped aside to allow the voice's owner to step forward. "And I, for one, have been looking forward to this day for ages. Congratulations, child. Now, are you going to leave an old woman standing outside on the sidewalk, or are you going to invite us inside to try out some of your fancy French baking?" The tiny Amish woman twinkled at Lizzie, who grinned back at her.

"Lydia! You're here too!" Lizzie stepped forward and gave Lydia Coblentz, a good friend who had gifted her with a tiny gray tabby kitten a couple of years earlier, a gentle hug, and she looked around for her friend Ruth, who usually wasn't very far from the old woman.

She spotted her pretty redheaded friend, also the recipient of a kitten from Lydia's cat's final litter, standing a few steps behind Lydia. "Ruth! I can't believe you all came! Where are Jonas and the *bopplin*?"

"Of course we came. How could we miss such an important event?" Ruth stepped up next to Lydia, taking the older woman's arm in hers. "Jonas and the *kinner* are already inside. Look!"

She pointed at the window behind Lizzie, who turned to see Jonas seated at a table by the window, his six-year-old daughter, Abigail, waving at them and mouthing, "Come inside! I'm hungry!"

Hearing a faint scratching, Lizzie raised her eyes higher, to the second story of her building, and smiled to see a curious feline face peering down at the crowd on the sidewalk. Following her friend's eyes, Ruth grinned. "Oh look, Little Mouse doesn't want to miss all the fun."

Lizzie chuckled. "Too bad the health department wouldn't appreciate a cat in the bakery!"

Lydia smiled up at the small gray cat and nodded with approval. "She looks *gut*! You are obviously taking gut care of my baby."

The pretty little cat was officially named *Petite Souris*, which was French for "Little Mouse." But she was more commonly known to Lizzie's friends by her English name. She was one of the kittens Lydia had gifted to a number of young single Amish friends a couple of years before. They were all from her beloved cat Hephzibah's last litter. Lydia maintained a keen interest in their welfare, stipulating that they had to be inside cats before she would allow the girls to take them.

Lydia gripped her young friend's arm. "But Lizzie, I'm beginning to feel faint! If I don't get one of those famous beignets soon, there's no telling what will happen."

Lizzie laughed. "We don't want to risk that!" She glanced at the Main Street director. "It looks as if this party better move inside, or I'll have a riot on my hands!" The director nodded, and they started moving toward the doorway.

"Don't forget me! I want one of these fancy beignets I've heard so much about too," Bishop Troyer said as he made his way toward the door, which he opened for Lizzie, standing aside so she and the other ladies could enter ahead of him.

The crowd cheered again as Lizzie led the way into her brand-new business, The Plain Beignet. Well-wishers patted her on the arm or back as she passed, congratulating her on opening her own business. Many followed her inside, and she turned to her parents and friends and said, "I'll talk to you all later. Thank you so much for coming! It really means a lot. But I'd better get behind the counter and help Eliza and Jane before they quit!"

A striking middle-aged woman with olive skin and dark curly hair stepped forward before Lizzie could escape behind the counter, smiling apologetically. "I'm sorry, I know you need to get to work, but if I could just have a couple minutes? I'm Philomena Jones, managing editor of the *Willow Creek Examiner*. I got a good photo of your ribbon cutting, but I need to ask a couple questions before I leave."

Lizzie nodded. "Sure! *Denki* for covering the story!"

The two women spoke for a few minutes, and then Philomena closed her notebook with a snap and smiled at Lizzie. "That should do it. Thanks so much for taking a couple minutes. This will be in next week's edition of the *Examiner*. Now I have to try some of your French baking!" With a wave, she headed to the sampling table, where folks were trying various pastries before hurrying to the counter to order a dozen of their favorites.

Lizzie breathed a sigh of relief. She hoped the stories in the two local papers were complimentary to her new business and brought in customers.

She hurried behind the counter and began serving her customers, many of whom were members of the local Amish community. But there were many *English* friends, neighbors, and fellow business owners there too, she noticed as she boxed half a dozen large croissants for Rebekkah, who owned a popular restaurant in town. Rebekkah's Kitchen was famous for its baked steak. "There you go, Rebekkah. Denki so much for coming!"

"Are you kidding?" The older Amish woman winked at her, tucking her purple-and-gold bakery box under her arm. "I wouldn't have missed it! You did good here, kid. Maybe we can talk later in the week, after things settle down? I'd like to discuss getting a regular order of these for my diner." She waved the box of croissants Lizzie's way, eyebrows raised in question.

Lizzie nodded quickly, her eyes wide. "Ja! That would be gut! I could do that."

"Great! Well, I'll get out of the way. Talk to you soon!" Rebekkah smiled at familiar faces as she made her way out of the shop, and Jane Bontrager, one of Lizzie's two employees and her best friend their whole lives, sidled up to Lizzie. "Whoa! A regular order for Rebekkah's Kitchen would be a coup! She has a great reputation. And it would be gut to have regular business right off the bat, *nee*?"

"Absolutely!" Lizzie agreed, smiling at Pastor Dan Williams from the Baptist church and his wife, Samantha, as they stepped up to the counter, closely followed by Father Bob from the Catholic church just down the street, who had a gleam in his blue eyes as he checked out the selection in the glass case. Lizzie knew the aging priest had a fondness for baked goods.

"Good morning, Lizzie!" Samantha said, smiling sweetly at the two young Amish women. "I'd say your grand opening is quite a success!"

Lizzie smiled and nodded. "Ja! I can hardly believe this day is finally here. It seemed as if it would never come."

"Well, all your hard work paid off, young lady, and now you have your New Orleans-style French/Amish patisserie!" Pastor Dan cast an admiring look around the space, which was decorated in a cozy style to encourage customers to linger awhile over a cup of delicious coffee and maybe order a second pastry before going about their day. "I always liked it in here when it was a simple Amish bakery, and it's even better now. You were smart to keep the Wi-Fi and cozy furniture, and I love your new color scheme. Very French Quarter! And I can't wait to try some of your scrumptious-looking pastries!" He leaned forward to study the offerings, his wife and Father Bob close beside him.

"As soon as you all decide what you'd like, I'll be happy to help you!" Jane chirped, nudging Lizzie to go circulate among her guests.

As Lizzie turned to make certain there were plenty of treats and hot coffee available for her guests on the sample table, a tall, slender man wearing a bespoke charcoal suit stepped into her path. He smiled at her kindly, his gray eyes twinkling above a regal nose and a rather magnificent mustache, which was carefully groomed and curled at the tips. Lizzie wondered how he got it to stay that way.

The stranger held out a manicured hand to shake, and Lizzie accepted his gesture, smiling at him in welcome. "Hello, and welcome to The Plain Beignet. I'm sorry, I don't believe we've met."

"Good morning, Miss Miller. I'm Mr. Valentine." He spoke with a cultured, possibly British, accent. "We haven't met, because I'm just here on a short holiday and heard about your grand opening." He leaned in and spoke conspiratorially. "I'm a big fan of French pastries, you see. So here I am! Congratulations! You've created quite a lovely ambience!"

"Denki. And please just call me Lizzie."

He smiled charmingly again and took an almost-militarily-precise step back, clasping his hands behind his back. "All right, Lizzie." He looked around the large space. "This is quite the historic building, so I'm told. It must have a lot of tales to tell."

She smiled. "Ja, I suppose so."

"Yes, I heard this was quite the destination back in the Roaring Twenties, and even before!" At her confused look, he clarified, "The 1920s. And famous people visited here. Intriguing! I imagine you occasionally discover some little trinket or other leftover from those days. It must be fascinating!" He looked at her almost expectantly, and Lizzie smiled and shrugged.

"I'm afraid I've only owned the building for a few months. We have found a few things, but I can't say how old they are. Nothing very interesting, though."

"Ah! You might be surprised what people find interesting. For example, I always think old family records and such are quite fascinating. Maybe you'll find something like that and get a glimpse into life in the past."

He waited for her to answer, staring at her intently, and she shook her head. "Well, we haven't turned up anything like that so far. There have been many owners since this building was built, I imagine, and probably anything from back in those days has either been tossed out or donated to the local museum."

At his look of disappointment, she quickly said, "If we do find anything, I'll be sure to take a look. I can see how such things would be interesting."

"I'd recommend it. Nothing like connecting with the past, eh?" He stared at her for a few more moments, then said, "No old papers, then? How disappointing! Well, maybe you'll stumble over some yet." He looked around. "So, I hear you live upstairs. How convenient! Just a short commute to work!"

Frowning uncertainly at his nosiness and wondering where he'd gotten his information, she nodded. "Yes. Very convenient. Well, if you'll excuse me..."

"Must be lonely, though. Do you have any pets for company? Maybe a dog? I don't suppose a dog would do well living upstairs in a small apartment, though, would it? Especially not a big dog." He peered at her keenly, but before she could answer, he glanced off to the side, and she followed his line of sight and saw Eliza King heading their way.

"Well, it's been enjoyable chatting with you. I won't hold you up. I'll just nip over to the counter and purchase some beignets and croissants, and then I'll be off. Have fun with your new business and home, Lizzie! Perhaps I'll see you again."

He gave a small bow, and despite the slight discomfort she'd felt at his probing questions, Lizzie had to stifle a giggle at his formal manner. She thought if he'd been wearing a hat, he'd have tipped it. Then he turned and walked toward the counter, disappearing into the crowd.

"Who was that?" Eliza King asked, hurrying up next to Lizzie.

"I'm not sure. A tourist, I suppose. A Mr. Valentine. It's probably nothing, but he asked some odd questions about the building and what old stuff we've found in here. He seemed interested in old family documents or some such." She shook her head. "So, how are the beignets holding up? Everyone wants to try one!"

"Not too bad. I think we made enough. And I doubt most days will be this crazy!" Eliza glanced over and saw that Jane was knee deep in people at the counter. "I need to get back over there and help Jane."

"I'll help Jane," Lizzie said. "But we'd better open the second register. Can you do that?"

"Ja, I'm on it!" Eliza hurried over to open their backup register. "I can help someone over here!" she called, and several customers turned and gratefully stepped up to the counter to place their orders.

The morning passed in a blur for Lizzie. Ruth and Jonas Hershberger had carried an order back to the table by the window to share with their three children, the bishop, and Lydia. Lizzie's parents stayed awhile and then blew her kisses and left.

Later, she heard Eliza call out to her brother, Dr. Reuben King, who was standing by a table where his pretty young wife, Mary, another old friend of Lizzie's, sat. Lizzie noticed in passing that the bishop, Lydia, and the Hershbergers had pulled their table over next to the Kings' and they'd formed a big, noisy, happy group, with young Abby earnestly explaining something to Mary, while the twin babies were passed around between the doting adults.

Lizzie smiled as she saw that Mary's pregnancy was just starting to show. "Ach, I'm so happy for her," she murmured to herself as she restocked a tray of Danish inside the glass display case. Mary, injured in a terrible buggy accident that had claimed the life of her father when she was a very young child, had recently had a surgery that improved her mobility and lessened her daily pain. She'd fallen in love with and married the town doctor, Reuben King, the year before.

And now they were expecting their first child. Lizzie was aware that there had been no guarantee that Mary would be able to have children. But according to her friend, everything was going just fine, and Mary had recently entered her second trimester and was glowing with happiness. Despite being a physician, Reuben was acting like a nervous papa-to-be, making sure his wife was comfortable and had everything she needed.

"Jane, watch the counter a minute, will you? I want to go say hi to Mary and Reuben."

Jane glanced over at the group of their friends and smiled. "Of course. Give her my love."

Lizzie grabbed a coffeepot and a couple of mugs and hurried over toward their table. On the way, she nearly collided with a small, fussy-looking man in a tidy brown suit who stepped into her path and stood with his arms crossed over his chest, glaring at her. When she apologized, he sneered. "You are a fool opening such a ridiculous shop. Who ever heard of a French patisserie run by an Amish woman?" He spoke in a heavy French accent but not the Cajun French mix she was used to hearing in the bayou.

Lizzie tilted her head, puzzled by his anger. She decided to try charming him, and smiled, holding out a coffee cup. In Cajun French, she offered him a cup of coffee, but he sniffed as if detecting a foul odor. "You should have left things as they were. You'll fail here, wait and see. And your French is atrocious." He turned without another word and exited the shop. Lizzie stared after him. She couldn't remember seeing him before. Why did he hate her so?

"That was odd. Are you *oll recht*?"

Lizzie glanced away from the door where the strange little man had made his angry exit, and saw that Jane's brother, John Bontrager, was standing nearby frowning in concern. "John! I didn't see you there. Ja, I'm fine. That was just so odd."

He frowned and looked out through the big front window, but the man was gone. "It was more than odd, Lizzie. It was rude and a bit threatening. Do you know who he is?"

She shook her head. "Nee. I've never seen him before." Squaring her shoulders, she gave John a nod. "I can't worry about it right now, I have too many people waiting on food and *kaffi*, and I really want to sit with Mary for a moment!" With a quick smile for her friend's brother, whom she'd known all her life, she hurried toward Mary and Reuben's table.

John watched his sister's vivacious and lovely friend hurry over to Mary and Reuben's table, a smile brightening her already-radiant face. He'd always thought Lizzie, who at twenty-five was a bit younger than he, was beautiful, but she hadn't seemed interested the few times he'd shyly attempted to talk to her outside their big, boisterous friend group—never mind asking her for something as obvious as a buggy ride or a singing. He couldn't even seem to get her to stand still and talk with him for more than a few seconds. He sighed. He had no trouble talking with his other friends. It was just Lizzie he froze up around—ironically the one person he really wanted to spend time with. "She probably thinks I'm a numbskull," he muttered to himself. "I can never put two words together around her."

"You were doing fine a minute ago. Who was that strange man, anyway?"

John turned to see who was talking to him and met the bright eyes of Lydia Coblentz, whose diminutive size was more than compensated for by her seemingly boundless energy. "Lydia! I didn't see you there. Um, I don't know that man. Neither did Lizzie."

Lydia nodded with a frown. "I didn't like what he said to our Lizzie. It almost sounded like a threat, nee?"

He nodded soberly. "I thought so too."

"Anyway, the point I was making was that you were talking to her the same as you're talking to me right now, intelligently. Not at all like a numbskull." Humor twinkled in her brown eyes.

He couldn't help but return her smile. "Well, denki, I guess. That was unusual for me, though. Generally when I try to talk to her outside our friend group I just stutter and fumble and forget what I wanted to say."

Lydia nodded wisely. "That happens sometimes. I'd say go sit down with her and listen to her, and comment when something intelligent occurs to you."

"Just that simple, hmm?"

"Ja, why not? You've known her all your life. It's not like she's a mystery."

He looked toward the lovely young woman, radiant today in a buttercup-yellow dress and crisp white work apron, who had found a way to make what many considered to be a pretty far-fetched dream come true. "I'm not so sure of that. She's pretty mysterious to me sometimes."

Lydia laughed and patted him on the arm. "Love will do that to the best of us!" With that, she sailed away toward the restrooms.

John did a double take, staring after the old woman who was considered a community treasure and had pretty much earned the right to say what she thought. What was that she'd just said? Love? He stood bemused, frowning at the closed restroom door. He wasn't in love with Lizzie; he just wanted to get to know her better, that was all!

"Best not to try and figure women out, son, especially that one," a gruff voice said. John turned and saw Bishop Troyer standing by his side, smiling knowingly.

"Did you hear what she said to me?"

"Ja, and like I said, don't spend too much time thinking about it. Just take her advice, and talk to the girl. It doesn't have to mean anything. You're not proposing marriage today, right?"

John shook his head, feeling as if he'd lost track of reality. His bishop smiled and pointed to where Lizzie was standing by Mary and Reuben's table. "Go sit down. Talk to your friends. I'm going to see if that old woman is ready to leave yet. I have things to do."

He wandered toward the restrooms, and John looked over at the table where Lizzie was laughing with her friends. "Why not? Nothing to lose. It doesn't mean anything." He walked over and smiled, hoping he wouldn't make an even bigger fool of himself.

"John! Sit down! Have some kaffi." Lizzie poured two mugs full and sat with a sigh in an empty chair beside Mary. "Oof! I don't think I've been off my feet since about four a.m. It feels gut to sit a minute! Are you sure you don't want any kaffi, Mary?"

Mary shook her head. "I've already had my daily allowance. I'll have to stick to herbal tea. My husband is a tyrant."

Reuben chuckled. "I absolutely am when it comes to your health, and the health of our *boppli*." He stood up. "I'll get you a cup of tea."

He walked to the counter, and his little sister Eliza hurried over to see what he needed.

Lizzie leaned toward Mary. "I can only stay a moment, but how do you feel? You look wonderful good!"

Mary smiled, and John thought her happiness couldn't be clearer. "Lizzie, I am the happiest and most blessed of women. I don't deserve so much happiness!"

"Oh, I think you do!" Lizzie said, patting her friend's hand. "Have you felt the boppli kick yet?"

"No, too early. When I do, I'll let you feel."

"Oh, I'd love that!"

The two women sat smiling at each other.

To John's relief, as he had nothing to contribute to a conversation about babies, Reuben returned with a cup of tea, which he set down in front of his wife. Lizzie held out her hands to Ruth Hershberger, who was seated farther down the table holding one of her six-month-old babies. "May I hold the baby?"

Ruth passed the child to John, who accepted him before he thought better of it. He looked down at the baby's sleeping face and thought how angelic he looked. Then he felt Lizzie poke him and turned to her questioningly.

"You have to wait your turn. Hand him over, please."

John handed the baby, who was sound asleep, sucking his thumb, to Lizzie, who squealed softly. "Oh, he's beautiful," she breathed, obviously afraid she'd wake him up.

"Don't worry, if the noise level in here doesn't wake him, nothing will!" Ruth laughed.

"Lizzie! We need you. We can't find the honey buns," Eliza called from behind the counter.

"That's my cue. Thanks for letting me hold him!" She handed the sleeping baby back to his mother, who looked adoringly into his angelic face.

"He won't look like such an angel soon," his father, Jonas, said to John. "He's got lungs on him when he wants something, and he's going to be hungry."

John nodded at Jonas, another childhood friend, and, looking to be sure Lizzie was out of hearing range, decided to fill him in on her earlier confrontation with the angry little Frenchman. For some reason it was really bothering him. "Jonas, did you notice a few minutes ago, when Lizzie first started to walk over here, a strange man stepped into her path and wouldn't get out of her way?"

Jonas frowned and looked around. "No. Is he still here?"

John shook his head. "No. He said some rude, even threatening, things to her, then stormed out. It's really troubling me."

"I can see why it would. Here comes Lizzie. I'll ask her about him."

"I'd be glad if you did. She brushed it off when I expressed concern."

Jonas nodded as Lizzie sat back down, but before he could introduce the subject, there was a tremendous crash, and several people screamed.

"What on earth?" Mary cried, grabbing Lizzie's arm. "The front window! It's broken. But. . .how?"

People were scrambling away from the large plate glass front window, which John couldn't clearly see yet because of all the people in the way. The shop cleared out in an amazingly short time as frightened customers hurried outside. He saw some Englisch customers on their cell phones, and imagined they were calling the police. Others were taking photos that would no doubt end up on social media. But what had happened?

Jonas, Bishop Troyer, John, and Reuben had hurried over to the front window, where they stood clustered around something on the floor. John saw Lizzie approaching, and stepped aside so she could see the broken glass scattered across the floor of her previously spotless shop.

"What on earth happened?" she asked, staring at what was left of the big window.

There was a huge hole in the center, jagged shards of glass dangling dangerously from the window frame and sticking out from the sides of the hole.

"I'm thinking it had something to do with that," John said, pointing to an object sitting underneath one of the abandoned tables.

Lizzie turned to stare at the object, frowning as if she couldn't believe what she was seeing.

"But that looks like a brick, wrapped in paper."

His earlier nervousness at being around Lizzie forgotten, John nodded, a grim expression on his handsome face. "Ja, I believe that's what it is." He moved the table and bent down to pick up the object.

"Careful there, it could have glass on it," Reuben cautioned. John nodded and picked it up carefully and set it on a table. Jane and Eliza joined them.

"What is it?" Eliza wondered.

The bishop gave John a searching look, then looked at Lizzie. "May I?"

She nodded, and he picked up the brick and carefully untied the string wrapped around it and the paper covering it. He set the string on the table and unwrapped the paper, placing the ordinary-looking red brick back on the table before smoothing out the paper.

"What can this mean?" he whispered, staring at the paper.

"What is it, Abram?" Lydia demanded. He looked at her sharply, then handed the paper to her. She took it and pulled a pair of reading glasses from her apron pocket. Slipping them on her nose, she took a few moments to look at the paper. "Interesting." She laid the paper down on the table so they could all see it.

It was covered in block letters, which spelled out, *You're not wanted here. This is a warning. Close your business, or next time someone could get hurt.*

They all stared at it for a minute, and then Bishop Troyer cleared his throat. "I think we'd better call the police. This was intentional vandalism. I'm so sorry, Lizzie. This has ruined your big day."

John decided it was time to speak up about Lizzie's threatening visitor. "Lizzie, you'd better tell them about that man and what he said."

"I don't have time to talk. I've got to board that window up and clean up all this glass."

"We'll get it taken care of after the police have a look at it," John said, putting a reassuring hand on Lizzie's arm and giving it a little squeeze. "But please tell our friends what that man said. They want to help, and they need to know someone threatened you a little while ago."

"Someone threatened Lizzie?" Ruth sounded outraged, and soon everyone was talking at once, wanting to know what John was talking about. Lizzie frowned at him. She knew he'd meant well, but she was sure the odd little man had nothing to do with the brick on the table in her bakery. Did he?

"Lizzie, what is he talking about? Someone threatened you?" Bishop Troyer put a hand on her arm. "You'd better tell us about it, quickly. I don't think we need to call the police. I hear sirens. They'll be here in a minute."

Lizzie listened to the approaching sirens. She wiped an angry tear from her eye. Someone had purposely thrown a brick through her window? A brick with a nasty note attached, moreover. Well, she might be a peaceful, God-loving woman who didn't want any trouble in her life. But she was also a woman who had waited a very long time for her dream to come true. And now someone had thrown a brick through it!

She felt her shock and fear turning into anger as she thought of how the brick could have hit one of the bopplin, or Lydia or Mary! Someone clearly did not want her or her lovely new business in Willow Creek. And they were willing to commit violence to try and frighten her into closing her doors the very day she'd opened them!

Well. Someone was going to find out they'd chosen the wrong peaceful, God-loving woman to mess with. She wasn't one to simply give up.

With no expression, because she feared if she let any emotion through at that moment she'd crack and burst into tears, she nodded once, then again as two police cruisers pulled up in front of her bakery, lights flashing, and several officers hurried inside.

"Is everyone all right?" the first officer asked, looking around, his eyes coming to rest on the brick lying on the table and then on the note hanging loosely from Lizzie's hand.

She took a deep breath and stepped forward. "Officer, I'm Lizzie Miller. This is my bakery. I need to report a crime. . ."

CHAPTER TWO

Lizzie sat alone in one of the sage-green armchairs situated on either side of a brown leather sofa in front of a gas fireplace in the back corner of her shop. She'd turned on the fire and was staring morosely into the dance of blue and orange flames, pondering her life choices.

The shop was closed, and she'd sent Jane and Eliza home after they'd all cleaned the place up.

Silently, she prayed. *Dear* Gott, *please help me to understand why someone would do such a thing. And am I where You want me to be? Or in my pride, did I misunderstand Your will, and this is the result? Please help me,* Vader. *I was so sure I knew what I was doing. Now, I'm not sure of anything.*

The front window was covered with wood until the glass could be replaced.

"At this rate, I'll be having a grand opening party and a going-out-of-business sale in the same week." Glumly she sipped from a cup of lukewarm coffee, the dregs of the pot she'd brewed after the police left a couple of hours earlier.

"I don't think it's as bad as all that." The deep voice spoke from the shadows of the darkened room behind her, and Lizzie jumped and spun around.

"Dat! Are you trying to frighten me half to death?"

He chuckled and sat on the leather couch. "Sorry. When you didn't come for dinner, your mother worried. I figured you'd still be here, cleaning up."

"We actually finished a while ago. I'm just sitting here thinking."

"I know you, *dochder*. You've been sitting here second-guessing yourself and wallowing in worry, nee?"

She glanced at him with a wry expression on her face. "You know me too well."

"Well, I did raise you. Besides, it's what I would do."

"Ja?"

He nodded. "But enough wallowing. This isn't going to stop you. Right?"

She heaved a sigh. "I don't know, Dat. It's kind of scary knowing someone wishes me ill to the point that they threw a brick through my front window. Someone could have been seriously hurt!"

"That's true." He peered at her cup. "What are you drinking? Got any more?"

She shrugged. "It's cold, stale coffee."

"Got any more?"

She snickered. "Ja. In the pot on the counter. You can grab a cup from—"

"Under the counter. I helped organize the place, remember?"

"I remember. Denki. And I'm very grateful. But now I'm—"

"Starting to wonder if you've made a mistake. And asking yourself every possible question about what you were even thinking to open your own business, let alone something as ambitious as a New Orleans–style French/Amish patisserie. Am I in the right ballpark?"

"I wish you wouldn't finish my sentences." She rolled her head enough to look at him. "Of course you're in the right ballpark." She pushed to her feet. "If we're going to sit here talking, I might as well brew a fresh pot of kaffi. And I have some cookies left over from this morning."

He followed her back to the kitchen. "Actually, you might rather get out some pop or iced tea if you have any. And some plates."

She stopped and turned to look at him. "Dat. What is going on? I'm really not in the mood for company tonight."

He gave her his signature charming grin—the one her *maem* said had won her over when she was fourteen and he'd moved to town with his folks and joined her for her last year at school. "Nothing's going on, exactly. Just a few of your friends want to sit down and have a little brainstorming session. You have to eat, right?"

She stared at him in disbelief. "A few friends? Who? And eat what? As much as I love pastries, I don't want them for dinner, Dat!"

"Of course not. That's why Abram and Lydia are stopping for pizza. And come to think of it, you don't need to worry about drinks. John and Jane Bontrager are picking up pop on the way over."

Her jaw dropped. "The bishop and Lydia are coming? And Jane and her *bruder*? But. . .why?"

Everyone wants to help you figure out who's out to shut you down, Lizzie. Your mother would have come, but I dropped her off at the Hershbergers so she could watch the kinner while Jonas and Ruth come over with Abram and Lydia."

"Jonas and Ruth too? Anybody else?"

Her father chewed his cheek, then nodded sheepishly. "Only Reuben and Mary and Eliza. That's it! Nobody else. Just a few of your gut friends. They want to help. You need to let them."

"I. . .I don't know what to do, Dat."

He walked over to her and held out his arms. She stepped into them, and he enfolded her in his warm embrace, making her feel safe, like she had whenever something had hurt or frightened her as a child.

"I know. That's why we're all going to talk it out tonight. We'll figure it out, *lieb*. But I have a suggestion."

She looked up into his dear face. "Ja?"

"Why don't we pray together before everyone gets here. Gott will help us figure out what to do about this to keep you safe, and your business thriving."

She smiled and snuggled her face into his shoulder, breathing in the reassuring scent of horse and leather and honest sweat that was synonymous with safety to her. "Ja, let's do that. You lead, please."

So he did. And then they got plates and napkins and glasses, and set them all on two tables they pushed together to make a space for friends to brainstorm.

An hour later Lizzie pushed away from the table, a hand on her belly. "Oh, I wish I'd skipped the third slice of pizza. I have regrets."

"I hear you," John said, patting his own flat belly. "Well, actually, my regrets are more based on the fact that I don't see any sort of dessert on the table. Do you have any cookies or something sweet?"

Lizzie looked at him in disbelief. "Do I have something sweet? I run a bakery! But didn't you get enough earlier?"

"Actually, I didn't have a chance to try anything. There were so many people, and then that man accosted you, and then the brick. . ." He gave her puppy eyes, and she snorted.

"I'll get some cookies. Anyone else want any?"

Lizzie headed behind the counter and put together a plate of assorted cookies, which she carried back to the table. "Here you go. Not very fresh anymore, but they'll have to do."

From the way everyone grabbed a cookie or two, she didn't think they minded.

Lydia pushed her reading glasses higher up her nose and picked up a list she'd made, acting as sort of a secretary for the group while they'd tossed around ideas as to who might wish Lizzie or her business harm. "Now then, back to business. Lizzie has given us a gut description of the man who threatened her, verified by John and me. The police said they'll have an artist sketch him and see if anyone knows who he is."

"He's probably not from Willow Creek, or one of you would have recognized him," Jonas said.

"But he was Englisch, so maybe not," Ruth pointed out.

"There was that other man, Lizzie," Eliza said. "The tall one with the waxed mustache and the British accent who asked you if you've found any interesting old records here."

"Oh ja, I'd forgotten him." Lizzie frowned. "He asked other odd things too. Like did I have a big dog upstairs."

"What?" Her father sat up straight. "That sounds pretty suspicious. What was his name?"

"Something different. A holiday name. Maybe Mr. Easter? No, that wasn't it. . ." Lizzie frowned again.

"It was Valentine," Eliza said. "You'd better write it down, and we can tell the police about him too."

Bishop Troyer waved a hand at Lydia. "Did you write down my suggestion of finding out if there were any other offers for the building? Maybe it's a disappointed real estate loser blowing off steam, or hoping to scare you off!"

"Please don't wave your hand in my face, Abram. I'm right here. Ja, I wrote down your suggestion. How do we follow up on that, though?"

"I could ask my real estate agent," Lizzie said. "She'd know the answer to that, for sure and certain."

Lizzie's dad nodded. "Gut idea. And why don't you ask the Petersheims whether anyone approached them privately about buying the building."

"That's a good suggestion, Dat! Lydia, please write that down," Lizzie said, nudging her elderly friend.

Lydia frowned at Lizzie. "No need to poke me, child, I'm writing it down."

Reuben stood and looked around at the group. "I think we've probably accomplished all we're going to tonight anyway, and it's getting late. Mary, it's not gut for the boppli if you don't get enough rest."

She smiled and grabbed her cane, pushing to her feet. "Ja, okay. If I think of anything else, I'll let you know, Lizzie."

"Denki all for coming. I was feeling pretty down before, but you've given me hope that we can solve this mystery before whoever wants me out of business gets their way." She stood and walked them to the door. Soon only John and Jane Bontrager and Lizzie's father remained.

"Lizzie, why don't you come home with me tonight? I don't like the idea of you being here alone," her father said with a worried glance around the large space.

"Dat, I've been living here for weeks, and tonight is no different."

"I didn't like it before either," he admitted with a wry smile. "But your maem and I realize you're an adult, and we didn't say anything. But the fact is, you could easily live at home and commute. At least until this situation is figured out." He gave her a beseeching look, and Lizzie sighed.

"I'll be fine. It's sweet of you and maem to worry, but I'd have to get up terribly early to drive into town every morning. I start work at four, and Jane and Eliza get here at five. Maybe if I were Englisch and drove a car it would make sense, but for me, no."

"But what if the person who did this comes back? You don't even have a dog to scare him away!"

Lizzie frowned. "You're the second person who commented on whether or not I have a dog today." She shook her head. "Besides, I've got Petite Souris. She's pretty fierce." Her attempt at reassuring her father fell flat, with the older man standing in the doorway looking unhappy, obviously reluctant to leave his daughter in what he thought was a potentially dangerous situation.

Jane raised her hand. "I could stay here for now. Then Lizzie wouldn't be alone."

Everyone stared at her, and then John stepped forward. "But Jane, that doesn't solve the problem. It just puts you in danger too. I don't like it, and I'm sure Maem and Dat won't either."

Jane rolled her eyes. "I'm twenty-two years old, and I am perfectly capable of taking care of myself. Tonight I can borrow a nightgown and toothbrush from Lizzie, if you have extras?" At Lizzie's nod, Jane smiled. "It's settled then! I'll stay tonight, and tomorrow after work, John, you can bring me my clothes and things, and don't forget to bring Secret and all her things, okay?" Then she turned to Lizzie with a look of sudden concern.

"Oh, wait! Do you think Little Mouse will mind having my kitty, Secret, here? That would ruin the whole plan."

Lizzie thought about it for a moment. "I don't think so. They are sisters, after all. And though they haven't seen each other for a couple years, it's a big place. I think they'll have room to get used to each other. You can shut her in your room for the first couple days so they can sniff each other under the door, ja?"

Jane nodded, satisfied. "Ja! That will work."

Lizzie smiled at her friend and then turned to look expectantly at the men. "Well? Are you both satisfied?"

John slowly shook his head. "You two think a couple of overgrown kittens are going to keep you safe?" He turned to Lizzie's dad for help. "Henry, this is no gut. Surely you see that?"

Henry shrugged. "I feel as you do, John, but after all, they are adults."

"Is there a lock on the door leading to your apartment?" John asked.

Henry frowned. "Nee. I meant to put one in but haven't gotten around to it. I'll do it first thing in the morning. Maybe you should come home until I get that done?" He looked hopefully at his daughter and Jane, but Lizzie shook her head.

"We'll be fine, Dat."

"You don't have a phone upstairs, do you?" John asked, frowning.

"Nee, of course not. We have the one down here for business. I've never needed one upstairs."

John grunted. "Ach, I wish you did have one up there. If anything happens, you won't be able to call for help!"

Jane rolled her eyes. "Nothing is going to happen, John. And if it did, I guess we could always open a window and yell for help."

John glared at her. "Look, you're my little sister. I just want to make sure you're safe."

Jane's expression softened. "I know. You're a gut bruder. We'll be careful, ain't so, Lizzie?"

Lizzie nodded. "Ja, and denki for worrying about us, but we'll be fine. It's already nearly ten. We have to get up in five hours and start the baking. So gut nacht, Dat. Gut nacht, John."

John still looked as if he'd like to argue, but Lizzie's father took his arm, drawing him outside. "Come, John, they'll be fine."

The two women locked the door and waved at the men, who climbed into Henry's buggy and pulled away down the street in the direction of both of their farms.

Lizzie looked at Jane and blew out a puff of air. "I wasn't sure they'd give in."

"Me either. I thought for sure and certain you'd be sleeping at your parents' house tonight!"

"I won't lie. I was tempted. Denki so much for volunteering to stay!

You're such a gut friend. I'm not afraid, exactly. But I have to admit I'll sleep easier knowing I'm not all alone here."

"I wouldn't leave you all alone. And just think, this will almost be like a sleepover! We'll have fun together."

Lizzie smiled at her friend and nodded. "We totally will. But it's late. Let's get upstairs and I'll get you set, and we can get some sleep. Tomorrow will come all too soon."

They turned off the lights except for one left on for safety, so the town's police officer patrolling at night could look inside and see that everything was as it should be. Then they headed upstairs.

At the top of the stairs the electricity ended, and there was a table with several battery-powered lanterns sitting on it. As Lizzie turned one on, her sleek gray tabby greeted her with demanding meows to let Lizzie know that she'd missed her dinner and wasn't amused.

"Okay, okay, Little Mouse, I'm sorry I forgot to come up and feed you. Things got a little crazy in the shop today." She moved toward the kitchen, which was located on the second floor of the three-story building. Jane, who'd been there many times, followed her in and took a seat at her 1950s teal Formica dinette set, which had come with the building.

"I love this table and chairs so much!" she gushed, running her hands over the cool, smooth teal tabletop. "You're so lucky the Petersheims left this set."

Lizzie finished preparing Little Mouse's dinner, and the cat dug in, making funny little chirping noises as she crunched her kibbles. Lizzie turned to her friend, who was watching the cat eat with a tired smile, and asked, "Would you like a cup of tea or hot chocolate before bed?"

Jane's eyes sparkled. "Of course! You know I can't turn down hot chocolate." Her smile grew devious. "Especially if you happen to have any cookies handy."

Lizzie rolled her eyes. "I can probably find a cookie or two." She pulled out her cookie jar, which was shaped like Elsie the Cow, and had also been left behind by the Petersheims.

She quickly had two mugs of hot cocoa on the table, complete with tiny marshmallows, and simply plopped the entire cookie jar down in front of her friend. "Go to town, Jane."

"Yay! Though I'm not going to ask when you found time for personal baking while you were getting ready for your grand opening."

Lizzie spoke through a mouthful of cookie. "I didn't. I brought a dozen upstairs last night in case I got hungry. I don't have much food in here right now. I haven't had time to shop."

"That makes more sense."

The two friends finished their snack, and then Lizzie led Jane to one of three bedrooms located on the second floor. "Here you go. There are even fresh linens on the bed. My room is across the hall, remember? And the bathroom is at the end."

Jane nodded. "Sure, I remember. I helped you move in, didn't I?" She plopped down on the full-sized bed adorned with a lovely pink-and-white quilt of appliquéd cherry blossoms on a white-on-white quilted background. "This quilt is so pretty. Didn't your grandmother make it?"

Lizzie nodded as she returned from foraging in the hall linen closet for a couple of clean towels. "Here, in case you want a shower. And let me grab you a nightgown."

She hurried down the hall to her room, lantern held high in front of her. She'd chosen the master bedroom because it had its own bathroom, which to Lizzie, who was used to sharing a bathroom with several siblings, was the height of luxury. She opened her pajama drawer and chose a warm flannel nightie. It was late April, and the nights still got pretty chilly. The steam heat from the boiler in the basement did a good job, but she liked sleeping with her windows open and a couple of heavy quilts piled on top of her. She went back to Jane's temporary room and handed her the nightgown. "Here you go! I hope you like flannel."

"Oh ja! It's so cozy." She looked around at the pretty pink-and-white room. "This room makes me feel pampered. The antique iron bed, the dressing table, the pink-and-blue braided rug. It's perfect. Denki."

"Why are you thanking me? You're the one doing me the favor! I'd be in my old bedroom at maem and dat's if not for you volunteering to stay here."

"You're right. It will be like sleepovers when we were kinner!"

"Minus the pillow fights and my maem coming in and telling us we'd better cut it out or we'd have to muck stalls the next day!"

They looked at each other for a moment, and then both burst into giggles. Lizzie wiped a tear from her eye and took a deep breath, holding her stomach, which ached from laughing too hard on a full belly. "I think I needed that laugh! It's been a stressful day."

Jane stood up and hugged her friend. "It'll all work out. You'll see. And tomorrow John will bring my kitty, and my things, and then we'll be roommates for a while! Honestly, I've been wanting to move out of my parents' house, so this will sort of give me a taste of that."

Lizzie looked thoughtful. "Who knows? Maybe we'll realize we can't live together."

Jane smirked at her lifelong friend. "Or maybe we'll find out we make great roommates, and I'll stay!"

"That might actually be a really good idea. Let's see how it goes and how Little Mouse and Secret get along, okay?"

She went back to her room and got ready for bed, then climbed under the covers and glanced at the novel she was reading. Deciding she was too tired to enjoy it, she picked up her Bible instead. Snuggling down into her soft winter flannel sheets, a gift from her parents when she moved out, she pulled the quilts up to her chin and read God's Word until her eyelids grew heavy. Marking her place, she replaced the treasured volume, an old Bible she'd inherited from her grandmother, on the nightstand and turned off the lantern.

Her last thoughts before drifting off were in the nature of prayers that things would get better rather than worse.

CHAPTER THREE

A loud crash from somewhere in the building sent Lizzie bolt upright in bed, blinking into the darkness. A second crash, followed by a cry from Jane and hisses and yowls from Little Mouse, had her kicking her way free of her sheet, fumbling her feet into her slippers, and rushing into the hallway, unlit lantern in her hand.

The cat's screeches and hisses had been joined by the sound of a man cursing and yelling threats at the cat, but it was too dark for Lizzie to make anything out. That's when she realized the staircase light was out.

Worried that someone might hurt Little Mouse, Lizzie fumbled for the switch on her lantern and switched it on, just as Jane came pelting out of her room, holding her lantern in one hand and a shoe in the other.

There was a final yowl from Little Mouse, then a cry, and the sound of someone falling down the stairs. The someone crashed through the door at the bottom, and then there was a groan and silence.

Lizzie and Jane stood frozen, lanterns held before them, staring at each other. Little Mouse was poised at the top of the stairs, back arched, fur puffed up, one paw extended, claws out. Before Lizzie could collect her thoughts and decide what to do next, the small animal darted down the stairs, and Lizzie cried out, "Little Mouse, no! Stay here!"

She approached the top of the steps and peered down, trying to see if the intruder was still down there on the floor. "Little Mouse?" she called softly. She couldn't see the cat. She couldn't see much of anything. If she turned on the light, she'd be able to see better, but if the intruder was still there, he'd be able to see her too. An angry yowl from below decided the issue for her.

"I'm turning on the light," she whispered, feeling for the wall switch in the dark. Finding it, she flipped it on, flooding the stairwell with light. Jane hurried forward and grabbed the sleeve of Lizzie's nightie.

"Lizzie Miller, don't you dare go down those steps! There's a burglar down there!"

Lizzie glanced back at Jane, knowing in her heart her friend was right. But her beloved cat was down there, possibly in danger! She took another step, and Jane grabbed her arm and pulled. "Lizzie! If you go down there, I'll tell your maem, and you'll never get to move out of your parents' house until you're an old grandmother! I'm not kidding!"

Lizzie looked at her friend, whose hair was coming out of its braid, flying around her face like a halo in the light of her lantern. Her eyes were fierce, and Lizzie knew she was not bluffing. "Really? You'd tell my maem?"

Jane nodded firmly. "In a heartbeat! That is a dangerous criminal down there. He broke into your home, and he had to know we were here! What was he doing? If not for Little Mouse, who knows what might have happened?" Jane glared at her, and her shoulders slumped. She knew Jane was right. On the other hand, their only way of calling for help was downstairs in the kitchen. Suddenly, she remembered the little-used back staircase. It came out right beside the back door in the kitchen, not far from the shop phone.

"Jane, we need to use the back stairs and go down to the kitchen to call for the police." She started toward the back of the building. The back stairs went up all the way to the top floor, and the access door was at the end of the hall.

Jane hurried to catch up, then paused as a thought struck her. "Wait a second!"

She hurried into Lizzie's room and grabbed Lizzie's bathrobe and a cardigan. She tossed the robe to Lizzie, who pulled it on, and shrugged into the sweater, buttoning it over her borrowed nightgown. "Lizzie, what if he's in the kitchen?"

Lizzie bit her lip as she paused by the back stair doorway. "I doubt it. I think he probably already left through the front door. And I'm worried that Little Mouse followed him out! Besides, if we don't go down, we can't call for help. We have no choice. Here, take my hand."

Lizzie turned on her lantern, then gripped Jane's hand. The two young women stared at each other with frightened eyes.

"Wait! Let's pray," Jane said, gripping her friend's hand hard. Lizzie nodded, and Jane whispered, "Father, please keep us safe. Please let the burglar already be gone. Please let Lizzie's kitty be fine too. Your will be done."

Lizzie smiled tremulously at Jane. "Gott will protect us, Jane. He has a plan for us, which hopefully extends past tonight."

Jane gave her a wry smile. "Ja, hopefully. Okay, let's go." They crept down the back stairs, listening for any sign that the intruder was waiting for them in the kitchen below. At the bottom, Lizzie wiped her sweaty palm on her bathrobe then gripped the metal doorknob, turning it very slowly and easing the door open. She peeked into the kitchen beyond, which was partially illuminated by a plug-in device her Realtor had given her as a housewarming gift. It supposedly emitted a sound too high in pitch for humans, or even dogs and cats, to hear, that repelled rodents. It also had a night-light. Lizzie didn't know about the supposed sound it made, but she had to admit she hadn't had any trouble with rodents—a real bonus in her bakery.

"I can't see anybody, and the kitchen door is closed," she whispered. She stepped into the kitchen, followed by Jane. They peered around, and then Jane made a beeline for the phone.

"I'm calling 911!" The operator picked up, and Jane told her their situation then hung up. "The police are on their way!"

Lizzie, who had tiptoed over to the door and was peeking through the small window into the front of the shop, put a hand on the door to push it open. But Jane grabbed her arm and pulled her away from the door.

"Elizabeth Miller, we are going to wait for the police before going through that door, *fashtay?*"

Lizzie looked at her best friend and saw that she was dead serious.

Slowly, she nodded. "Ja, I understand. I just hope they hurry. I'm worried about Little Mouse."

Jane heaved a sigh of relief. "Well, I'm worried about us. Come on, let's hide in the stairwell until we hear the police, in case he comes in here." She pulled her friend back toward the stairs, and Lizzie went willingly, pulling the door nearly closed so they could see and hear through the crack. She sent up a silent prayer for her cat's safety, and plopped down on a stairstep to wait for the police.

They didn't have to wait long. Within minutes, red-and-blue flashing lights sliced the night, and two cars pulled up in front of the building with a screech of tires.

"They're here!" Lizzie cried. She burst through the door and hurried through the kitchen, pushing through the swinging door into the front of the shop and flipping on the light switch that illuminated the space behind the bakery counters. Moments later several officers entered the shop. It appeared the front door was open wide to the night.

"Hello! Police! We had a call about an intruder!"

Lizzie held up her hands. "Yes! I'm the owner."

"Are you the one who called, ma'am?" One of the officers, a tall man with graying hair, stood just inside the door, looking at her while his two companions, a man and a woman, stood nearby, looking searchingly around the inside of the shop.

"I made the call!" Jane said as she arrived, breathless, behind Lizzie. "You got here really fast!"

"Just let me turn on the rest of the lights." Lizzie flipped the switches for the restaurant, flooding the large space with soft light. She looked around. Other than the door standing open, everything looked normal.

The first officer took a step forward. "I'm Sgt. Hernandez. Do you mind if we look around and make sure the intruder is gone?"

Lizzie's eyes widened. "Nee! Please, do." Then a thought occurred to her. "Little Mouse! Jane, do you see her anywhere?"

The female officer paused in her search of the space. "You saw a mouse?" She glanced around. "Down here or upstairs?"

"The big bad mouse won't get you, Anderson," the third officer teased.

"If you see it, let me know and I'll rescue you."

Throwing a deadly glare at her companion, Officer Anderson turned back to Lizzie and Jane. "I'm just trying to figure out the situation."

Lizzie bit back a smile. People were afraid of odd things. Who was she to judge? "Nee, Officer Anderson, not a mouse, a cat. My cat is a gray tabby named Little Mouse."

The police officer, a middle-aged woman with graying brown hair pulled back in a ponytail, looked relieved. "Ah, good to know. Um, I may have seen her just outside, crossing the street."

"What? Oh no!" Lizzie looked at the door and tried to think how long her fearless cat, who never usually even tried to go outside, might have been gone. "She's an indoor cat! I need to go find her."

"Anderson, have a look in the kitchen," Sgt. Hernandez, who seemed to be in charge, told her as Lizzie hurried to the front door. As she stepped outside, she heard the third officer, whose name she hadn't yet caught, snicker and warn Anderson to watch out for mice in the kitchen.

"Miss, please don't go far. It's still dark, and we don't know where your intruder went," Sgt. Hernandez called to Lizzie from inside.

"I won't go far. I just want to see if I can see her out here."

Outside it was cold and misty, with the dew settling on the ground as morning neared. Dawn had not yet broken, and it was still dark outside. Lizzie looked around, but she didn't see her beloved cat. "Little Mouse, where are you?"

A nearby streetlight shone down on the city tree lawn, and Lizzie saw something that puzzled her. Creeping nearer, she realized she was looking at the outline of a shoe in the recently mowed, dew-covered grass. Glancing at the two police cars pulled up out front, she realized that the officers had crossed the grass farther down.

Looking across the street at the small, shadowy park next door to Stutzman's Furniture, she thought she could see more footprints, vanishing into the darkness. She started across the street, but a hand on her shoulder stopped her.

"Lizzie! Where are you going?"

"Look! There's a footprint here in the grass, and more across the street. You can see them in the dew by the light of that lamppost. But we have to hurry. They'll soon disappear."

"Miss, that would be our job." She spun around, and there was Sgt. Hernandez, looking at her as if she'd lost her mind. "What footprints are you talking about?"

She pointed first at where he and the other two officers had crossed the grass by their police cruisers. Then she pointed at the clearly visible single footprint in the grass in front of her, a little ways to the right of her front door. Hernandez took off his hat and scratched his head. "Well, I'll be. I didn't notice that our shoes left tracks, and I didn't notice this one." He gave her a look of respect touched with a bit of embarrassment. "But you're not going out into the dark looking for someone who broke into your store."

When she opened her mouth to protest, he raised a hand. "I didn't say we wouldn't investigate. I said you won't." Turning, he shouted into the building. "Anderson! Jakes! Get out here. We've got a clue."

"There's nothing of note inside, Sergeant," Anderson said as she preceded her partner out of the bakery.

"Well, I noted a lot of really tasty-looking pastries," Jakes said with a hungry backward look.

"Jakes, get the black bag out of the car. Anderson, look at this footprint." Hernandez pointed at the print in the grass. She approached and studied the print, then looked at her superior.

"There are more across the street. You can just make them out in the light of that lamp."

She peered across the street and nodded as Jakes hurried up with a black bag in his hand. He handed it to Hernandez, who opened it and started rummaging inside. "You two go see where those footprints lead. Be careful. He's probably long gone, but don't get complacent."

He pulled out a measuring tape and measured the shoe, then jotted something in a notebook. "Hmm. About an 11 medium." As the two officers jogged across the street, he took out his cell phone and shot a couple of pictures of the print. Then he started walking back and forth, looking for anything else they'd missed.

Lizzie, meanwhile, had noticed something else in the wet grass. Stooping down for a closer look, she drew in a sharp breath. Next to the footprint, fainter, but visible, were little paw prints. "Little Mouse!"

"Where? Do you see her, Lizzie?" Jane asked, looking around.

"No, look, paw prints! They have to be hers. And they're heading across the street. She was following that burglar!" Lizzie started across the street at a fast clip, ignoring the calls from both Jane and Sgt. Hernandez. She heard them following, and hurried to the edge of the grass in the little park. She stopped to examine the grass. "I can't see anything."

Remembering she carried a lantern, she switched it on and held it low over the grass. "There! Look! More paw prints!"

Hernandez and Jane had caught up, and they peered down at the grass. "By golly, you're right," Hernandez said. "Your cat is following the perp."

"You should have seen her go after him before!" Jane said. "She was hissing and yowling and carrying on. I think she made him fall down the stairs. She may have clawed him. He was cursing and yelling something wonderful. I'd be surprised if he wasn't pretty scraped up!"

"I have to find her." Lizzie again started forward, but Jane's hand on her arm stopped her. "Lizzie, be sensible. It's dark yet. Let's wait for morning, and then we'll look. She won't go far. She's never been outside before."

"She won't know how to behave! She doesn't know about cars or dogs or anything! She could get hurt!" Lizzie felt tears rising in her eyes and blinked furiously.

"She'll be okay, Lizzie. We'll find her, you'll see. You must have faith."

Lizzie swallowed hard and nodded. Jane was right. Gott would keep Little Mouse safe until Lizzie could find her and bring her home.

Just then, the two officers came into view on the far side of the park, walking briskly, and Officer Jakes appeared to be carrying some sort of bundle. As they drew near, Lizzie heard a disgruntled meow, and she gave a glad cry and hurried forward. "Oh, you found Little Mouse! Thank you so much for bringing her back!"

She took her cat from the officer's arms and cuddled her close. "You naughty girl! You could have been lost or eaten by a coyote or something!"

"That's not all we found," Anderson said, reaching into her pocket and pulling out a sealed plastic baggie, which she handed to her superior.

"What's this?" Hernandez asked, holding the bag up and peering at it in the light cast by the nearby streetlight.

"It's a blood-stained handkerchief!" Anderson said. "The cat had it!"

Everyone turned and looked at Little Mouse, held secure in Lizzie's arms. She looked back and chirped with what seemed like satisfaction, as if to say, "Yep! I found you a clue!"

"What do you mean, the cat had it?" Hernandez demanded, looking at Jakes and Anderson.

"Just that, sir," Jakes said, shaking his head. "I've never seen anything like it. We came around a corner about a block off, and there sat the cat, holding that handkerchief under a paw on the sidewalk. She let Anderson pick her up, and I used tweezers to put the handkerchief into that bag. Nobody has touched it. Well, except for the cat, that is."

Little Mouse began washing her fur, unconcerned.

"Unbelievable," Hernandez murmured. "Let's go inside. I want to look around some more before heading back to the station."

They turned and headed for the bakery, Lizzie cradling the cat in her arms. Once inside, she sat down and examined the cat closely, making sure she hadn't come to any harm. "Well, you seem okay, you silly thing. And you were very brave, chasing off that burglar and finding us a clue!"

The little cat reached out and patted her cheek with a paw, a gesture Lizzie had learned could mean anything from affection to hunger. She smiled and scratched the cat under her chin. "You'll be wanting your breakfast, nee? Come on then and I'll feed you." But before she could stand, Sgt. Hernandez stepped closer. He'd been standing a couple of feet away while she examined the cat. "Miss Miller, if you don't mind, I thought I saw something just now, when your cat reached up its paw. Do you mind if I have a look?"

Lizzie shook her head, and the policeman squatted down in front of her and gently took one of Little Mouse's paws in his large hand. Anderson, Jakes, and Jane all crowded in to have a look. He turned the paw over, and there were several gasps of surprise. The bottom of the cat's paw was bloody.

"Little Mouse, you're hurt!" Lizzie cried. But Sgt. Hernandez shook his head. "I don't think so. Look at her claws." Lizzie looked more closely and saw what he meant. The tips of the cat's claws had dried blood caked on them. "She's not the one who's hurt," the policeman said softly. "Looks like she marked our perpetrator. That should make it easier to identify him."

"Which the bloody handkerchief seems to corroborate," Anderson pointed out. "We can do a DNA test, see if he's in the system."

"That'll take months," Jakes muttered.

"Yes, but if we make an arrest, it'll help convict him," Anderson returned. "And getting a blood type won't take much time."

"True," Hernandez said, pushing to his feet. "Well, ladies, let's get your statements, and then we'll let you get back to bed for what's left of the night."

Lizzie snorted indelicately. "Sergeant, this is a bakery. I'm already late for starting the day's baking. There won't be any more sleep tonight."

With that, Lizzie and Jane gave the officers their official statements about what had happened, and Sgt. Hernandez rose to leave.

"Anderson, Jakes, I want you to stay here until morning, just to be sure our perp doesn't get any idea about coming back for whatever he was looking for. Maybe it was just your garden-variety break-in, but after what happened here earlier, I doubt it. Obviously, he's after something, and until he finds it or we catch him, you ladies aren't safe here. I'd recommend sleeping elsewhere until this is over."

He nodded at his officers and left, talking into his radio as he headed out to his car.

"Well, I was really hoping it was just a random thing," Jane said, frowning. "There's no way your folks or mine will let us stay here now."

Lizzie gave her friend a stubborn glare. "I refuse to be driven out of my own property! Oh, I'm having very un-Christian thoughts right now."

Officer Anderson smiled. "Understandable. Look, why don't you two go upstairs and get dressed, and then maybe we could talk you into making a pot of coffee?"

Lizzie and Jane looked at each other in dawning horror. "Oh goodness, I'd totally forgotten we're in our nightgowns and bathrobes!" Jane cried. She hurried over to the stairs and disappeared up them.

Lizzie stood more slowly and tucked a flyaway strand of hair behind her ear. "Ja, of course. Um, the coffeepot isn't hard. If you'd like, go ahead and get a pot started. And help yourselves to any pastries that look good behind the counter. I'll be back down in a few minutes."

She left the officers heading behind the counter to figure out the coffee and forage for breakfast, and went up to officially start her second day in business. She had a feeling it was going to be a long one, especially once word of what had happened got out, and she sent up a silent prayer for a clear head despite little sleep.

"And Gott, if you could help us figure out who wants my business closed down sooner rather than later, I'd be most grateful!"

CHAPTER FOUR

Agnes Miller put a plate of bacon down on her wooden kitchen table with a bit more force than was strictly necessary. "Well, I don't like it! I don't want my daughter sleeping in a building where people are breaking in at night! What's to stop that man from returning? He could hurt you!"

Lizzie took a deep breath, searching for calm. It was two days after her grand opening. After the police had left the day before, she and Jane had gotten to work, prepping for the day. By the time Eliza had arrived at work everything was in place—everything except the boarded-up front window, that was.

Lizzie hadn't been surprised when a locksmith showed up at one point, sent by her dat, to install new locks on both the exterior doors and the door up to her apartment.

They'd worked all day, and then when Jane's bruder, John, showed up near closing time, telling them he was there to take them to their respective homes as their respective parents wouldn't hear of them spending that night in the bakery after what had happened—even with the fancy new locks. They'd decided it was easier to go home, talk to their folks, and then regroup. They even had a pretty good plan, but now Lizzie's *mudder* wasn't giving her a chance to reveal it.

"Maem. I don't mean to argue with you and Dat. I don't really want to stay there right now either. But I'm frustrated. How can I make a go of my business if I'm not there? And I really hate to be driven out of my home."

Agnes frowned and gestured weakly around the cozy kitchen where they all sat. "Lizzie, this is your home. That's just a temporary place for you to live while you run the bakery. An apartment above a bakery is not a home!"

"The Petersheims lived there for decades. They raised all their kinner there."

"Well, ja, I know. But surely you want to marry eventually, and then you'll give up this bakery and move into your husband's home."

Again, Lizzie had to reach for patience. "I don't know what the future holds, but this bakery is not a passing fancy. It's been my dream since I was fifteen! I won't marry a man who expects me to give up my dream. Would you?"

Her mother looked troubled, and Lizzie knew that she'd never fully understood her daughter's odd ambition to own and run a New Orleans–style French patisserie in Amish country. But she'd always been supportive, even going so far as to allow Lizzie to do an internship at a French bakery in New Orleans when she was eighteen—an internship that had started out as a six-week position and had turned into a two-year intensive learning experience.

She'd returned home at age twenty, ready to go after her dream. Her first step was to talk to a financial planner about how to go about it, an unusual step for an Amish woman. But she wanted what she wanted, and she wasn't going to lose her dream through ignorance of business practices.

So upon the advice of the financial advisor, a woman she had met through the Holmes County business incubator, she'd gotten a job and started saving money.

Five years later, she had considered her savings account adequate for a down payment on a building and all the things she'd need to furnish her bakery business. She'd increased her knowledge and experience by working in a bakery in Willow Creek all that time and was starting to look around for a suitable location for her business when the people who owned the bakery where she'd worked since returning from New Orleans approached her and asked if she would be interested in purchasing their business—lock, stock, and barrel.

She'd jumped at the chance, and due to all her preparations and her savings account, things had moved forward quickly.

Fast-forward to the ribbon cutting, and Lizzie had thought she'd had the world at her feet.

"Guess I have feet of clay," she mumbled.

"Now, lieb, no such thing. This is just a small setback," her father said, putting a comforting hand on her shoulder.

Reluctantly, her mother nodded. "Your father is right. The Englisch police will certainly figure out who is behind the vandalism and break-in before long. I do wish you'd consider staying with your vader and me until then, though. I can't help worrying. You're my boppli, no matter how old you are."

Lizzie smiled fondly at her mother. "Maem, how about a compromise?" At her mother's raised eyebrow, Lizzie went on. "Eliza King, Mary King's sister-in-law, has invited Jane and me to stay with her in her apartment above her bruder's doctor's office. She has an extra bedroom, with two twin beds. It's only a couple blocks from the bakery, so the commute would be reasonable, and Jane and I agreed that it would be smart not to stay in the apartment above the bakery until the intruder is caught. And we can walk to and from work together every day, so you won't have to worry about me walking alone in the dark."

Her parents exchanged a quick glance, and her mother nodded reluctantly. "Ja, if I can't have you here, then I'm satisfied that you'll be safe with Eliza King above the doc's office for now. Why didn't you just tell me you'd decided to do that instead of giving me a hard time?"

Lizzie shrugged. "I'm sorry, Maem. I guess an Englisch girl would say you'd pushed her buttons. You got my Amish up!"

"Is that even a thing? Never mind. When are you moving in then?"

Lizzie tilted her head to the side, watching a small spider make its way across her mother's kitchen ceiling while she considered her answer. "She invited us to come tonight, but we both decided to spend another night at home with our parents and start fresh tomorrow, after work. Eliza's bruder, Doc Reuben, will bring his truck and help us move what we need." She shrugged. "Though it won't be much. I'm obviously leaving my furniture there, and neither of us has a lot of clothes. We probably could have walked."

"It was nice of him to offer," her father said.

"Ja, very nice," her mudder seconded. "So that's settled. Now, eat your breakfast. It's nearly time for you to leave for work."

Lizzie jumped up from the table, finishing off her orange juice and carrying her dishes to the sink, where she washed them up and placed them into the dish drainer. Then she kissed her maem on the cheek and hurried up the stairs, calling out as she went, "Denki for breakfast, Maem! It was *appenditlich*, as always. I've got to brush my teeth, then I'll be ready to go."

Later that morning Lizzie was sipping a cup of kaffi during a lull after the morning rush. She'd worked at the bakery long enough to anticipate about an hour's quiet time before the lunch rush began. Usually she'd spend the time restocking the shelves and cleaning. But she was still exhausted from her recent adventures and just wanted to take a few minutes to recharge.

She sank gratefully into a comfy chair and propped her feet up on the coffee table in front of her. Holding the cup of coffee on her lap, she leaned her head back on the chair and closed her eyes. "Just for a minute," she murmured, listening to the hum of the old building and relaxing into the deep armchair.

"When Jane said you were asleep in front of the fire, I didn't believe her, but here you are."

Lizzie jumped, sloshing cold coffee onto her work apron. "John! What? Asleep? No, no, I just closed my eyes a moment ago."

He stood smirking down at her. "A moment ago, huh? Do you know what time it is?"

"Ja, sure, it's about ten, right?" She leaned forward and peered at the clock hanging on the wall across the room. And gasped. "Eleven thirty? No! It can't be! Why would Jane and Eliza let me sleep? I probably have drool on my dress." She jumped up, bobbling the coffee cup she'd forgotten on her lap, just managing to catch it by the rim before it fell onto the floor. "Oh, *sis yuscht*! I've wasted the morning, and the lunch crowd will be in any minute. Excuse me, John, I don't have time to chat!"

She darted behind the counter and through the door leading into the back of the shop, unaware that John followed on her heels. "You must really have needed the nap. And who can blame you after the week you've had?"

Eliza and Jane, both working in the back prepping for the lunch crowd, exchanged a quick look. "Uh-oh, time for a reckoning, I bet," Eliza said.

Jane grinned. "Ja, look how grumpy she looks."

"I'm right here. Don't talk about me as if I weren't, please. What were you thinking, letting me fall asleep for more than an hour? Now we're behind!"

John leaned against the door and stuffed his hands into his jacket pockets, a small smile on his handsome face as he enjoyed the show.

"We're not behind." Eliza lifted a tray of croissants filled with egg, tuna, and ham salad and headed toward the front of the shop. John opened the door for her and stood aside as she sailed through. He let the door swing closed as Lizzie rounded on his sister.

"Not behind? We must be." She rubbed her eyes and looked blearily around her kitchen, obviously still fighting off the effects of her impromptu nap.

Jane picked up a second tray of sandwiches and handed them to John, indicating with a point of her chin that he should carry them out to Eliza, before she turned and picked up a large tureen of soup, which she carried to the door, turning and pushing it open with her shoulder after first looking through the window to be sure nobody was coming the other way.

Lizzie followed Jane into the front and watched, bemused, as she and Eliza set everything up. She had to admit that they seemed to have it all under control. "That's lentil soup?"

Jane nodded. "Ja, as we discussed. And assorted sandwiches on our own croissants. We've got you covered, boss."

Lizzie frowned in thought. "Did you remember the oyster crackers?"

Eliza nodded. "Ja."

"Did you write the menu on the whiteboard?"

Jane nodded, pointing to the whiteboard hanging on the wall next to the counter. "Ja. All done. Relax, Lizzie. It's not going to kill you to let someone else do the work once in a while."

Lizzie knew her friend was right. But she felt like a slacker anyway. And she was grumpy.

She glanced at John, and something about the little smile on his familiar face as he observed her postnap snit grated on her. She shook it off. She'd known John all her life. He was her best friend's bruder, after all. Why should she care if he was amused by her behavior, even if he had really pretty green eyes that she somehow hadn't noticed before were the exact color of an empty Coke bottle. She growled in frustration at her own wayward thoughts.

"Well, gut," she conceded. "But don't let me do that again. If I see that we can regularly get by with only two people working, I might have to rethink having three of us here all day." With a smile for her two friends, whose jaws had dropped at that, and a glare for John, who only looked even more amused, she turned and sallied back into the rear of the shop to start the dough for the next day's breads. That would teach them.

CHAPTER FIVE

A few days later, Lizzie stood on the sidewalk in front of her bakery as two workmen, one an Amish man she knew from her church district, Zeke Yoder, finished setting the new plate glass window into the front of her building.

"That'll do it!" the man she didn't know said, using a red bandanna to wipe off his brow. He stuffed the bandanna into the back pocket of his jeans, then looked at the window one more time and gave a satisfied nod. Turning to Lizzie, he grinned. "Good thing the name of your shop is stenciled on the other window. At least you don't have to pay for that again!"

She smiled. "Ja, the silver lining for sure and certain. Denki for getting this done."

Zeke finished packing up their tools. He walked over to Lizzie and his partner. "Okay, Jake, I've got everything. Thanks for the appenditlich pastries, Lizzie. I think I prefer good old-fashioned Amish baking, but there's something to be said for that fancy French stuff you make."

"Well, we've got both, Zeke, so come back anytime you need baked goods."

"Actually, my girl, Evelyn, will be here this weekend visiting her *dawdi*, the bishop. I think I'll stop in Saturday morning and get a box of the Danish Bishop Troyer likes so much."

"Gut idea! Soften him up!"

"Can't hurt." He waved, and Lizzie watched the two men saunter to their truck, climb in, and drive away.

"That's one thing out of the way," she muttered.

"Well, that looks much better than the plywood!" The perky voice from behind Lizzie caused her to jump a tiny bit. "Oh, I'm sorry! I didn't mean to startle you!"

Lizzie smiled at the Main Street director. "Good morning, Anita! You're out and about early."

"Yes, well, I have a breakfast meeting with the mayor, the police chief, and the editors of *The Budget* and the *Examiner*, and I saw you out here and decided to say hello." She glanced at her watch. "In fact, I only have a couple minutes. How's business?"

"Pretty good, considering. I suppose people are curious, either about the new business, or the break-in."

Anita chuckled. "Well, either way, they're spending money in your shop, right? Win-win."

Lizzie nodded. "I guess so. Although I could have done without the break-in."

"That's what my meeting is about, actually. This may have been an isolated incident, but I want to be sure our businesses are protected in case whoever it was comes back to chuck any more bricks."

"I'd love to find out it wasn't actually aimed at me, no pun intended," Lizzie said. "Who would want to toss a brick through my window?"

"Much less one with a nasty note. What did it say again?"

"Something about not belonging here, and I should leave or I'll be sorry." Lizzie grimaced.

"Not the way we like to welcome new businesses to the community generally," Anita said, patting Lizzie on the arm.

"But who would want me to leave? There's been a bakery here for, what, thirty years? Why is it suddenly a problem for someone?"

Anita frowned and glanced across the street at Stutzman's Fine Amish Furniture. "Well...I can think of one possibility, though I don't like to gossip, you understand." She looked at Lizzie expectantly.

"Of course not. Gossip is wicked. I don't approve of it either." Lizzie raised an expectant eyebrow at the Main Street director, waiting for her to dish up her gossip, albeit reluctantly, of course.

Anita looked around and stepped closer to Lizzie. She leaned in, and Lizzie leaned instinctively closer to hear what she had to say. "The Stutzmans were not happy that the Petersheims decided to sell this building to you, you know."

Lizzie hadn't known. "Really? But why? They already have a business. Were they interested in expanding into the bakery business?"

"Oh, no. They wanted to shut down the bakery and expand their furniture business over here."

Lizzie raised an eyebrow and tucked a strand of light brown hair back into her *kapp*. "Huh. Mr. and Mrs. Petersheim didn't mention that to me. I didn't know anyone else was interested in this building. They came to me one day and offered to sell it. I didn't expect it. I thought I'd have to move somewhere else, maybe Berlin, and open a bakery in a couple years."

"You were fortunate. I guess you were in the right place at the right time. It didn't hurt that you'd worked for them for years, and they knew you wanted to get into the business, though, I expect."

Lizzie nodded. "So, the Stutzmans wanted the building?"

Anita nodded emphatically. "Oh, yes! In fact, I was walking past the furniture store one evening after closing with my little dog, and I heard them inside, having a terrible argument with Mr. Petersheim about it. Oh my, was Mr. Stutzman angry! He threatened Mr. Petersheim. I may have sort of paused outside a moment—you know, so my dog could sniff the grass—and that's when Mr. Petersheim left, and Stutzman stormed outside after him, shouting that this building was being wasted as a bakery, and even more by being sold to some young woman who wouldn't utilize the space efficiently, where he would. Something about Mr. Petersheim would be sorry, blah blah blah. Of course, as soon as he came out, I grabbed Moxie and hurried away. I don't think he even saw me, he was so angry. He nearly got run over by a FedEx truck!"

Lizzie was astonished by this news. "But, you never said anything before. Did you tell the police about this?"

Anita looked blank. "No, why would I?"

Lizzie stared at the other woman. "Because someone just vandalized my building, and you just told me about someone who might have a good motive!"

"Hmm. You may be right. I'll mention it to the chief at our meeting." She glanced at her watch. "Oh! I'm going to be late. Talk to you later, Lizzie! Glad to have you as a member!" She hurried away, throwing a kiss behind her as she went. Lizzie turned and studied the front of the Stutzman's furniture store, and she wondered.

"It's time I called the Petersheims and got their take on all this," she mused as she stared at the building across the street.

"See something you want?"

Again taken by surprise, Lizzie spun to face the man who'd come upon her unnoticed. When she saw who it was, her lips curved upward in a welcoming smile. "John! What are you doing here?"

John Bontrager took off his hat and ran his hand through his thick brown hair, which he wore cut a little shaggier than the traditional bowl cut common to many Amish men. "Well, I just delivered a dining room table and chairs to Stutzman's across the street there, and I thought I'd stop in and see how you're doing."

"How I'm doing?"

"Well, you and Jane and, er, Eliza. All of you. Not you in particular. Necessarily." John mentally rolled his eyes at his awkwardness. What was wrong with him? He suddenly couldn't talk to a girl he'd known since before they both started school. And she was just standing there, looking at him patiently, probably thinking she needed to be careful as he'd obviously lost his mind.

"Got it," she said, turning and looking at the newly replaced window. "Well, my window was replaced, so I'm pretty *froh* about that."

He looked at the new window and felt enormously relieved that there was something intelligent to talk about. "Ah, ja. It looks gut. And they got it in pretty quick."

She nodded. "Ja, they had to custom order it. Now let's just hope nobody tosses another brick through it."

"From your lips to Gott's ears," he said. "So, why were you standing there staring across at Stutzman's shop?"

She turned back from her shop, hand on the doorknob, and frowned across at the furniture store. "It's probably nothing."

He waited to see what obviously wasn't "nothing" to her. When she just kept staring, a small frown on her face, he decided to prod her a bit. "Nothing?"

"The Main Street director was here a little while ago. She mentioned that the Stutzmans had tried to buy this building and weren't very happy that the Petersheims sold it to me instead."

"Huh. I didn't hear about that." Now John stood frowning across the street. "Are you thinking that maybe they're mad enough to toss a brick through your window?"

She shrugged. "Who knows? I'm thinking the only way I'll find out is if I talk to them. It hadn't occurred to me—probably because I've been so busy remodeling and moving in—but they never came over to congratulate me or welcome me to the business community like most of the other downtown Willow Creek business owners have done."

He thought about it and realized they hadn't been at the grand opening, at least not when he was. "Hmm. They didn't come to your opening either, did they?"

She shook her head. "Nope. And I'm pretty sure every other person in town did, if only to score some free baked goods and check out the crazy Amish woman who's *narrish* enough to think she can bake French pastries. . ."

"New Orleans style!" They both finished together.

She grinned at him. "Ja, that's right."

He laughed. "From what I've tasted, you're not foolish at all. Your baking is absolutely appenditlich. I'm especially fond of the éclairs."

She gave him a shy little smile. "You like my éclairs?"

He nodded emphatically. "Oh ja. That Bavarian cream is the best I've ever tasted!"

She grinned. "Well, denki! I developed it myself during my internship in New Orleans." She looked around then leaned in as if about to reveal a huge secret. "I'd tell you what's in it, but I'm sworn to secrecy."

He smiled into her lovely, Wedgewood blue eyes, not able to recall when he'd enjoyed himself more than he was right at that moment, bantering with Elizabeth Miller. "Sworn, huh? I didn't think we Amish did that."

She pursed her lips as if considering it. "You may be right. I'll think about it. But I might rather confess before the congregation than reveal the secret ingredients in my Bavarian cream. It could be bad luck."

"I didn't think we did luck either."

She shrugged. "I spent two years in New Orleans. Those are some superstitious people. A little of it may have rubbed off." At his look of alarm, she laughed. "I'm kidding. I believe in Gott's grace, not luck. But it's fun to pretend."

She looked back at the furniture store, and her smile faltered. "But I am going to have to go talk to the Stutzmans. Not today. I've spent enough time out here when I should be in there as it is. Soon, though."

He put his hand on her arm when she would have finally opened the door and gone inside. "Let me go with you when you talk to them, okay?"

She gave him a puzzled look, and he shrugged. "I just feel like it would be a gut idea for you to have someone with you. You know, to witness what they say. It'll lend you credibility later if you need to report them or something."

He grimaced, thinking she'd never go for that argument, but she surprised him. "Ja, okay. You can come with me. Do you have time tomorrow?"

He thought about it. "As a matter of fact, I have a couple more things I need to deliver to them. So tomorrow works for me. What time?"

She bit her lip, and his eyes were drawn to her pretty mouth. He snapped his attention back to her eyes when she said, "How's two o'clock?"

Mentally chiding himself for letting his attention wander yet again, he nodded. "Okay, that works. You will wait for me, ja?"

"I said I would."

He smiled. "Okay, then. Let's go inside. I need an éclair and a cup of kaffi."

Before she could answer him, movement in the park across the street caught her eye, and she leaned around John to get a better look. "That's odd."

He turned to look behind him and saw only the front of the furniture store across the street. He looked at her curiously. "Who did you see?"

She frowned. "Well, I thought it looked like the man from the grand opening—the one who asked odd questions about what we've found here, and whether we have a dog. I thought he was in the park. That Mr. Valentine."

"What?" He turned and stalked across the street, walking all around the little park. Lizzie stood staring after him in astonishment. When he returned a few minutes later, she raised an eyebrow. "Find anyone?"

"No. Nobody. Are you sure it was the same man?"

She shook her head. "Nee. I only caught a glimpse. But it could have been."

"Hmm. "Did you tell the police about him?"

She nodded, and he frowned. "Ok, but now we need to tell the police he was skulking around again today." He opened the door for her, and she preceded him inside.

"Okay, gut idea. And you can have that coffee and éclair."

He followed her in, but before closing the door, he gave Stutzman's and the park an uneasy glance. When she called to him, he shook his head and went inside for that snack. He could really use it.

CHAPTER SIX

Shortly after closing time that afternoon, Lizzie, Jane, and Eliza were busy clearing up clutter from tables recently vacated by the mommy group that had descended upon them midafternoon, when a banging on the locked front door made all three women pause and stare apprehensively to see who was there.

"Ach! It's only Anita!" Lizzie said, heading over to open the door. Anita spilled inside, arms overloaded with bundles of plastic-banded magazines which she plopped onto the nearest table before slumping exhaustedly into a chair and fanning herself with her hand.

"Those are heavy!" Anita gasped. "Be a dear, Elizabeth, and get me an ice water, would you? I'll tell you what these are as soon as I can catch my breath."

With a small grin at the Main Street director's dramatic flair, Jane went behind the counter and filled a glass with ice and water, which she carried out and handed to Anita. "Here you go."

"You're a dear, Jenny!" Anita gulped half the glass and sat back.

"It's Jane," Jane said before returning to the task of closing the shop for the afternoon.

"Oops, sorry, Jane," Anita said. Then she winked at Lizzie and patted the chair next to her. "I know you're probably in a hurry to get home, but sit a minute and let me show you these wonderful publications!"

Lizzie sent an apologetic look to Jane and Eliza and sat down. Before she could say anything, Eliza had put a glass of cold water on the table for her, then made her escape into the kitchen, hiding a grin as she went.

"Oh, what nice employees you have!" Anita gushed. "You didn't even have to ask!"

Lizzie nodded. "Ja, they're my friends. We take care of each other. So, what have you got here?"

Immediately brightening up, Anita pulled a magazine out of one of the bundles. "This is the Holmes County Community Guide. The Holmes County Tourism Bureau and Chamber of Commerce makes these." She flipped through until she came to a section of restaurants, and turned the magazine on the table so Lizzie could see it. "Look! You're listed! I didn't say anything in case it was too late to get you in, but it wasn't. This will help bring customers into your store. More than a hundred thousand of these books are printed and distributed annually. Tourism is our biggest industry here in Holmes County! You're also in the member's section. But this listing with a photo of the historic building is the real boon. The Petersheims had actually paid for it, and said to leave it in but to change the name if I could. Isn't this thrilling?"

Lizzie admired the listing for her bakery. "It is really nice," she admitted. There was a photo from the ribbon cutting. You couldn't really make out her face as she wielded the scissors. And that was fine with her.

Then she squinted and peered more closely at the photo. Wasn't that the strange little man who had spoken so angrily to her that day? She picked up the magazine and looked again. Yes! It was him.

"Anita, may I keep a copy of this?"

"Of course, honey! In fact, these are all for you. Every business in the chamber gets some of these to hand out. You'll put them on that stand over by the door."

Lizzie glanced over and remembered that every year, magazines like this were placed in that stand. She'd simply forgotten.

Opening another bundle, Anita showed Lizzie a second magazine. "This is the Willow Creek Main Street Business Directory. You're listed in here too."

Lizzie nodded, but her attention wasn't really on Anita anymore. She had a photo of the angry man from her opening day! She could show it around and find out who he was. Jumping to her feet, she picked up the chamber guide. "Denki, Anita! But I really need to run. Please come back another day, and we can have a cup of kaffi and a nice chat."

"Oh, well, okay," Anita said, obviously disgruntled at having her visit cut short. "I'll just put these magazines in the rack by the door for you on my way out, okay?"

Lizzie nodded. "Ja! But I'll keep this one. Have a gut day!"

As soon as she locked the door behind Anita, Lizzie hurried to the back where Eliza and Jane were washing up dishes. "Look, look!" She slapped the magazine down on a countertop and opened it to the page with her listing. Jane came over, drying her hands on a dish towel, and gave the page a curious look.

"Okay, we've got a listing in the tourism book. That's gut, Lizzie! Congratulations."

Lizzie rolled her eyes at her friend. "No! I mean, ja, it's gut, but that's not what I want to show you. Look closely at the photo of the ribbon cutting." She pushed the magazine toward Jane, who gave her a curious look before bending to study the page.

Eliza strolled over and leaned over Jane's shoulder. Immediately she squeaked, "Oh my goodness! It's him!"

Lizzie nodded. "Ja! You see him, Eliza. Jane, don't you see?"

"Where?" Lizzie pointed, and after a moment Jane gasped, "Oh! Sis yuscht! It's the man from the first day! The one who was so unpleasant!"

"Ja! He was lurking around outside during the ribbon cutting watching us. It's creepy!" Eliza shuddered.

Lizzie nodded. "It sure seems like it. He must have been there the whole time, waiting for a chance to yell at me." She peered closer. "I don't see a brick in his hand. In fact, his arms are crossed over his chest. He's obviously not carrying anything big."

"Doesn't mean he didn't have it stashed somewhere. The note could have been in his pocket, and he put it on a brick he found in the street or something before tossing it through your window," Jane pointed out.

Eliza nodded. "He has a really unpleasant face. Sort of weaselly.

Makes him look suspicious, like someone who would do something mean, don't you think?"

The other two looked at the man again. "I don't know," Lizzie said. "If he smiled, maybe he wouldn't look so sinister."

Jane giggled. "Ja, that's probably true. Well, what are you going to do about this, Lizzie?"

Lizzie looked at her friends. "I guess I need to tell the police. But I also want to ask around and see if anyone knows who he is."

"You should ask Anita. She knows everyone," Eliza pointed out.

"Why didn't I think of that when she was here?" Lizzie wondered, feeling stupid.

"Well, to be fair, she's a bit of a gossip. . ." Jane began.

"A bit?" Eliza smirked.

"A big gossip, then," Jane conceded. "Lizzie probably didn't want her talking about this all over town before we got a chance to look into it."

"Ja, that's right. Meanwhile, girls, there's something else I found out today—from Anita, as a matter of fact."

They looked at her expectantly, and she continued. "Did either of you know that the Stutzmans wanted to buy this building?"

Eliza looked blank, and Jane frowned. "The Stutzmans from across the street with the furniture store?"

Lizzie nodded. "Mm-hmm. Anita said they put in an offer, but the Petersheims told them they were selling to me. Isn't that interesting?"

"In what way?" Jane asked.

"Lizzie must be thinking that they could be angry at not getting the building," Eliza said, glancing at Lizzie for confirmation.

Lizzie nodded. "Exactly. The question is, how upset are they? Have either of you noticed that they didn't come to the opening, and they haven't been by since to wish us well?"

"Well, maybe they're busy," Eliza said. When the other two looked at her in disbelief, she laughed. "Hey! Don't give me that look. I'm just trying to be objective. There are other possibilities for them not coming by than that they wish you ill, Lizzie."

Lizzie scrunched her mouth to the side while she pondered this.

Then she nodded. "Ja, of course there are. But tomorrow I'm going to go talk to them and find out."

"Lizzie! That seems rash!" Jane squealed, and Eliza nodded emphatically.

"Ja, Lizzie, just in case they are the ones who threw the brick, you should be careful! They could be dangerous."

"Or at the least, very unpleasant," Jane pointed out.

Lizzie crossed her arms over her chest and frowned at her friends. "So, you two don't think I can take care of myself?"

Jane patted Lizzie on the arm. "We just want you to be careful. Why borrow trouble? Nothing's happened since last week. Maybe it was a one-time thing."

"But it wasn't," Lizzie pointed out. "Someone broke in that very night! Should I wait around for something else to happen? Maybe next time they'll burn down the building."

Eliza and Jane looked at each other helplessly. They knew Lizzie. When she got something stuck in her craw, there was no dislodging it. Jane sighed and squared her shoulders. "Fine. But you're not going alone. Eliza and I will go with you."

"We will?" Eliza asked, looking doubtful.

"Ja, we will," Jane said firmly, glaring at the younger woman.

"Denki, but there's no need," Lizzie said. "I'm not going alone."

"Who's going with you?" Jane demanded.

"Well, actually, your bruder, John, offered to go. I said yes."

Jane stared at Lizzie. "He did? When did you have a chance to arrange that?"

"He happened to come by just after Anita left the first time, and I mentioned that I was planning to go talk to them. He insisted on going with me. We're going tomorrow at two, after he drops off a furniture order."

"Well, that sounds fine, doesn't it?" Eliza asked, looking from one friend to the other.

"Hmm, yes, I suppose so," Jane conceded. "But it's interesting to me that you didn't mention it before now. You've had this planned all day, and you didn't tell us. I wonder why?"

Lizzie wasn't sure herself. "I don't know. Honestly, I came inside, and he came in too, remember? And I almost forgot! We were standing outside, and I thought I saw that man from the grand opening! The tall one with the mustache, Eliza, you remember."

Eliza blinked. "And you're just thinking to mention this? Where was he?"

"He was in the park. But John went straight over there and couldn't find him. He disappeared."

"I don't like this, Lizzie!" Jane said, looking uneasily toward the door.

"Oh, we're probably making too much of it. But I'm going to tell the police about seeing him here again the next chance I get," Lizzie said.

Jane still didn't look satisfied. "John doesn't usually get involved in things like this. Especially since the Stutzmans are customers of his, he wouldn't want to risk that relationship. They sell a lot of his furniture."

Lizzie frowned. "I hadn't thought of that. Maybe I should tell him not to come after all."

Jane thought about it for a moment, and then a strange smile crossed her face, and she shook her head. "Nee. I think it's fine. Just go over and introduce yourself as their new business neighbor. You don't really know them, do you?"

Lizzie shook her head. "No, since they belong to another church district and they're quite a bit older than I am. My parents may know them. I'll ask."

"Well, just do that then. It's honest enough. You can feel it out from there, see if they say anything. See if they're polite."

Eliza nodded. "Ja, that seems like a gut plan. And while you're there, look around for loose bricks."

"Very funny," Lizzie said, picking up her magazine and looking around. "Let's lock up and walk back to your place, Eliza. I'm starving. And I have some thinking to do about all this."

John wasn't sure what had prompted him to climb into his buggy and head to The Plain Beignet right about the time he knew the girls would be heading home. He told himself it was just the neighborly thing to do. No, the brotherly thing, since Jane was his sister.

He pulled his buggy up in front of the bakery and saw that there were still lights on inside. He settled down to wait for a few minutes. *It'll give me time to figure out what to say about being here.*

After a few minutes, the door opened, and he sat up straight in his seat, but instead of Jane, Eliza, and Lizzie, out came an Englisch woman John thought he recognized as having something to do with tourism. Alice? Angie?

"Anita!" he remembered as the woman hurried past, barely glancing at his buggy. "Must have had some touristy stuff to talk about with Lizzie." He settled down to wait for a few more minutes. After fifteen, when the girls still showed no sign of coming out, he grew impatient and climbed down from the buggy. He tethered the horse to a hitching post out front and walked up to the door, which he tried. It was locked. "Well, that's smart, anyway." He knocked, and momentarily his sister opened the door.

"John! Well, isn't this interesting?" She glanced at Eliza and Lizzie, who exited the store behind her, carrying their bags. Lizzie locked up and then turned to give John a puzzled look. "*Guder nammidaag*, John. *Wie ghets?*"

He glanced at his sister, who was wearing a strange, smug smile, and returned his attention to Lizzie. "I was driving by and thought I'd see if you girls would like a ride home. It's getting dark."

"It's a while until dark, but I won't turn down a ride!" Eliza hurried over to the buggy and climbed into the back. "Come on, I'm getting really hungry."

"Well, denki, John, this is nice of you," Lizzie said. She stuffed a magazine into her bag and walked to the buggy with Eliza, while John hurried around to the driver's side.

Lizzie started to climb into the back with Eliza, but Jane put a hand on her arm and stopped her. "No, I'll sit in the back. You sit up front with John."

She scurried into the back, leaving Lizzie standing awkwardly beside the buggy. John settled into the driver's seat and took up the reins. He looked at her, one eyebrow raised, and she realized she was standing in the street making everyone wait. "Oh! Sorry. I was woolgathering." She climbed up beside John and he snapped the reins. The drive to Eliza's was very short, only about three blocks.

John pulled into the doctor's office parking lot and looked at the three friends. "Well, I hope you have a gut evening."

Jane rolled her eyes. "Don't be narrish, John. You're here, so you might as well come up and eat supper with us. Unless you already ate?"

He shook his head, looking sheepish. "No, actually I came straight from work."

"I thought you were driving by," Eliza said with a smirk.

"Well, I just sort of found myself driving by there, so I stopped," John admitted. "I guess I'm a little worried about you guys and this business with the break-in, and then Lizzie thinking she saw the odd man from the grand opening. Did she tell you about that?" At their nods, he continued. "Until they find out who is behind all this, maybe I'll just come by and pick you up every night. It'll make me feel better."

Lizzie opened her door and climbed down, followed by Jane and Eliza. John climbed down from the other side and secured the horse. He tied a feed bag to his nose and patted him on the rump. "That'll hold you for a while, Mike."

"Oh, look!" Eliza cried, pointing at an upstairs window. John looked at the window and was amused to see two feline faces peering out at them. "Little Mouse and Secret have been waiting for you to get home, I see."

Lizzie laughed and Jane said, "Oh ja, they know we get home about this time every evening, and they want to be sure to let us know they're ready for their supper!"

He followed his sister and the others up the steps.

"You really don't need to pick us up every night, John. We're all big girls," Jane said, continuing the previous conversation as Eliza unlocked the door.

He waited until all three women were inside before following them in and closing and locking the door behind them. Then he followed them upstairs to Eliza's apartment, above her brother Reuben's medical practice. Reuben had lived there before he and Mary Yoder had married the year before. Eliza had come for a visit, and ended up liking Willow Creek so much she'd stayed. Her mother back in Lancaster, Pennsylvania, hoped she would find a husband soon. But Eliza, not yet nineteen, was enjoying just working and being part of the local Amish community.

Both cats greeted them enthusiastically at the top of the stairs, winding around and between all of their legs as they headed back to the kitchen.

"Just be patient once, and we'll get your supper!" Lizzie scolded Little Mouse, bending down to scoop her up as Jane did the same with her cat, Secret.

In the kitchen the women busied themselves feeding the cats and taking care of other small chores. Soon both cats were contentedly tucking into their food in a corner of the large space.

John looked around the kitchen, which was big enough for the vintage chrome-and-Formica dinette set, with six chairs, to fit comfortably and still allow plenty of space to move around. He noticed the nice antique Hoosier cabinet against one wall and strolled over to check out the piece, which he figured dated to the 1920s. "This still has the flour dispenser! And it's got flour in it!"

Eliza looked over and laughed. "Well, ja. How else am I going to bake bread?"

"But this is a really nice piece. Solid oak, and in pristine condition!" He opened and closed the door on the bread box. "Look how smoothly this works!"

"I guess the original owners took good care of it," Jane said. "John's really into antique furniture," she told her friends. "Probably because he makes beautiful furniture himself."

"Denki, Jane. I guess I do get kind of weird about it. Sorry."

"No, I totally get it," Lizzie said, walking over to admire the piece. "I mean, this dates back to when our *grossmammies* were kinner, and it looks new." She ran a hand over the smooth oak. "It wonders me about what it's seen in this kitchen, if it's been here all these years."

"Exactly!" John cried, turning to look at Lizzie as if he were seeing her for the first time. "That's exactly what I mean. This piece was made to last, and it's been part of the life of more than one family over the years. It's seen happiness and sadness, love and anger. And it's endured. It makes me feel gut, like things can last, you know?"

Lizzie smiled up at him. "Ja, I know just what you mean. It's like Gott's love for us. It lasts."

He found himself caught in her gaze, his smile slipping away, and took a step toward her. Someone loudly cleared her throat, causing both John and Lizzie to jump and turn to look at Eliza and Jane, who were both grinning like fools at them.

"You should see the pair of you!" Eliza hooted. "Going gaga over an old piece of furniture."

John stuffed his hands into his pockets and stepped back from Lizzie. "Well, it is a very gut piece of furniture, though."

Lizzie looked a bit embarrassed, but she quickly recovered. "So, what's for supper tonight? I'm starving!"

The three women began bustling around the kitchen, fixing a meal, and John sat down and watched. He found himself admiring the way Lizzie moved, with no wasted motions as she set the table and prepared a salad.

She's so graceful. How have I not noticed before how her movements flow like water slipping around the bend in a stream?

"John? John!"

He started, then looked away from Lizzie at Jane, who was standing with her hands on her hips. "Sorry to break into your daydream, but do you mind filling up the water glasses? We're about ready to eat."

He nodded and hurried over to fill up the glass pitcher from the sink, thinking he'd better get his head out of the clouds. He stole a glance at Lizzie, who was putting the finishing touches on her salad, and shook his head. Was he interested in her in a new way? Or did he just want to keep her from doing something reckless and possibly getting herself into trouble? He would have to think about that. But not when he was in a room full of women—especially his very observant younger sister, Jane.

CHAPTER SEVEN

Officer Jakes drained his coffee and eyed the carafe Lizzie had set on the table when he and Officer Anderson arrived, along with a plate of pastries she was experimenting with.

"Do you mind if I refill my cup?" he asked, looking at Lizzie hopefully. "This week has been more exciting than usual, and my batteries are low."

"Of course." Lizzie refilled Officer Jakes' cup and turned to Officer Anderson. But the officer held a hand over the top of her cup and shook her head. "No thanks."

"So, you found something you wanted to show us?" Officer Jakes carefully sipped his hot coffee, hissing when he burned his tongue. "I never can wait for it to cool."

Lizzie pushed the tourism guide toward them, and they both glanced at it before lifting their eyes and giving Lizzie a questioning look.

Lizzie leaned forward. "Do you see anyone out of place in the picture of my ribbon cutting?"

He pulled a pair of cheaters from his breast pocket, perching them on his rather large nose. They gave him a studious air. He picked up the book and looked intently at the photo. "Hmm. Maybe. Anderson, take a look at this." He handed the magazine to his partner.

She gave it a cursory look, and then her eyes sharpened and she put the magazine down on the table and tapped the strange man's image with a blunt-tipped fingernail. "This guy. I don't know him. And he looks angry."

Jakes nodded. "That's what I thought." He looked at Lizzie. "Do you know this man?"

She felt encouraged that the officers seemed to be taking her seriously. She'd been afraid of being brushed off. "No, but I can tell you where I've seen him before I noticed him in this magazine. He was at my grand opening. He came inside, and he confronted me, telling me my business would fail."

"He was more specific than that, Lizzie," a voice spoke from behind her, and she turned to see John Bontrager standing there, frowning down at the photo in the magazine.

"John! I didn't see you come in," Lizzie exclaimed. "Is it already two o'clock?"

"I'm a little early. Thought I'd have a cup of coffee and maybe. . .a pastry?"

She smiled at him. "For sure and certain. Help yourself."

He helped himself to two pastries, and she poured him a cup of coffee while he looked at the picture in the magazine. "When did you get this? Why didn't you mention it to me?"

Lizzie raised her eyebrows. "I just got it last night, from Anita Frederickson. Not that I'm apologizing for not mentioning it to you, since I don't report to you as far as I'm aware."

John had the grace to look contrite. "I'm sorry, it's just that I thought since we're going to talk to the Stutzmans together, you'd have let me in on something having to do with this situation. I didn't mean to imply, um, anything."

Lizzie worried the strings of her prayer kapp, and felt like a jerk for being rude to John, who was only trying to help.

"Who are the Stutzmans, and why are you two going to talk to them about the case?" Officer Anderson asked, looking at them both pointedly. "You're not thinking about poking your noses into this matter, are you?"

Lizzie took her eyes from John and looked at the officers, both of whom were frowning at her. "I didn't plan on interfering, exactly. But I heard that the people who own the furniture store across the street wanted to buy this building, and they're supposedly still angry that the

Petersheims sold it to me instead. John and I were just going to go over and sort of feel them out, see if they might be mad enough to throw a brick through my window."

Officer Jakes sipped his coffee and looked at Lizzie cooly. "And if they are? Did it occur to you that they might also be mad enough to escalate the violence if you confront them? Maybe throw the next brick at your head?"

Lizzie blinked at the officer. "No, I admit that didn't occur to me."

"Officer, they're Amish," John said. "I don't think they'd hurt us. And Mr. Stutzman sells furniture I make in his store. I figured we wouldn't go right in and confront them. We'll deliver a piece of furniture and see if Lizzie's presence startles them into saying anything incriminating."

The two officers looked at each other, communicating without words in the way of longtime partners of any kind. Jakes turned back to them. "That actually has merit. But the fact that they're Amish is no guarantee that they won't commit violence. People are people, no matter what church they belong to."

"Have you ever heard of someone Amish committing an act of violence against another person?" John asked curiously.

"Oh yeah." Jakes nodded. "It doesn't happen as often as out in the general population, I'll admit. But it's not unheard of."

Lizzie looked at Officer Anderson, who nodded. "He's right. Please be careful. It goes against my instincts to let you two get involved in this, but if you keep it to what you said, it could prove useful. You'll need to call us and tell us how they reacted."

John and Lizzie nodded. Then Officer Anderson tapped the photo of the man in the picture again. "You were about to elaborate on this man's behavior last week?"

"Oh, just that he didn't just say her business would fail, but specifically that she was foolish to think that an Amish woman could run a French patisserie, and that she should have left things as they were when the Petersheims owned the business."

"I remember you told us about this guy that day. And I recall when we first interviewed you, you said he spoke with a heavy French accent?"

Officer Jakes asked, squinting down at the photo of the odd little man.

"Ja, but not a New Orleans accent. I think he was from France. Not that I've been there, but I know he didn't have an accent you'd hear in New Orleans."

"Interesting. I'm glad you called about this, Elizabeth. It was the smart thing to do. Mind if we take this with us?" Officer Anderson picked up the magazine and looked at Lizzie for permission. When Lizzie nodded, she rolled it up and stood. Officer Jakes gulped the rest of his coffee and stood as well. "Be careful this afternoon, and let us know what happens. Meanwhile, we'll see if we can identify this man. Shouldn't be too hard. Frenchman in Amish country, with some sort of grudge against Amish bakers. We'll be in touch." The two officers stood to leave, but Lizzie suddenly remembered seeing Mr. Valentine again, and asked them to wait a moment while she told them about him and about how she might have seen him across the street the night before.

"Even more reason for you all to be very careful until we get to the bottom of this, understand?" Officer Jakes asked, looking at each of them before the officers took their leave.

John looked at Lizzie. "You were going to tell me about finding a photo of that guy, weren't you, Lizzie?"

She fidgeted in her chair, again playing with her kapp strings and not meeting his eye. He reached over and lifted her chin with a finger. "Lizzie?"

She sighed in frustration. "Well, I wasn't aware you were all that interested, John. And you're not my brother, you know, even if you are my best friend's."

He studied her intently, a small frown marring his brow, before he nodded as if he'd just come to an important decision. "Well, it turns out I am interested in this case, and in your welfare, Lizzie. We've been friends for a long time. Is it so strange that I want to help ensure your safety? And incidentally, my sister's as well, since she works here."

Lizzie considered what he had said. She couldn't see any harm in John taking an interest in helping figure out who was out to shut down her business. And she knew for sure and for certain that she could trust him. John Bontrager was as honest as the day was long. And she couldn't help thinking he was pretty easy on the eyes too—even if he was her friend's brother.

"Okay, I guess that makes sense. But don't tell me what to do as if you were my dat, okay? I'm my own person, John, and I'm not looking for a man to order me around."

He raised a brow at that, and Lizzie felt a tiny bit foolish for her outburst. Most Amish women, while perfectly capable of running their own businesses without the help of a man, were happy to share that responsibility with the men in their lives. But those men were generally family members—husbands, fathers, brothers, even sons. John was none of those things to Lizzie, and being the brother of her best friend and an old friend of hers in his own right didn't give him license to interfere in her life. She had parents happy enough to fill that role already, she thought with an amused smile.

"What are you smiling about now?" John asked, and she realized she'd been sitting there lost in thought.

"Oh! Sorry, nothing." She stood. "I guess if we're going to go talk to the Stutzmans, we might as well get it over with."

"I've got the piece of furniture I'm delivering in the wagon, out back. Do you want to ride over with me? I need to take it around back to their loading dock."

John prayed that he and Lizzie were doing the right thing by confronting the Stutzmans. After all, they regularly purchased pieces from his family to sell in their store, and he really didn't want to mess up that arrangement. On the other hand, it bothered him that they hadn't welcomed Lizzie to the downtown business community. They were one of the bigger employers in the area and, as Amish folks, should really be big enough to overlook disappointments like not getting real estate they'd had their eye on and welcome a young woman into their community when she set up in business across the street.

But John wasn't naive enough to think all Amish were friendly, welcoming people. And though his own experiences with the Stutzman family had been positive, that might be because the relationship went back to his father and the older Mr. Stutzman's day. Since they attended another church district, he realized he really didn't know how they treated people they viewed as competitors in business—in other words, people who inconvenienced them or got in their way.

"Let me grab my bonnet and wrap. We can go through the kitchen and use the back door."

John waited while Lizzie told Jane and Eliza where they were going, and then he followed Lizzie out the back door into the warm spring day.

"Mmm, look! Dandelions are in bloom. I need to gather them to make jelly. I love dandelion jelly," Lizzie said, stooping to pluck a yellow blossom on her way to John's wagon. She stopped to scratch John's big Percheron, Mike, on his velvety gray nose, and when the horse nosed the flower with interest, she laughed and let him eat it from her palm.

"I can pick another one for myself!" she told John as she climbed up onto the wagon seat.

He chuckled. "Well, Mike thinks you're wonderful for feeding him one of his favorite treats! He ate all the ones he could reach."

"Do you like dandelion jelly?" Lizzie asked John as he steered Mike and the wagon across the street and down the alley behind Stutzman's Fine Amish Furniture.

"Who doesn't?" he replied, turning Mike and directing him to back slowly up to the loading dock. When the wagon was in position, he set the brake, hopped out, and gave the horse a fond slap on the rump. "Gut boy! We won't be long, old fellow."

Lizzie climbed down as two men came outside and one shook John's hand. The other man held up his right hand with a grimace. It was bandaged and he wore a wrist brace.

"Sorry, can't shake your hand today, John!"

"Tucker! What happened to you?" John asked with concern.

"My own clumsiness! I dropped a piece of furniture, and it caught my wrist just so. Nasty scrape and a sprain. It'll be good as new soon,"

Tucker Stutzman said with a glance at Lizzie. "And who have you got there?" Tucker was above average height, nearly six feet tall, with black hair and dark eyes. His beard was short, telling Lizzie he'd only been married a short time. He eyed Lizzie, who stood slightly behind John, and raised an eyebrow. "Do you have a new helper, John?" The man laughed. "I don't know how much she could carry, but she's *schee* enough to make up for it!"

Lizzie's cheeks flamed at being talked about as if she weren't there, and called pretty by the strange man, and John frowned. He found himself stepping slightly more in front of her. "This is Elizabeth Miller, the new owner of the bakery across the street. She's not an official helper. We wanted to take a ride, and I told her we needed to deliver this sofa table I promised your dat first."

At the mention of Lizzie's name and occupation, Tucker's eyes widened a bit, but he quickly schooled his expression and smiled at Lizzie. "It's gut to meet you, Elizabeth! I'm sorry I haven't gotten over there to say hello. My brother and I are always working, it seems. We even eat lunch on the fly. And my parents, well, they're not really fans of baked goods. Um, lately." He had the grace to look uncomfortable as he said this.

The second man came forward. He was pretty much a carbon copy of Tucker, though a few inches shorter, with dark blue eyes. "Did I hear you say this is the *maedel* who bought the bakery building from the Petersheims?" He held out a hand, and Lizzie shook it, disarmed by his welcoming smile. "Nice to meet you! I'm Isaiah Stutzman, Tucker's younger brother. It's gut to meet the maedel responsible for my vader not getting something he wanted for maybe the first time in his life!"

"Isaiah!" Tucker hissed, but Isaiah just chuckled. "I know, I know, I'm fraternizing with the enemy and all that. But she's such a schee enemy! And you've got to admit it's funny, bruder. She's just a little thing, and she got the best of dat!"

"I didn't mean to get the best of anyone, actually," Lizzie said. "I didn't even know your dat wanted to buy the bakery until yesterday."

"Oh ja! He's had his eye on that building for quite a while. Had this big plan to expand this place over there, and for Tucker and me to live there so he could keep us handy all the time. Maem and Dat live out on the family farm outside Berlin, so they really liked the idea of us living right across from the furniture store." He chuckled again. "I can't speak for Tucker, there, who pretty much always does what Dat wants without any regard for his own true wishes. But as far as I'm concerned, I'm happy as a pig in mud that the Petersheims decided they wanted the place to stay a bakery and sold to you instead of to Dat. I've got other plans that don't involve living across from this store for the rest of my life."

Tucker's face had grown darker and sterner as his brother talked, and finally he bit out, "Isaiah! You're talking out of turn! This is family business!"

Isaiah shrugged, not looking the least bit repentant. "I know, Tucker. But let's be honest—our parents have not acted like gut Christians toward this woman, and neither have we. Did we go welcome her to the business community? No. And even though we belong to different church districts, we're all Amish, and we're supposed to support each other. I'm ashamed of myself. I apologize, Elizabeth. I hope we can be friends from now on. Someday I'd like to hear the story of how you came to open a New Orleans–style French patisserie in Holmes County! It must be a gut story!" He threw back his head and laughed.

Obviously disgusted, Tucker shook his head. "My bruder will help you unload that bench, John, and then you and Elizabeth can be on your way."

John nodded, and he and the younger Stutzman brother carried the heavy oak bench that had a back and a seat that lifted for storage, off the wagon and inside the back of the store. They were back outside in a minute, just in time to see that Isaiah had moved closer to Lizzie and was asking her if she'd like to go for a buggy ride the following weekend.

John's mouth dropped open as he overheard, and a quick glance at Tucker verified that the older Stutzman brother, at least, did not think the idea was a good one. No doubt it would infuriate his father—which, come to think of it, was probably part of the appeal for the younger, and somewhat feckless, Stutzman brother.

But before either John or Tucker could say anything, Lizzie smiled prettily at Isaiah and shook her head regretfully. "I'm so sorry, Isaiah, but I've got plans for Sunday afternoon."

Isaiah's smile faltered for a moment—no doubt he was used to girls jumping at his invitations, as he was both good-looking and from a wealthy Amish family.

Then he looked at John, and his eyebrows rose. "Ah, it's like that, is it? Well, I guess I'm too late, but if the two of you don't work out, the offer stands."

John glanced at Lizzie, and he thought she looked confused. Before she could correct Isaiah's conclusion, he stepped in and took hold of Lizzie's hand. "Don't hold your breath, Isaiah."

For a moment the two young men stared hard at each other, and John worried that Isaiah might act on his disappointment. But he needn't have worried. Isaiah smiled, then chuckled. "I won't. I think I'd only turn blue and fall down. You two have a gut ride!" He turned and went back inside, leaving his brother alone on the loading dock with Lizzie and John.

"Well, denki for the bench, John. It's beautiful, like all your work. How's that lighted china cabinet coming along? Dat will want to know."

"I expect it to be completed in another week or so."

Tucker nodded. Then he looked back toward the open door into the furniture store. Seeing no one, he turned and looked at Lizzie, frowning as if trying to make up his mind about something. Suddenly he leaned in and spoke in a loud whisper. "Listen, Elizabeth, my parents weren't the only ones who wanted that building. And I won't have you thinking any of us would throw a brick through your store window." At her surprised look, he nodded. "Ja, we heard about that. Shameful, cowardly thing for someone to do. I want you to know that we had nothing to do with that."

Lizzie stepped forward, a look of curiosity on her face. "Denki for telling me that, Tucker. But who do you suspect? Who is this other person who wanted the building?"

He shook his head, looking frustrated. "That's just it. I'm not sure!"

A gruff voice from inside called out, "Tucker! You outside, boy?"

"Ach, that's my dat! Listen, talk to the people at the historical society.

There's something about that building—I don't know what."

Another call of "Tucker!" had him hurrying toward the back door of the store. "Go! Better he doesn't see you here together. You wouldn't want to lose his business, John."

Lizzie grabbed John's hand and pulled him to the wagon. "Come on, John. Let's go!"

John glanced back once and saw Tucker disappearing into the store and pulling the door closed behind him. He went to help Lizzie up onto the wagon, but she scrambled up on her own. He unhitched Mike and they drove away. But he glanced back, and he thought he saw a darkly frowning face peering at them from the window beside the loading dock door. It looked like Obadiah, Tucker and Isaiah's dat. And he didn't look happy. John suspected Isaiah, who never kept quiet when it would do everyone the most good, had told him exactly who was outside his shop.

He only hoped he didn't lose the account.

"No help for it now," he muttered.

Lizzie seemed to have something else on her mind. "John, are you aware that those men think you and I are, well. . ."

"Dating? Ja. Sorry about that, but there didn't seem to be another gut explanation for us riding together in the wagon to deliver furniture."

She turned on the bench seat and looked at him. "John, we can't go around pretending to be dating! People will get the wrong idea! Next thing you know, they'll be expecting a wedding. After all, I'm no spring chicken."

He frowned over at her. "You're not exactly old, Lizzie. What are you, twenty-five?"

She rolled her eyes at him. "Ja, I'm twenty-five. And for an Amish woman, that's old to be single. My maem is always asking me when I'm going to find a nice young man and give up this silly idea of owning a business. I can't seem to convince her that the bakery is not a passing whim. You'd think the two years I spent learning the business in New Orleans, or the next five years I spent working for the Petersheims, would have done the trick, but she's not convinced. Now when she hears we're dating—and she'll hear, don't fool yourself—she's going to get her hopes up that soon she'll have grandchildren!" She slumped back on the bench. "Oof. This is not gut!"

"I guess I didn't think it through."

She gave him a disbelieving look that had him squirming a bit. "You think? Well, think it through now, John. Because if you're not careful, we'll find ourselves planning a wedding!"

He chanced a sideways glance at her. She didn't look amused. And John, usually the personification of an easygoing young man, felt his temper ignite. What was so terrible about people thinking they were dating? Was there something wrong with him? She acted as if the very idea of marrying him was the last thing in the world she could ever imagine or consider. He gave a disgruntled huff, and she turned to look at him.

"What?"

He glanced at her. "What *what?*"

"You huffed. What was that about?"

"I didn't huff." He glared at the road ahead then turned to look at her, and she flinched at his obvious anger. "But if I had huffed, it would be because you're so insulted at the idea that people might think we're dating, as if I'm some kind of. . .of leper or something!"

She stared at him, and he couldn't tell what she was thinking. Then she covered her face with her hands, and he was horrified, thinking he'd scared her with his temper and made her cry. He pulled the wagon over to the side of the road and called out, "Whoa, Mike." Then he turned to Lizzie and saw that her shoulders were shaking. Oh no! He had really upset her!

He lifted a hand to touch her but drew it back. He couldn't touch her! He. . .realized he wanted to touch her. Where had that come from?

"Lizzie, I'm sorry, I didn't mean to upset you. Please, don't cry."

She raised a hand, in a staying gesture, and he paused. She lifted her face from her hands, and he realized that he'd been wrong—she wasn't crying at all. In fact, she was laughing! She was laughing so hard, she had tears rolling down her face, but they were tears of mirth, and at his expense, apparently. Huh. How did he feel about that?

He wasn't sure.

CHAPTER EIGHT

"Wait, you let the Stutzmans believe you and Lizzie Miller are dating? Without even asking her first? Ach, John, what were you thinking?"

John took off his straw hat and let his head fall back, closing his eyes. He and his best friend, Noah Lapp, were hauling a load of lumber to his father's shop, and John had confessed his indiscretion to Noah on the way back to the shop.

"I wasn't thinking. Tucker and Isaiah came outside to help unload the bench we finished for them, and Isaiah got a little. . .flirty. So before I realized what I was doing, I just blurted out that we wanted to go for a buggy ride, and she came along with me to deliver the furniture. She didn't bat an eye, which impressed me since I was basically panicking inside. But I've noticed she's pretty cool in a crisis."

Noah, who was driving the wagon, turned and looked at John. "Really? When did you have the chance to do that?"

"Oh, I was at the grand opening of her bakery last week. My sister works there, so I went to support them. And eat pastries." He grinned at his friend.

"Ach, ja, I heard about someone tossing a rock through her window. Crazy!"

"It was a brick, and yes, crazy. But that wasn't the only thing. Earlier, a very strange man got in her face and said nasty things about her business. And she stayed calm."

"Wow. I really don't know her well. I mean, I see her at church, but that's it. I've never really talked to her."

John shrugged. "I've always liked her. She's a gut friend to my sister, and that's gut enough for me."

Noah cast him a wicked grin. "You've always liked her, huh? Interesting."

"Now, Noah, don't you start too!"

Noah laughed at John's discomfort. "So, you didn't finish telling me what happened after you stumbled and put your foot in your mouth."

"We were driving, and she sort of casually mentioned that the Stutzmans now think we're dating. I apologized, and she said something about how her maem was going to start planning a wedding, and how she isn't ready to settle down because her business is more important, or something like that. Like she was trying to let me down easy, Noah!" John heaved an embarrassed sigh and pulled at the collar of his shirt. Then he sheepishly admitted, "And that's when I lost my mind."

"Oh ja? What happened?"

John squirmed a bit on the hard bench seat, hating to admit that he'd lost his cool. "I got a little salty and said it wasn't as if dating me would be the worst thing in the world. Like I was doing a complete about-face and trying to convince her she should want to date me!"

"Ach, John!"

"That's not the worst of it. Then she put her face in her hands, and I thought she was crying so I pulled over to apologize again! But Noah, she wasn't crying. She was laughing! Laughing at me!"

Noah chuckled a little and shook his head. "It is a pretty funny situation, you have to admit."

"I hope her father thinks so when he hears that his daughter and I are supposedly dating, and I didn't even ask his permission."

"I mean, she's twenty-five, right? And you're even older. You know, maybe this isn't a bad thing. It's time you got married. Settle down. Live above the bakery. Grow a big belly from all that delicious baking your *fraa* will feed you!"

"Very funny. This just proves she was right. All people need is to hear we might be dating, and they start growing celery."

Noah turned the wagon carefully off the road onto the gravel drive leading to John's father's furniture shop. His eyes grew round as he saw something over by the shop that John didn't see. "Well, looks like you're not going to have to wait long to find out how her father feels about it."

John looked curiously at his friend. "What? Why's that?"

Noah pointed with his chin. "Because there he is, talking to your dat now."

He pulled the wagon up to the shop and drew back on the reins. "Whoa, Mike. Gut boy. Thanks for letting me drive, John. I really like the feel of him. Maybe I need a Percheron. I'll think about it."

John wasn't listening. He couldn't believe his eyes. Lizzie's father was there, all right, and when he spotted John in the wagon, he said something to John's father, then turned and started walking toward the wagon, a serious expression on his face.

Noah grinned at John. "I'm glad I'm not you!" He jumped down, nodded at Lizzie's dad, and headed to the back to start unloading lumber.

John sent up a silent prayer that he wasn't in very hot water and jumped down to face Lizzie's father.

John stood up straight and stuck out his hand, which Henry shook. He spoke through a suddenly dry mouth. "Afternoon, Henry. Did you need to talk to me?"

"Ja, ja, I heard you've been keeping an eye on the girls, driving them home from work in the evenings. I appreciate that, what with this nonsense going on. Denki, John. I know Jane is your sister, but you don't owe anything to Eliza or my Lizzie."

John's eyebrows flew upward, and he struggled to find his footing. Henry wasn't there to call him out for inappropriate behavior? He was there to thank him? "It's no problem, Henry. Was that what you came here for today? To tell me that? Because there was no need."

Henry shook his head. "Nee, I had another matter to discuss, but first I wanted to thank you for your help."

"Another matter?" Suddenly it was too much for John. He cracked under pressure. "Henry, I imagine you've heard the rumor that I asked Lizzie to date me without speaking to you first. It was an accident. I would never disrespect you that way."

Henry blinked. "You accidentally asked my daughter to date you?" John knew he was making a mess of things. He held up both hands in a placating gesture. "Nee, nee. I meant to say I didn't ask her to date me. I just let the Stutzmans think we were dating, to explain why we were taking a buggy ride together yesterday."

Henry crossed his arms over his chest. "You took my daughter for a buggy ride but didn't intend to court her? You just wanted other men to think you were?"

Feeling desperate, John threw up a quick prayer for wisdom and the right words to explain what had happened. "Let me start over."

"I think that's a gut idea."

"Okay. Here's what happened." John explained the situation with the Stutzmans and Lizzie's bakery building. He explained how he had to come up with a reason for her to be with him delivering furniture, and the conclusion the Stutzmans had reached. When he'd finished, Henry nodded his understanding.

"I understand. So, to be clear, you're not interested in dating my daughter?"

John started to answer in the negative, but he stopped and frowned as he realized he wasn't sure of the answer to the question. He tugged on the collar of his shirt again while considering his reply. "Um. . ."

Henry's mouth turned up at the corner. "It's a simple question, son."

"Well, I would have thought so last week. But this week, I'm not sure."

Henry smiled fully and slapped John on the back. "If you decide in favor of courting Lizzie, I would appreciate you coming to me first. Ja?"

John smiled sheepishly. "Denki for not being angry about all this. It was just a ridiculous misunderstanding, because we were trying to find a clue to what happened."

At that, Henry frowned again. "As to that, don't you think it would be wise to leave the seeking of clues to the police?"

John bit his lip and nodded. "You're right."

"Okay then. Well, it was nice seeing you, John."

"I'm sorry you had to come all the way here to talk to me about this, Henry."

Henry looked surprised. "What? Oh, that's not why I came here. I didn't know anything about this. I came to commission a piece of furniture from your dat for my Agnes' birthday. She's been wanting a pie safe for all the years I've known her, and it's high time she got one, don't you think?"

John nodded mutely, and Henry waved as he strode to his buggy.

"I just made a fool out of myself for nothing," he muttered. Shaking his head, he determined not to get dragged into any more detective work by Elizabeth Miller. Although in light of his newfound interest in her—and he admitted to himself he was interested in the independent, headstrong woman—it might be hard to say no to her.

"I'll just have to do my best, while I figure out whether she and I could get along well enough to have a future together. And since I know she's serious about keeping her bakery, I need to consider whether I want to marry a businesswoman and live above a business in town. Guess I've got some thinking, and praying, to do."

That evening as Lizzie and Jane were winding down for the day, John came quietly through the front door and took a seat out of the way. There were a few diehards still pecking away at their laptop computers and one teenaged Englisch couple sitting with their heads close together, obviously exchanging important secrets, but for the most part the place had cleared out.

John picked up that week's edition of *The Budget*, which he hadn't seen yet, and settled into the cushions of the comfy couch. He was partway through a story about what was happening in a town in Colorado when Lizzie spoke from behind him, startling him.

"Evening, John! We're about done here. Are you hungry? We've got a couple sandwiches left over from lunch, and they won't make it until Monday."

"I can always eat."

Lizzie laughed a bit. "Well, you're a big guy. It takes fuel to keep you going strong." She handed him a plate with three egg salad sandwiches on her own croissants, while mentally imagining slapping herself on the forehead, wondering whether calling him a big guy sounded weird. She shrugged. Oh well. It wasn't as if he'd just met her. She'd known John Bontrager all her life. If he thought she was weird, it was way too late to hide it now!

But he didn't appear to notice. He took the plate with a light in his eye and smiled up at her. "Wow, denki, Lizzie. These look appenditlich."

She handed him a big glass of milk. "I figured you'd need to wash them down."

He nodded, his mouth already full of sandwich, and took the glass from her. Their fingers brushed briefly, and Lizzie felt an odd zing that made it all the way to her toes. Whoa! What was that? She chanced a peek at John, but he didn't seem to have noticed anything, so she decided to pretend she hadn't either. "Well, I need to do a few last-minute things, and then Jane and I will be ready to go. It's Eliza's day off, so just the two of us tonight."

She turned and hurried back to the kitchen. She looked at Jane, who was getting ready to haul the garbage bags out back to the dumpster, and bit her lip, wondering whether she could tell Jane about what she'd felt. "Nee, Jane is John's sister. That would definitely be weird!"

She finished her end-of-day chores and was about to go see what was keeping Jane out back when the door to the kitchen opened and John pushed through, carrying his dirty dishes. "Oh, denki," Lizzie said, hurrying forward to take the plate and glass from him. "You didn't have to do that."

"What, was I going to leave them out there for you to deal with?" He swung them up out of her reach when she would have taken them. "I'm capable of washing a plate and a glass."

She watched as he did just that, drying them and returning them to their proper cabinets—after a brief search.

"Denki."

"It's nothing." He looked around. "Where's my sister?"

"I was about to go see what's keeping her. She took out the trash a few minutes ago and hasn't come back inside." Lizzie hurried to the back door and pushed it open, peering out into the alley behind the row of businesses. She looked down toward the dumpster, but didn't see Jane.

"That's odd. Where would she have gone?"

"What do you mean? Isn't she there?" John sounded alarmed, and he shouldered past Lizzie to examine the alleyway. He looked both ways, then turned to Lizzie. "Where could she have gone?"

Lizzie stepped outside and peered in both directions, starting to grow uneasy. "She shouldn't have gone anywhere! Just to the dumpster and right back inside."

John strode down to the dumpster, and around it. "She's not here!" He trotted to the end of the alley and looked both ways up and down the street. Then he turned and jogged back to Lizzie. "Lizzie, I'm worried. I'm going to go look in the other direction."

"I'll go back inside in case we missed her. Maybe she went upstairs for something."

John nodded and headed the other direction in the alley, and Lizzie hurried back inside, looking around the kitchen as if Jane would just materialize, then out into the restaurant. "Jane? Jane! Where are you?"

When there was no answer, she hurried to the door that led upstairs and took the steps as fast as she could to search their living space. She even went up to the third floor and looked around. No Jane.

Back downstairs, John had returned. He'd taken off his straw hat and was running one hand through his hair, a nervous habit. "Lizzie! I went all the way to the end of the alley. No sign of her anywhere."

"I went all through the building. She's not inside. What do we do now?"

He stood and stared at her, but she didn't think he was actually looking at her—more like *through* her. Then he blinked and made eye contact. "Is there any chance she had other plans? Maybe she caught a ride at the end of the alley?"

Lizzie glanced over at their pegboard, and she shook her head, pointing at it. "Nee, look, her wrap and bonnet are still here. And there's her bag, hanging under the wrap. She wouldn't go anywhere without those. And besides, she didn't say anything to me about having other plans. We talked about what we were making for supper tonight when we got home. Eliza is trying a new recipe for chocolate cake." She put a hand up and covered her mouth, suddenly afraid. "What if something has happened to her?" Tears flooded Lizzie's eyes at the very thought, and John awkwardly patted her on the shoulder.

"Okay, okay, we're not going to panic. Maybe she suddenly got ill, or...something."

Before they could decide what to do next, the back door opened and Jane came inside, looking a bit disheveled, but otherwise just fine.

"Jane! Where have you been?" John stormed over to his sister. "You had us worried sick!"

Jane looked from her angry brother to her teary friend, and an expression of dismay crossed her pretty features. "Oh, I'm so sorry! I didn't think!"

"Didn't think?" John ran both hands through his hair, making it stand up in crazy disarray. "What were you even doing? We thought you were just taking the trash out."

Lizzie walked over and placed a calming hand on each of her friends' arms. "Okay, Jane is fine. Eliza will be expecting us, and it would be ironic if we made her worry because we were running late. So let's close up and head over there. We can talk on the way."

The siblings looked at each other, both still noticeably upset. But first Jane nodded, and then John did.

"Gut!" Lizzie pulled Jane clear of the back door, shut it, and locked it. "I'm ready. Let's go."

They grabbed their things and walked through the shop, turning out lights and making sure everything was secure. John reached the front door first and opened it for his sister and Lizzie. Jane sailed through without a look for her brother, but Lizzie paused, and again lay a hand on John's arm. She looked up at him and smiled. "Please don't yell at Jane. You know how stubborn she can be. We'll find out faster if we stay calm, ja?"

He frowned but nodded tersely. She squinted at him, trying to figure out if he meant it, then decided to leave well enough alone. "Let's go. I'm starved."

"What's for dinner? I could eat again."

"Third supper?" Lizzie laughed. "Why not? We'll stuff your mouth, and then you won't be able to talk."

John snorted out a laugh, and then Jane, who had obviously been trying to hold on to her mad, snorted too. "Oh, very ladylike!" her brother said, and Lizzie laughed at their silliness. Soon they were all laughing, and the tension was broken.

As they pulled up into the parking lot at Eliza's, Lizzie turned to Jane. "Nobody is angry. We were worried. Where on earth were you?"

Jane blushed. "Well, looking back it was pretty stupid. I saw a kitten, and I followed it down the alley to the street."

John frowned. "But I went to both ends of the alley and looked down both streets. I couldn't see you anywhere."

They climbed the steps to the porch, and Jane pulled out a key Eliza had given her and unlocked the front door. "Well, the kitten ran inside the open doorway of a business down the street. I followed it inside."

"You did? Which business?" John asked as they trooped upstairs to Eliza's apartment.

"The saddlery. You know, the one owned by Frank Gerber?"

John nodded. "Ja, I know it. In fact, he's made me tack for my buggy. He does gut work. The kitten was his?"

Jane frowned. "I'm not sure. It disappeared in the store, and I was going to just say hello and tell Mr. Gerber what I was doing, when I saw he was with a customer. It was Samuel Mast." She darted a look in Lizzie's direction, and Lizzie suppressed a smile. She knew that Jane had nursed a huge crush on the buggy maker for years.

"Ach, ja. Samuel is a gut man," John said, clueless to his sister's feelings. "I suppose he was ordering some fittings for a buggy he's making."

Jane shrugged. "I couldn't say. But when he saw me, he asked about the store and whether we had any idea who had thrown the brick or broken in. That started a conversation, and then I suddenly realized I'd been gone maybe fifteen minutes, so I hurried back. Again, I'm sorry I didn't think about worrying you both."

Lizzie smiled as they went into the kitchen, where they were greeted by delicious scents and Eliza's cheerful hello. "So, did you talk to Samuel much?"

Jane bit her lip and frowned at Lizzie. "Nee. He just asked about you and your shop, and then he said he hoped the police caught the vandal soon."

"He asked about Lizzie?" John frowned.

"He was just making small talk while he waited for his order." Jane shrugged, then bent down to pick up her cat, Secret, and snuggle the brown tabby beneath her chin. "It's the talk of the town, after all. It's not as if he was interested in talking to me in particular. I'm going to go wash up. Be right back." She hurried from the room, and Lizzie glared at John.

"Are you clueless?"

He held up both hands. "What did I do now?"

She sighed and shook her head, exchanging glances with Eliza.

"John, your sister has a big crush on Sam Mast. She has for years," Eliza explained as she started carrying food to the table.

"No she doesn't," John said, sounding very sure of himself. "I'd know if she did."

Lizzie and Eliza exchanged looks again, and both giggled. Lizzie bent and picked up Little Mouse, who was mewing piteously for attention.

"You think so?" Lizzie asked. John's face darkened, and Lizzie decided it was time to stop teasing. "John, everyone knows about this, except, apparently, you."

"And Sam," Eliza added.

"Right, he's clueless too," Lizzie said with a shake of her head.

Jane reentered the room and looked around. "Are you discussing my business?"

"Maybe a tiny bit, but only because we all love you," Lizzie said, going over and hugging her friend.

"Well, I remembered something else Sam said, but I'm not sure I want to tell such a bunch of gossips." Jane flounced over to a chair and sat down, petting her cat and ignoring them.

The others took their seats, and Jane and Lizzie set their cats, who had already been fed by Eliza, on the floor. Then they all bowed their heads for the silent prayer. Afterward, they started passing the food around.

"We're not really gossips, you know, Jane," Eliza pointed out cheerfully, handing her the Chow Chow. "We were just sharing information about a friend we all care about. That isn't malicious. Doesn't something have to be malicious to count as gossip?"

Jane waved a hand. "Semantics." She dished up some mashed potatoes and handed the bowl to John, who took it with a smile of appreciation.

"What a gut meal, Eliza! Denki!" John accepted the platter of pot roast and scooped a generous portion onto his plate.

Lizzie's eyebrows rose in disbelief as he added green bean casserole. "John, this is your third meal in, what, two hours? Where are you going to put it?"

"Hey, you said that it takes a lot of fuel to keep me going." He gave her a wicked grin. "You weren't wrong!"

They all laughed, and again the tension was broken. Lizzie glanced at Jane, wondering whether it would be a good idea to press her for information on what Sam Mast had said. Before she could decide, Eliza broke into the conversation, pointing a fork at Jane.

"So, Jane, what were you saying about Sam?"

Jane looked confused for a moment, and then she nodded, a look of sudden excitement on her face. She put her fork down and placed both hands flat on the table, leaning forward. "He told me something very interesting about your bakery building, Lizzie!"

Lizzie exchanged looks with John and Eliza. "He did? What did he say?"

"Did you know your building used to be an inn?" Jane asked, looking at each of them in turn. When Lizzie shook her head no, Jane smiled. "I didn't think so! I'd never heard that!"

"Okay," John said. "That's interesting, but what does it have to do with anything?"

Jane sat back, a smug look on her face. "It was an inn for maybe a hundred years! According to Mr. Gerber, the Petersheims were only the second owners since it closed less than fifty years ago!"

"That's interesting, but is it really relevant?" John asked, forking mashed potatoes into his mouth.

"Wait, it gets better. It turns out several famous people stayed there over the years," Jane said.

"So?" John asked.

Jane deflated a bit. "I thought it was interesting."

Eliza wiggled her fingers in front of her face. "Did he say the place is haunted by one of them? That would be interesting."

John rolled his eyes. "We don't believe in ghosts, remember?"

She shrugged. "Ja, but it's fun to pretend."

"Thanks all the same, but I'd rather not think of the souls of departed hotel guests wandering the halls of my home," Lizzie said with a shudder.

"It's fun," Eliza insisted. "I love reading ghost stories. Chilling!"

"Ghost stories aside, what else did Sam say?" Lizzie asked, hoping to turn the conversation away from spooky things involving her place of residence. Even though the Amish didn't believe in ghosts as a rule, it could be easy to forget that when one was alone in a strange place listening to noises of unknown origin.

"Oh, he thought he remembered hearing something once about someone famous staying there and doing something that made the inn famous. But he couldn't remember exactly what."

Jane resumed eating, and the others stared at her in disbelief. "All that lead-up, and that's all you have?" Lizzie asked. "Maybe someone famous did something there sometime, but he doesn't remember who or what?"

Jane looked up and met all their gazes. She hurriedly swallowed the bite of pork roast and blotted her mouth with a napkin. "Sorry! I was kind of distracted. But maybe it'll help you think of some new questions to ask about the place."

"Speaking of questions, I've got to remember to call the Petersheims!" Lizzie knocked her fist against her forehead.

"I thought we agreed we're done asking questions, right?" John said, giving Lizzie a significant look.

Feeling heat crawl up her face, Lizzie gulped. "Oh ja, maybe John is right. Maybe we shouldn't get involved. After all, we're supposed to remain separate, not go poking around into Englisch police business."

Eliza looked from John to Lizzie, a suspicious frown creasing her brow. "Okay, you two, what's going on here?"

"Nothing?" Lizzie said, hoping Eliza would drop the matter. But there was small chance of that.

"Nothing? I think it's definitely something," Eliza said, pointing her fork at Lizzie. "Don't you, Jane?"

Jane nodded. "Oh ja. Sounds like something to me."

Lizzie sighed. "Okay, fine." She explained what had happened at the furniture store, with the result that there was probably going to be a rumor circulating in the community that she and John were dating.

Jane threw back her head and laughed. Eliza smiled and cut another piece of meat, which she ate with a considering expression on her face.

John glared at his sister. "What's so funny, Jane?"

"Oh, John, it's just so gut! You, the original hard-to-get man, caught in the wily net of our very own too-busy-to-date woman! You're right—this is too good for people to ignore, true or false. It's going to be hot news on the Amish grapevine."

Lizzie sighed. "What's wrong with being focused on my business right now? I'm only twenty-five. I have plenty of time to marry."

"Said nobody's Amish mother ever," Eliza muttered. Lizzie smiled at her friend.

Jane picked up another roll, broke it precisely in half, picked up a butter knife, and carefully spread butter on it in a smooth wave. "John's the sensitive type," she said before biting into the roll.

His mouth dropped open. "I am not!"

Jane shrugged. "Why else would you care whether people think you and Lizzie are dating? It's nobody's business."

"Really, I'm not sensitive. I don't know why I acted that way. You're right, Lizzie, we never have thought of each other that way. Before."

Lizzie paused with a forkful of potatoes halfway to her mouth. "Before? What does that mean?"

He looked panicked. "Did I say before? I meant, you know, we didn't think that way before, so why would we now?"

Her eyes narrowed, Lizzie nodded and ate the potatoes.

"This is more interesting than Englisch television," Eliza commented.

"When did you watch television?" Jane asked curiously.

"When I moved here, Reuben had one. We watched a couple shows. They were full of drama. I liked them."

The conversation turned to other things, to Lizzie's relief. But she snuck a few glances at John, who was studiously not looking her way, and wondered what he'd really meant by that word. *Before*. Because now that he'd planted the idea in her head, she was starting to wonder about him in a whole new way.

And she wasn't sure she liked that.

CHAPTER NINE

The next morning, after the breakfast rush, Lizzie was washing up in the kitchen. She was alone, as it was Jane's day off and Eliza had run to the post office.

She found herself returning over and over to the dinner table conversation of the night before, and to John's cryptic statement.

"What did he mean by *before*? Ach! I can't stop thinking about that."

Lizzie and Jane had been best friends since their school days, and John had always been mostly in the background.

She'd been comfortable with things just as they were—as they'd always been. "So why did he have to throw a wrench in the works?" she fumed as she dried a dish and slammed it into the cabinet.

"Whoa, save the pieces!"

At the sound of her dear friend's voice, she spun around, a grin splitting her face. "Lydia! Oh, you're just the person I needed to see! Come, sit, I'll get you kaffi and cookies."

She hurried to her friend and guided her to a chair at the table in what Lizzie thought of as the employee lunch area—basically, a small round table and four old chairs.

"I didn't come to get free food, but if you insist, dear, I'll accept, just to be polite."

"Oh ja, I insist!" Lizzie set a mug of coffee before her friend and then put out cream and sugar—plenty of sugar—so Lydia could doctor it up the way she liked it, light and sweet. "But it's not free. I need your ear, so think of the food as payment for your wise counsel."

Lydia chuckled. "You could have had my ear for nothing, child, but I am a bit peckish, so I'll just indulge while you talk to me."

Lizzie sat down and took a hot, comforting sip of her own coffee.

"Go ahead and say your piece, child. I'm listening," Lydia prodded gently.

Lizzie nodded and took a deep breath, unsure of where to begin. "Well, you know Jane Bontrager and I have been close friends since we were kinner, right?"

Lydia nodded. "Closest two girls I've ever known."

Lizzie continued, "And then there's Jane's bruder, John."

Lydia looked up alertly. "A handsome boy. And another gut friend of yours, I think."

"Ja, he is. Not as close as Jane, of course. But he's always been there, sort of in the background, you know?"

Lydia nodded and selected a second cookie. "Go on."

Lizzie sighed. "Well, just recently, things have gotten a bit. . . complicated, you might say. . .between John and me."

The elderly woman chuckled. "Complicated, hmm? Sounds promising. Go on."

Restless, Lizzie stood and walked over to the door looking into the alley. She drew back the ancient curtain and peered outside, then turned and walked back to the table. "It's just that in the last week or so, I've noticed that he's grown quite tall and handsome." She stared off into the distance, absently taking another cookie and nibbling it around the edges in a circle. "I don't know how I didn't notice that happening. And suddenly he's talking to me more than he used to."

She paused and looked at Lydia, who just nodded. "Mm-hmm. Go on."

Lizzie blew a puff of air from her cheeks. "He seems to be noticing me more too. He helped me out recently with the, well, the mystery I guess you'd say, of who threw a brick into my store window and broke into my place last week." She cleared her throat. "And we took a ride together."

"Better and better. Go on."

"It wasn't supposed to mean anything. When we went to ask the Stutzmans a couple questions about their parents trying to buy my building before I did, they wanted to know what I was doing with John in his wagon. So he kind of accidentally implied without actually saying it that we were riding out together, and just stopped there first to deliver a bench." She stopped and looked expectantly at her friend.

"He accidentally implied that, did he?"

Lizzie nodded. "Accidentally. I'm certain of it, because he wouldn't actually want to ride out with me, would he?"

Lydia sat back, put her hands on her knees, and grinned at her young friend. "That's the million-dollar question, isn't it?"

"Lydia! If he was interested in me, he would have said something before. He's no green kid. He's at least twenty-eight!"

"So a mature man, and sure of himself."

"Exactly!" Lizzie gave her friend a pleased nod. "So? What do you think?"

Lydia tipped her head down to regard Lizzie over her half-moon reading glasses. "I think you need to explore this question yourself and not ask other people to somehow divine John's intentions. If you're going to ask anyone, ask John."

Lizzie sighed. "Ach, I know! But you've been around and I figured you'd have some insight."

"As it happens, I do."

Lizzie perked up, and Lydia raised a hand. "Not about your romantic life. About the case!"

Lizzie blinked. "The case? The case! You have information? Something new?"

Lydia took another sip of her coffee and set the cup down on the table. She gave Lizzie a satisfied smile and picked up her bag. Reaching inside, she began to dig around inside the voluminous bag, which had a picture of a frazzled tabby cat on it and the saying "I'm fine. Everything is fine."

"Now where did I put that?" she muttered under her breath. Suddenly, her face lit up. "Ah! Here we go." She pulled out her hand.

"An old mug?" Lizzie cried in dismay. "Lydia, what can that possibly have to do with the case?"

Lydia set the mug down on the table and slowly turned it so Lizzie could see the image and words on the mug. Lizzie leaned forward. "The Willow Creek Historical Society. Um, okay?"

Lydia held up a finger and rotated the mug some more, bringing into view an image.

"Hey! That's my building!" She picked up the mug as Lydia sat back, a satisfied expression on her face.

"Read the caption."

"The Old Willow Creek Inn, founded in 1870 by Jeremiah and Elizabeth Parker. Designated an Ohio Historical Site in 1984."

She looked up at Lydia, puzzled. "Okay, that is interesting and fun, but I don't see what it has to do with anything. I knew this was a historical building and had even heard it was once an inn."

Lydia waved a hand at Lizzie. "Think about it. If this is a historical building, then there's history here. And where there's history, sometimes there's intrigue."

"Hmm. I hadn't thought of that. So, how would I find out what has happened here over the years? I never heard the Petersheims talking about anything." She closed her eyes in dismay. "I have got to remember to call Mrs. Petersheim!" She shook her head at her forgetfulness. "Of course, with a building this old, there are rumors of ghosts, but that doesn't bother me."

"No, but maybe there are other rumors, child. Rumors you haven't heard, but maybe someone else has. Someone who believes them and wants something rumored to be in this building."

Lizzie's mouth dropped open. "Huh! That's an interesting theory, Lydia!"

"What theory is that?" a deep voice asked from the doorway into the shop.

Lizzie sat up straight, unconsciously smoothing her apron over her teal dress. "John! I didn't hear you come in!" She held up the mug Lydia had brought and showed it to him. "Look at this. Lydia found it—um, where did you find this, Lydia?"

"Believe it or not, in the cabinet in my own kitchen. It was way up high on a top shelf I never use. I decided to clean that out, and there it was."

"Lydia, you didn't climb up a ladder or step stool, did you?" John frowned at his elderly friend. "That's a gut way to break your new hip!"

"Of course not. I'm not stupid." She took a sip of coffee and smiled at John over the rim. "I asked Jonas to climb up there for me. Such a gut boy!"

"I wonder when this was made? I haven't seen another one. You'd think there would be at least one here in this building, wouldn't you?" Lizzie asked, pondering the old mug.

Lydia shrugged. "Such things get broken in time. But I can think of two or three possible places you can get more information on the mug, and on the building."

"The Willow Creek Historical Museum!" John suggested.

"Are we going on a field trip?" Eliza asked as she pushed through the back door. "Sounds fun. I went there one rainy afternoon last summer when my sister was visiting from Lancaster and I needed somewhere to take her. It's got a surprising amount of stuff for a small museum."

She dropped a small pile of mail onto the table, and Lizzie picked it up and absently started sorting through it.

"We were just talking about places where we could learn about the history of this building," John said, going over to the cabinet and getting himself a mug, and then pouring a cup of coffee. He sat at the table and picked up a cookie, which he ate in two big bites. "Mmm, gut!"

"Denki," Lizzie said as she separated the mail into bills and junk.

"How about the newspaper office?" Eliza suggested, getting herself a glass of cold water from the sink and sitting in the last remaining chair at the table. "*The Budget* has been around for years, and so has the *Willow Creek Examiner*, which is right here in Willow Creek. We'd have to go to Sugarcreek to talk to the people at *The Budget*. Or we could call, I guess."

"Gut ideas, Eliza," Lizzie said, half listening. Suddenly she stopped sorting mail and peered intently at a long white envelope. "What have we here?" she murmured.

"What is it?" John asked, craning his neck to see the envelope. Lizzie turned it around and everyone looked at it. It was a regular, windowless number 10 envelope, the likes of which could be found in every office and many homes in America. On the front, printed in block letters, was Lizzie's name and address. There was no return address.

"I don't like the look of that," John commented. "Don't open it, Lizzie."

Lizzie laughed nervously. "Now we're starting to see danger where none probably exists."

Eliza plucked the envelope from Lizzie's hand and held it up to peer through it with the ceiling light behind it. "No, John's right, Lizzie. I watched enough crime dramas on television when I first got here to know this drill. You can't open it, because there could be a bomb inside! Or poison powder that you'd breathe when you tore it open. We need to call the police. This is a clue."

Everyone stared at her in disbelief. John gave a nervous chuckle. "Well, that's going a little farther than I was thinking, honestly. I just thought it looked a bit suspicious. Not like a bomb or anything."

Lydia stood. "Eliza is right, though. It looks like a clue, and there could be fingerprints."

When everyone stared at her, she smiled. "I sometimes watch television when I spend the winter down in Pinecraft. I like detective shows." She walked over to the wall phone and picked up the receiver, holding it out toward Lizzie. "You'd better get the po-po here."

"Po-po?" Lizzie choked on a cookie crumb. John thumped her on the back.

Eliza smiled smugly. "It's Englisch slang for *police*." She turned to Lydia. "I like detective shows too. And detective books. I have a gut collection, if you want to borrow any."

"Denki, child. I just might. Now, let's make that call. I have other places to go, you know."

———————— ⚓ ————————

"You did the right thing, calling us," Officer Anderson said, holding the envelope up to the light on the kitchen ceiling. "Hmm. Can't see anything, but that proves nothing."

She tucked the envelope into a brown paper bag that went into her messenger bag. She looked around apprehensively, and John, who was standing next to Elizabeth, recalled that she had a mouse phobia.

"I haven't seen any mice here, Officer," he said reassuringly, and Anderson shot him a smile.

"Ah, of course not. Just checking. Place looks good. How's business?"

"Actually, pretty good, considering. Denki," Lizzie said.

"I expect business may have gotten a boost from all the excitement," Lydia piped in from her seat at the kitchen table. "You know how people are. Amish or Englisch, everyone wants the scoop!"

Officer Jakes chuckled. "That's God's honest truth, ma'am."

"So, Officers, have you had any luck identifying the man in the photo I gave you?" Lizzie asked. John thought he detected a tiny bit of impatience in her voice, and he realized this entire situation must be very stressful for her. Instead of worrying about running her brand-new business, she had to worry about what was going to happen next to sabotage it.

Officer Jakes shook his head. "We've been asking around, but so far nobody recognizes him."

"Can't you just input his photo into your computer and his name will pop out?" Lydia asked. John, turning to look at the officers, caught Anderson rolling her eyes a bit at Jakes.

"Are you a fan of detective books, ma'am?" she asked.

Lydia grinned and nodded sheepishly. "Well, ja, a bit."

Jakes smiled. "We understand. All the police shows and detective books make it sound so easy. But the truth is, there is no magic computer program. We tried that, of course, but came up blank. So now it's just a matter of beating the pavement, knocking on doors, and asking a lot of people if they've seen him. We've got a couple of people who saw him here but don't know who he is."

Lizzie slumped a bit, and John felt sympathy for her plight. "Well, denki for working hard to solve this, Officers," he said.

Lizzie worked up a smile and nodded. "Ja, denki. And please, let me know what's in the envelope right away, okay?"

"Of course," Anderson said. "Any fingerprints on the outside will be obliterated by the US Postal Service and you all, but inside might be a different story, since you were smart and didn't open it. Good job, there!"

"We were leery of letter bombs and poison powder," Lydia piped up.

Jakes kept a very straight face as he nodded at her. "Wise, ma'am. Always wise to be cautious."

"It's not my first rodeo," Lydia said, and John wondered what that meant and where she'd picked it up.

"No, ma'am, obviously not," Anderson said, her lips quirking a bit as if holding back a smile.

"Hmmm," Lydia said, pushing to her feet. "Well, I have to go. Abram has a dentist appointment. Sore tooth. If I don't pry him out of his house, he'll 'forget' to go."

"Oh! That reminds me," Lizzie said, getting up to walk the older woman to the front door. "I saw Zeke Yoder, the young man who is dating his granddaughter from Lancaster, Evelyn? He fixed my front window. He mentioned that Evelyn will be visiting soon."

Lydia smiled. "Ja, the girl has settled down. She was a challenge a couple years ago—boy crazy. But I think all she needed was time to grow up. And admittedly, attention from a good bu hasn't hurt. I'll remind Abram she's coming, just in case it's slipped his mind."

Lizzie held the door for her and then turned back into the bakery. Officers Jakes and Anderson were approaching from the direction of the kitchen.

Anderson stopped and nodded at Lizzie. "Well, we'd better be getting back to the station and look into this letter you got. We'll be in touch." She touched her cap and headed out the door, Officer Jakes behind her.

Glancing at the front, she saw a line forming at the counter and Eliza hustling to meet customers' needs.

"I've left Eliza on her own long enough." Lizzie heaved a tired sigh. "Time for me to get back to work."

CHAPTER TEN

"Here it is." Lizzie stopped on the sidewalk in front of what looked like a typical house built sometime in the early part of the last century. A sign out front read WILLOW CREEK HISTORICAL MUSEUM, along with the hours and a little note saying it was owned and operated by the Willow Creek Historical Society.

"It's open," John said. "Let's go inside. Do you have the mug?"

"Right here." She held up a little brown shopping bag. "I wrapped it so it wouldn't get broken." She started up the path, John right behind her.

At the front door, she hesitated. "Do we just walk right inside?"

He reached past her and tried the handle. It opened, and Lizzie felt a bit foolish. "Ah, denki."

"No problem." He grinned at her, and she shook her head and preceded him into the building. In the front hall there were several pieces of antique furniture. On a lovely maple sideboard was a guest book.

John admired the furniture. "Wow, this stuff is beautiful. Look at the workmanship in this table." He ran an appreciative hand over the beautifully maintained wood. "Ach, that's lovely."

"I see you appreciate fine craftsmanship, young man," a creaky voice said from behind them. John and Lizzie both turned toward the voice and beheld a tiny, wizened old man with mere wisps of white hair decorating his pink scalp. He really looked like an ancient baby, and Lizzie felt a completely inappropriate mirth bubbling up inside her. She squelched it and offered him a smile.

"Good afternoon. I'm Lizzie Miller, and this is John Bontrager." John offered his hand, and the elderly man leaned on a cane and stepped forward to shake it. "I do appreciate fine craftsmanship. I'm a carpenter and furniture maker by trade."

"Ah! Well, that explains it. I've noted that Amish carpenters and furniture makers are among the finest these days, with a real attention to detail and love of the craft. It is most gratifying."

John hazarded a glance at Lizzie, who gave a tiny shrug. "Well, thank you, Mr. . . . I'm sorry, I didn't catch your name."

"Of course! Sorry about that. I'm Mr. Rumpkin. I'm the head curator here at the Willow Creek Historical Museum. Are you here for a tour? Or is there something else you need help with?"

Lizzie peered curiously at the tiny man. Remembering why they had come, she held out the brown shopping bag. "Would you mind taking a look at this, Mr. Rumpkin? My business was recently vandalized and broken into, and I'm trying to figure out who would do that, and why."

"Ah! You must be the new proprietor of the bakery on Main Street. It's a pleasure to meet you!" He accepted the bag and reached inside. He spoke as he unwrapped the mug. "I did hear about your misfortune the day of your grand opening. I'm sorry I wasn't there, by the way. I was here, as we were open. So please accept my heartfelt felicitations in regards to your new business venture. An Amish woman opening a French patisserie! Extraordinary!"

"A New Orleans–style patisserie," she pointed out as he carefully withdrew the mug and began curiously examining it.

"Aha! I recognize this, although it's been some time since I held one." He tipped his head back and studied the ceiling for a moment. "Right, we had five hundred of them made back in, hmm. . .1970, perhaps? I'd hazard a guess that not many survive to this day. They weren't meant to be heirlooms, after all."

"Why did you make them?" Lizzie asked eagerly, leaning forward and fiddling with her kapp strings nervously as she listened.

"Well, as a fundraiser, of course, for the 100th anniversary of the Willow Creek Inn, which was built in 1870." He smiled at her expectantly.

When she said nothing, he frowned. "As you're the new proprietor of the Willow Creek Inn, I'd expect you to be a bit more impressed with that."

"Oh! I am impressed Mr. Rumpkin. It's just that I haven't given much thought to the history of my building." Lizzie bit her lip. "I recently learned it had been an inn, but it's been a bakery for so long—longer than I've been alive."

Mr. Rumpkin nodded. "Of course! The purpose of the fundraiser back in 1970 was to keep the building from being demolished."

"Demolished!" John said, surprised. "But it's in great shape. Why would they do that?"

Mr. Rumpkin shrugged. "It was the seventies. Everything was about out-with-the-old and in-with-the-new! I recall hearing—although I was a young man at the time and not paying much attention, I'll admit—the village wanted to tear it down and put in a new police station. The location is good, very centrally located you know, and the building was vacant and deteriorating. Not many people cared."

"Well, something stopped that from happening," John commented, coming over and standing next to Mr. Rumpkin.

The old man smiled up at John. "It was a fierce old lady who stopped the whole thing in its tracks," he reminisced. "She saved the local community theater from being demolished in favor of a parking lot for City Hall too. Ha! That made a few people mad."

"Wow," Lizzie said. "One old lady? She must have been amazing."

The old man nodded, a fond smile on his face. "Oh, she was amazing all right. In fact, I admired her spunk so much that I married her! Of course, she wasn't old at the time. But my oh my, could she get people to do what she wanted. That's how I became so interested in local history. It was a love of hers, and I loved her, so it became a love of mine." He nodded again, a faraway expression clouding his faded blue eyes.

John and Lizzie looked at each other, and Lizzie could see that John shared her reluctance to break into the man's memories. After a few moments, the old gentleman seemed to come back to himself.

"Oh, forgive me. When I think about my Lisa, I can fall into memories and get carried downstream to a deep pool of reminiscing. Sometimes I forget I'm in the middle of a conversation. Now, where were we?"

"You were telling us about the mug, and how your wife saved the building that houses my bakery," Lizzie reminded him.

He nodded. "Of course, of course!" He handed the mug back to Lizzie and walked slowly through the lobby and into an adjoining room. Lizzie and John followed him, and he crossed the room and stopped before a large, lighted china cabinet filled with an eclectic assortment of knickknacks, tchotchkes, and odds and ends. He studied the contents for a moment, then grunted to himself. He opened the door and reached inside, then turned, and Lizzie saw that he was holding a mug just like the one Lydia had given her. "Here we go! This is the same mug, from our collection." He turned it over and peered at the bottom. "Yep, see, it's dated 1970. Just like yours. So these two mugs are from the original printing, the first year of the fundraiser to save the old inn."

He handed it to Lizzie, who looked at it, then handed it to John. "It's just the same," John remarked, handing it back to their host.

"Actually, your mug is in better shape. This one has a tiny chip on the handle." He shrugged. "Doesn't hurt a thing since nobody is going to be drinking out of it, right?" He replaced it in the cabinet and closed the door.

"Now then, I wish you could talk to my wife, but I'm afraid she's already gone to heaven to be with Jesus." His eyes again turned inward and misted up a bit. "It's been ten years already. Hard to believe."

He shook off his melancholy and turned and started walking. "Come with me. We can sit and talk."

They followed him into a kitchen, where he indicated they should take a seat at a table much like the one in the bakery kitchen. He then took a teapot from the counter and gathered three colorful Fiestaware mugs from a cabinet. "These are the newer ones. No lead in the paint." He poured tea into each, setting one in front of John and the other in front of Lizzie before taking a seat himself and lifting his own cup to his nose. He inhaled the vapor and sighed. "Mint tea. Always soothes me—and my stomach!"

"Oh, denki! We didn't expect you to serve us tea, Mr. Rumpkin," Lizzie said.

"Nonsense. I'd just set it to steep when you arrived. I enjoy company. In fact, have a cookie." He pushed a cookie jar shaped like a fat red tomato toward them. John smiled his thanks, opened the lid, and selected a gingersnap. He held the jar for Lizzie to see inside, and she chose a peanut butter cookie. She nibbled around the edges in a circle, and John ate his in two big bites.

Mr. Rumpkin started talking to them about his late wife, whom he had clearly adored. They let him talk, and eventually his talk turned to the old building. "Interesting place, that inn," he said, chasing his words with a sip of tea. "It was a well-known and popular place back in the day. We're talking the early 1900s, mind you, when things were good in this country, and in this town. Famous people stayed in that hotel, and they had big parties! There were movie stars, politicians, and writers. Lots of writers. I guess the peace of the town inspired them."

"Really? How interesting," Lizzie said.

"Yes, I've always thought so. Of course, it gets even more interesting. You see, there was the murder, and the mystery."

Lizzie's mouth dropped open. "A murder?" She squeaked. "In my bakery?"

"Oh my, yes. A nasty murder. And the mystery arose from the murder."

"Are you certain?" John asked, reaching for Lizzie's hand without even thinking, and grasping it to comfort her. She was clearly shocked by this news.

"Yes. It was the talk of the town. Of course, I wasn't even born yet back then, but there are a number of newspaper stories detailing the murder and the arrest."

"They caught the killer?" Lizzie asked. "Well, that's good, anyway."

"They did," Mr. Rumpkin nodded. "But they never solved the mystery, to this day."

Lizzie's lips parted, and she leaned forward. "What was the mystery?"

Mr. Rumpkin sat back and surveyed his audience, a small smile playing about his thin lips. "Why, what happened to the manuscript, of course. It was never found. It would be worth a fortune today." He leaned forward and looked intently into Lizzie's eyes. "There are folks who always believed it was hidden somewhere in that hotel. And that the ghost of E. W. Fingle walks the halls of that building still, guarding the secret of his lost manuscript."

Lizzie felt a tingle of fear skitter down her spine. Even though she didn't believe in ghosts, the old man told a compelling tale. She couldn't help but be affected.

John was more pragmatic. "So, if there were rumors back then that this E. W. Fingle— I'm assuming he was a famous author of the time?"

Mr. Rumpkin nodded, and John continued. "Okay, assuming this man was murdered and his book was never found, what makes you think the killer didn't take it himself?"

"Because the man who killed him, another famous author at that time, a Mr. Gregory K. Liptak, reportedly walked right into the lobby of the inn where E.W. Fingle and some cronies were enjoying an after-dinner chat one evening and confronted Fingle, claiming he'd sent a telegram ahead of time, saying he was on his way and was going to shoot Fingle dead for stealing his idea for the great American novel. People heard him tell Fingle he wasn't surprised that a man who would steal another author's ideas wouldn't be bothered believing he might have to pay for it someday, and that day had come. Then he supposedly pulled out a pistol and shot Fingle dead in front of numerous witnesses!"

Lizzie gasped. "No! That's terrible! The poor man!"

Mr. Rumpkin nodded. "Yes, unless you buy into the claim that he'd stolen another author's idea for a book he turned into a bestseller." He shrugged. "Anyway, after he shot Fingle, he threw down his gun and turned himself over to the hotel manager, who held him until the police came. He had no time to search for the manuscript."

John's eyes were wide, and he clasped Lizzie's hand in his own. "Did he say anything after he did it?"

Mr. Rumpkin sat back and sipped his tea. "The story goes that he started laughing. He supposedly laughed for a full minute, while his unfortunate victim bled on the floor. And then, he was reported to have wiped the tears from his eyes, and smiled a satisfied smile before saying, 'Well, he won't be stealing any more ideas from me, will he?'"

There was a long silence while John and Lizzie processed what they'd heard. Then John asked, "But what about the telegram?"

Mr. Rumpkin shrugged. "It was never found. If it existed at all, I'd say Fingle never received it."

In a small voice, Lizzie asked, "But, what about his manuscript? Wasn't it up in his room?"

Mr. Rumpkin smiled and shook his head. "Nope. Seems that during all the excitement, someone nipped up to his room and made off with it. Or. . .maybe he hid it somewhere." He watched John and Lizzie's reactions of disbelief and dismay, then shook his head. "I love telling you two this story. You're great listeners. Maybe because you're Amish and your heads aren't already filled up with nonsense from the television. It's all new to you! Does my old storyteller's heart good." He sipped more tea, then continued his tale.

"The police didn't care much about a missing manuscript, which wasn't even missed until Fingle's agent arrived to take possession of his things. Sadly, Fingle was estranged from his wife, who didn't care enough to show up. Anyway, the story goes that the first thing the agent did was look for the author's current work in progress, his manuscript."

He sipped his tea, and John shifted in his seat, impatient. "So, he didn't find it?"

"Nope. No sign of it. Well, that agent caused quite a stir. Said it was his property now, and whoever took it better give it back. But nobody came forward. And the killer didn't have it. Not unless he'd gone up to the room first, stolen the manuscript, and then stashed it somewhere before killing Fingle."

"Do you think that's what happened?" Lizzie breathed, totally caught up in the old tragedy.

"No way of knowing for certain," Rumpkin said. "Except that there were eyewitnesses who claimed to have ridden in on the train with Liptak and walked down from the station into the hotel lobby, looking for a room. They say he went straight there, with no stops." He shrugged. "So unless he had an accomplice working with him—and none was ever turned up—he didn't take it."

"Wow." Lizzie sat back. "That's quite a tale. And it's disturbing to know that someone was murdered in my building. Goodness! The lobby must be where my café space is." She shuddered. "I don't like thinking of someone violently dying there."

Lizzie wondered if there was any trace of that old death on the floor of the building. But the floors had been sanded and refinished. There would be no physical trace. But did murder leave a stain, as some of the mysteries she'd read claimed? She shuddered again. She hated to think of it! And it didn't matter. That building and all it represented was hers now, and she had to deal with it—good, bad, and ugly.

John didn't like seeing Lizzie looking so pensive. She was clearly very disturbed by the tale of old violence Mr. Rumpkin was feeding them.

He squeezed her hand, and she looked down. That's when they both realized they'd been holding hands for several minutes while they listened, captivated, to Mr. Rumpkin's tale. They pulled apart as if burned, and both folded their hands in their laps. John bit his lip. Would Lizzie be angry at him? Think him bold and inappropriate? He hadn't even realized he'd taken her hand! Closing his eyes a moment, he prayed for guidance. *Lord, please help me know how to act and what to say to make Lizzie feel better about all this. I know we had to learn these things, but I never expected anything like this! And I'm sure Lizzie didn't either.*

If Mr. Rumpkin noticed anything odd about their behavior, he didn't indicate it in any way. He just sipped his tea and thought his thoughts. Lizzie took a sip of her own tea, which John suspected had, like his, grown cold. She cleared her throat and asked, "Mr. Rumpkin, what do you think happened to that manuscript?"

The old man scratched his head and then peered at Lizzie. "Well, missy, that's the million-dollar question, isn't it? No telling. Some think it's hidden somewhere in that building to this day."

John didn't like that. It could explain why people were breaking in and trying to scare Lizzie off her own property. "Wouldn't it have been found when the building was renovated?" John asked.

"You'd think so, wouldn't you?" Mr. Rumpkin said. Then he shook his head. "Except that while there were extensive renovations done on the first floor, the second and third floors were in very good shape. There was no water damage, as the roof didn't leak—old slate. Good for decades. So the plaster walls were intact. Nobody had any reason to bust into them. And no old rumor was going to get my Lisa tearing out those historic walls, I'll tell you that!"

John and Lizzie looked at each other in dismay. "So, there might be people today who think there is a valuable lost manuscript from some long-dead author hidden inside my building?" Lizzie cried.

"Yep, that's a possibility," Mr. Rumpkin said.

John shook his head. "Nee, Lizzie, it doesn't make sense! If someone thought that, why didn't they try years ago? The Petersheims lived there for decades and ran it as a bakery. If someone was going to break in to search the place, wouldn't it have happened during all that time?"

Mr. Rumpkin shrugged. "You'd think so, wouldn't you?" He took another cookie and took a bite. "I expect it might have been the newspaper report a couple of years ago that stirred things back up."

Again, John and Lizzie stared at one another. "Newspaper report?" John finally asked. "What report?"

Mr. Rumpkin looked at him in surprise. "Why, the report in the *Willow Creek Examiner* about the 100th anniversary of the murder, and the subsequent mystery." He frowned, thinking, and said, "I guess it's more than a few years. Must be ten years ago now." He nodded. "Yep, that's right. Hard to believe it's been ten years, but 2014 was the hundredth anniversary of the murder. The editor, Philomena Jones, likes a good mystery. She interviewed me about the old story, and I was happy to talk to her. Brought in a lot of tourists to the town and to the museum here for a couple of years. Then it sort of died away again." He looked at them both. "Don't you remember the story? It was a pretty big deal."

Lizzie shook her head. "No, I read *The Budget*, mostly. Besides, I'd only have been fifteen at the time."

John nodded. "And I'd have been eighteen. And I don't read the *Examiner* much either. We don't pay much attention to the Englisch news." He shrugged. "So we didn't know anything about it. Sorry," he added when Mr. Rumpkin gave a disgusted snort and drank more tea.

"I'd think the Petersheims would have known about it," Mr. Rumpkin said. "And you worked there, didn't you, young lady?"

Lizzie thought a moment. "Yes, but not ten years ago."

Mr. Rumpkin looked surprised for a moment but then nodded. "Huh. Right. But if you talk to the Petersheims, they'll probably be able to tell you about some of the folks who visited the bakery, looking for information on the missing manuscript. There are some who figure the Petersheims must have found it and sold it privately. You know how rumors start."

"Then why would they come looking for it now?" John asked.

"Well, there are those who think it's never been found. That it's still in there somewhere. It's a big building, with lots of hiding places. Now, I'd love for you to come back another day, and I'll show you memorabilia about the restoration of your building. Give me a couple days to gather it together. But now I'm tired. An old man needs his rest." He pushed to his feet, and John and Lizzie reluctantly stood too.

Lizzie carried their cups to the sink and started washing them out.

"Well, thank you, young woman," their host said. "You both come back in a few days, and I'll have more to show you."

He showed them to the door, and they stepped onto the porch. Before they could leave, he reached out and grasped John's sleeve. "Young man, I wonder if you'd ever be interested in doing a little community service? I have a couple of pieces of furniture here that could use a little TLC from someone who knows furniture. I think you might be the man for the job. We don't have much of a budget, you understand."

John smiled. "Sure, I'd be happy to restore a piece for you now and then. I couldn't do many. Maybe one or two a year. I have to earn my living too."

Mr. Rumpkin grinned. "That's fine! That's just fine! I'll show you a beautiful table that needs work when you come back. I'll see you both in a couple days. Not Thursday. We're closed Thursday. Goodbye, now." He went back inside and closed the door, and they heard the lock snick shut.

They walked down the steps and slowly back to the bakery, each lost in their own thoughts. Outside the bakery, they stopped and faced each other.

"Wow, that was a lot," Lizzie said. "Do you think he's telling the truth?"

John pursed his lips, thinking about it, then nodded. "Ja, I think he believes it all. I think we should find the newspaper article from ten years ago and read up on this from another point of view. What do you think?"

Lizzie's eyes lit up at the suggestion. "John! That's a really gut idea! I wish we could go right now and talk to that editor, Philomena Jones. But I really have to get back to work. I've been gone more than an hour. How about tomorrow morning? We could go early when they open up." She bit her lip. "Can you find out what time?"

He nodded. "Sure! Probably eight or nine, but I'll look it up on our shop computer as soon as I get back."

"You've got a computer?"

"Ja. It's how my dat takes orders." He shrugged. "It's how we do business these days."

She nodded. "Maybe I should consider getting one. It would make ordering supplies a lot easier, that's for sure and certain. Well, denki for going with me. That was very interesting." She bit her lip, and he found himself staring at her mouth, thinking about how they'd unconsciously clasped hands while they listened to that harrowing tale. She peeked up at him, and he smiled down at her, thinking about how cute she looked in her eggplant-purple dress and black apron.

"I'll see you tomorrow, John. And please, remind me to call the Petersheims!"

He shook his head. "I'll see you tonight, when I come to get you after work, Lizzie. And I'll have the time the newspaper opens when I get here."

She nodded. "Ja, of course. Well, goodbye for now."

"See you later, Lizzie." He tipped his hat, turned, and walked jauntily down the street to where he'd parked his buggy. He snuck a look back at her and found her staring after him.

He blew out a puff of air. "Oh boy. This is all getting a lot more complicated than I expected! Well. Nothing to do about it right now except go back to work. Tomorrow will take care of tomorrow."

CHAPTER ELEVEN

"Good morning!" Lizzie gave John a cheerful grin as she climbed up onto the seat of his wagon in front of the bakery the next morning. She settled into her seat, and he set the wagon into motion. "Denki for picking me up."

He turned the corner just past the bakery. "I have to drop off these dining room chairs this morning, so I needed to use the wagon anyway." He shrugged. "Two birds, one stone."

"I know you said the newspaper opened at eight, but with the morning rush, I just couldn't leave before now."

"It's okay. If I deliver these chairs, my dat won't mind me taking a little side trip. It's just a couple miles to where we need to drop off the chairs. Do you mind? It's a bit out of our way."

"Of course not." She glanced behind them, but the chairs were covered with a blue tarp in case of rain. "Dining room chairs? Who are they for?"

"An Englisch couple we made a table for when they got married about five years ago. Their family has expanded, so they've decided they need more chairs now."

Lizzie laughed, and he smiled at her as they rumbled down the road. Suddenly, a thought struck her. "Wait a minute," she said, staring at a road sign at an intersection they'd just crossed. "We're on Old Inn Road?"

He looked at her, then turned his attention back to the road. "Ja, what about it?"

"I must have seen these signs for my entire life, but I never thought about it. Don't you see? Old Inn Road intersects with Main Street, at the corner by my bakery! It might have been named for my building in the first place!"

He rubbed his jaw, looking thoughtful. "Hmm. I wonder we didn't think of that before."

"Ja! Main Street is the principal route through town, but Old Inn Road heads out toward the state route that connects Willow Creek to bigger towns to the north and south. Maybe a hundred years ago, it was the more important road."

"Makes sense." He turned into the driveway of a one-story brick house with a lot of toys in the yard. A young woman in a kelly-green sleeveless blouse and jeans carrying a baby on her hip came to the door and waved. "Good morning, Mr. Bontrager! I'm so excited to see our new chairs!"

"Gut morning, Mrs. Barrows!" He set the brake on the wagon and jumped down. An older child in blue jeans and a yellow-and-green-striped T-shirt followed his mother out of the house and stood behind her, clinging to her leg. John shook her hand and introduced her to Lizzie, who smiled. "You have beautiful kinner, Mrs. Barrows."

"It's Cynthia. Thanks!" She smiled at the toddler, who gazed back at her from big brown eyes. She had an amazing head of curly black hair, like her maem's, and two little gold stud earrings in her tiny earlobes. Her deep brown skin was set off by the sweet little butternut sundress she wore. She gave Lizzie a shy smile.

Cynthia gently tousled her son's hair, which was cut very short. "They're a handful, but I wouldn't trade my life for the world. My Tony works hard so I can stay at home with them and we don't have to put them in day care." She nuzzled her daughter's neck, making the toddler giggle. "I'm the luckiest mom in the world."

John smiled at her. "I'll unload these chairs, and you can show me where you want them."

"Oh, thanks! I really appreciate that."

John soon had the four chairs inside the cozy little house, and they waved goodbye to Cynthia Barrows and her two adorable children. As John guided Mike back out to the road, Lizzie looked back. The children were playing in the driveway while their mother sat in a wooden Adirondack chair, sipping tea.

"What a blessed family," she murmured.

"What's that?" John asked as he turned the horse back onto the road back to town.

"Oh, I just said the Barrows family is blessed. Such lovely children, and she can stay home and care for them. She's not so different from most Amish wives and mothers I know."

"Ja, they're a nice family," he said. "Soon she'll be calling for us to make her a couple table leaves. We offered this time, but they're spreading out the expense, I think."

Lizzie just nodded, her eyes on the road. She was quiet, lost in her thoughts. Sometimes she yearned for what Mrs. Barrows had. The life of a stay-at-home mom, kinner of her own, a husband. But then she thought of how hard she'd worked to get her bakery, and she felt torn. Could she have both? Was that possible?

John glanced at her. "Why the frown?"

She bit her lip, then turned and looked at him. "John, we've been friends for a long time."

He looked at her as if he wasn't sure where she was going and nodded slowly. "Okay."

She huffed impatiently. "Well, I feel like I can talk to you. You're almost like my own brother."

He slanted her a sidelong look and said, "Not like a brother, I hope. I don't think of you as a sister, for sure and certain."

She gulped and decided to ignore that for the moment. "Okay, like a gut friend, then."

He nodded again, so she continued. "When I see a family like the Barrows, I get all confused. I really want my bakery, and I also want to get married eventually and have kinner. But I don't know if I can have both!"

He stared at her. "Well, the Petersheims did, didn't they?"

Her mouth dropped open, and then she closed it and nodded. "Well, ja, they did. But they were always there, together."

"Of course they weren't," he replied as they turned back onto Main Street. "At some point, they were young newlyweds just starting a business and family. Who knows what they did before buying the bakery? But in the end, they worked together and made their dream come true. Maybe you should ask Mrs. Petersheim how they did it."

She stared at him. "I could do that when I call her about the history of the inn."

He turned into the parking lot of the newspaper building and drove the wagon down to the end, where there was a hitching post. "Right! I'm supposed to remind you to call them. Consider yourself reminded." He hopped down and secured Mike while Lizzie climbed down from the wagon.

"Oh, denki!" she laughed. "Well, let's see what the folks here can tell us about this business."

The inside of the newspaper office was dated, and a bit dark. Knotty pine paneling covered the walls, and the floor was an odd pinkish-red color, with chips and divots here and there where decades of rolling desk chairs had taken their toll.

Rather than giving a gloomy impression, however, the office was cheery, with interesting odds and ends hanging on the walls that Lizzie could only assume were bits of newspaper memorabilia. She peered closely at something hanging on one wall while John rang the bell on the ancient glass display case, which was full of an assortment of office supplies for sale. Some of them looked as if they'd been there for a very long time.

"Coming!" came a call from the back of the shop, accessible through a swinging door which was pushed open at the moment. Through it Lizzie could see a fascinating machine she imagined was some kind of printer, possibly dating to the opening of the newspaper.

Before she could speculate more, a short, curvy woman with a golden-olive complexion and piles of curly brown hair hurried in from the back. Lizzie remembered the newspaper editor, Philomena Jones, from the ribbon cutting. "Sorry! Sorry! Our newspaper cat, Arthur, caught one of those awful water bugs and left it stranded on its back in the bathroom." She shuddered visibly.

She finally took a good look at them, and a smile blossomed on her pretty face. "Oh! You're the new bakery lady. Um, don't tell me. . . Elizabeth! Lizzie. Lizzie Miller." Looking pleased with herself, the woman put her hands on ample hips and nodded in satisfaction. "Rough start you've had! Intruders breaking in at night, rocks through the window. What next?"

Before Lizzie could comment, a plump orange-and-white cat hopped up on the counter and demanded attention from Lizzie and John. "Oh, you have such a pretty cat!" Lizzie exclaimed. "I love cats. I have one too, but she can't come into the restaurant. Or at least not when we're open and food is out."

"I think your friend, Lydia Coblentz, mentioned that she'd given you a little gray tabby a couple years ago?"

"You know Lydia?" Lizzie was surprised. Although considering Lydia, she shouldn't have been. Lydia knew everyone and everything that happened in Willow Creek.

"Oh, sure. I've done stories on her quilts. It was such a shame when her home burned down a few years ago during that awful blizzard! All her quilts, and a couple from her mother and grandmother." Philomena shook her head in sorrow. "But I understand she is quilting again now that her hips are in good shape."

Lizzie nodded. Lydia had broken a hip, and subsequently had both of them replaced. Now she claimed to be good for another fifty years with her titanium hips. "She's something, all right."

"So, how can I help the two of you?"

John looked at Lizzie, who gestured for him to go ahead and tell their story. "Well, Lizzie and I have been trying to figure out who might want to scare her into leaving her property."

Philomena's head snapped up at that, and Lizzie watched as her eyes changed from laid-back curiosity to alert newspaperwoman. "You think someone is actively attempting to frighten you away? But who? Why?" She looked around and grabbed a notebook and pen and jotted down a few notes. Lizzie gave John an alarmed look, but he shook his head and continued. "Well, Mrs. Jones. . ."

The editor waved a hand at him and said, "Phil. Mrs. Jones was my mother-in-law, and a terrifying woman she was."

John bit back a smile. "Okay, Phil. So, the brick that was thrown through Lizzie's window had a note wrapped around it telling her to leave. And an odd little man at the grand opening made no secret of the fact that he wanted her gone too."

"He as much as said so!" Lizzie added, still a bit outraged at his audacity.

Phil nodded. "Okay, yes, the police have been by with what I assume is the man's photo. I didn't recognize him, so he's not from here. I asked for a copy to show a couple friends of mine who live in nearby towns. Maybe one of them will recognize him."

"Gut! Denki!" Lizzie gave her a bright smile.

"Is there more?" Phil asked, placing the notepad down on the glass counter. The cat immediately sat on it.

"Well, yesterday Lizzie and I went to the Willow Creek Historical Museum and spoke with Mr. Rumpkin, the curator. He told us about an old murder that took place in Lizzie's building back when it was the Willow Creek Inn."

Phil's eyebrows rose. "Really? Interesting." She scrunched up her nose and glanced to the left, thinking. "Oh, of course. I remember now. I did a story on the, what, hundredth anniversary of that? Maybe five or ten years ago."

"Yes! That's what Mr. Rumpkin said. It was ten years ago." Lizzie and John told the editor everything they could recall from their conversation with the museum curator. When they finished, Phil leaned on the counter. "There's motive in there somewhere, but the crime is one hundred years old! Talk about a cold case!"

"We were hoping you might have some articles about the murder in your archives," Lizzie said.

Phil popped upright. "Great idea! Of course, there's the one I did a few years ago, but it seems to me that I used some old stories for background on that. Sorry, ten years ago might as well be fifty. I write so many stories, I can't keep them straight. Come on back. Let's look." She led the way into the back of the newspaper building. Lizzie and John looked around at machines from the past, racks holding huge, thick books containing who knew what, and a little kitchen area.

Phil stopped in front of one of the tall racks holding about twenty large black books, tilted her head back, and looked up toward the top of the rack, hands braced on her hips. "Hmm. We need the edition from, what—1914, right? Of course, the newspapers from back then are at the top of the rack." She glanced at John. "You're taller than I am—anyone is!—can you reach the books at the very top?"

John stepped forward and reached up. His fingers brushed the edge of the book he was going for, but he couldn't get hold of it. "Not quite."

"Drat. Then we need a stool. Now, where is it?" She looked around, and Lizzie spied a step stool tucked away under a nearby counter.

"Is that it?" she asked, pointing.

"Yes! Good eye." Phil hurried over and grabbed the stool, then brought it back and placed it at the bottom for John to step onto. "Now, I'm right here. If you start to slip, I'll brace you with a hand on your back."

John smiled. "I'll be fine." He hopped up onto the stool and easily reached the book, which he took down with care.

"Perfect. Give me that one, and get the one next to it too, because I'm not sure which one we need."

John handed her the first book and grabbed the second before carefully hopping down from the ladder.

"Okay! Bring it here, please," Phil said, walking to the counter that had been concealing the stool. She laid her book down and took the one John had. "Now, these newspapers are really old, and they'll break just like a cracker. You have to very carefully take hold of the outer edge, touching as little as possible, and turn the pages. We really ought to be wearing cotton gloves." She looked around. "But as usual, they're nowhere to be found. So please just be gentle. Start at the beginning. You can be sure of one thing—when you find the story, you'll know. A murder will be on the front page, so you won't need to look at each page. You'll want to start at the week following the date of the murder, since it was a weekly paper back then too."

She scanned the front page of the newspaper at the beginning of the book, which was dated in January, 1914. "Okay, as I recall, the murder took place on May 4, 1914. You'll need to flip through until you find that week's edition. Oh, I just remembered another source of potential information for you. Hold on, I'll be right back."

John and Lizzie carefully flipped through the enormous book until they came to the April 27th edition.

"John! I think May 4 was a Monday! It'll be the next edition!" Lizzie gasped. John nodded and carefully turned the pages. Before he reached May 4, Phil came hurrying back, a book in her hands.

"This is a history of Willow Creek by Norman Cliff. Published just about twenty years ago, so all the early stuff is in here. And here's an accounting of the murder story you're looking for! It'll give you additional information to what's in the newspapers."

Putting the book on the counter, she watched as John flipped the last few pages in the big book. "Ah! There it is, May 4! See? What did I tell you? They were really melodramatic back in those days. A murder in this little town would have been big news. Huge! It still is. Look at that screaming headline! And the black-and-white photo of the suspect. When you read this, it'll be full of grisly details we'd never print these days, so be prepared for that."

Lizzie looked across at John, who looked a bit dismayed. "Uh, okay," he said. "Denki for the warning." He glanced at Lizzie. "How's the book account?"

"Not grisly, so that's gut!" she said, eyes scanning the page. "This is amazing! John, there's a photo of the room where it happened in my building! Oh, there's paint or something in the shape of a body on the floor!"

Philomena leaned in for a look. "That's a chalk outline, Lizzie. Police used to trace a dead body with chalk or tape just before it was taken away by the coroner. But few people know that the reason for this wasn't to preserve evidence. It was done so the newspaper photographer could get a dramatic photograph of a crime scene without the upsetting image of an actual body in it. Cool trivia, huh?"

Lizzie thought the editor looked very pleased with herself, so she smiled. "Interesting. And I'm perfectly happy not to be looking at a photo of the dead man." She shuddered. "It's bad enough to be looking at the chalk outline and knowing right where that is in my bakery!"

John was reading the newspaper account. He turned the book slightly so she could see better. "Look, there's a photo of the man who was arrested for the murder. He doesn't look very repentant, does he?"

Phil looked, then shook her head. "Nope. I'd have to agree."

Lizzie looked up from the history book. "That could be because he did exactly what he came here for, and never expected to get away with it. It says here that he confessed to the crime as soon as the police got there. He didn't even have a suitcase, and he traveled all the way from New York!"

John finished reading the story from the week of the crime. "Would there be a follow-up story the next week?"

"Oh, I imagine so. Probably for several weeks. Let's look," Phil said. "But first, let me take photos of this page for you. I'll print them out so you have a copy." She took out her smartphone and quickly took several photos of the front page, including one of the photograph of the victim and one of the photo of the murderer. Then she put her phone down and turned to the next Monday. "May 11. Here you go."

She turned the book back toward John, who let out a low whistle. "Goodness, that was fast. He's been sentenced to life in prison, and they're already shipping him out to serve his sentence."

"Justice on the frontier was swift. Discouraged such things as murder as much as possible. He's lucky they didn't simply hang him from a tree. Probably helped that he was famous. The judge probably didn't want any more scandal than absolutely necessary."

"But I don't see any mention of a missing manuscript," Lizzie murmured, peering at the newspaper article. "Maybe in this book." She returned to reading the account in the history book.

"Missing manuscript?" Phil asked John. "Now this is getting more interesting."

"The murdered man was a famous author at the time," John said. "There were rumors that he was working on a new book, but nothing was found in his room, amongst his personal effects."

"I'm starting to remember hearing about this. It's been a long time, though, and I've forgotten the details," Phil said. She took photos of the follow-up story from May 11, then turned carefully to May 18 and scanned the front. "Aha! Here you go, Lizzie. It took them a couple weeks to get the story, I guess, but they got it in the end."

She gestured for Lizzie to join them and stepped out of the way. Lizzie hurried around the counter and stood next to John, who was already reading the account of the suspected missing manuscript.

"The killer denied having any knowledge of any manuscript," he said, reading further.

Lizzie moved closer to him so she could see the story better. As her eyes scanned the printed words, she became aware of the scent of soap and...wood chips? She sniffed a bit and realized it was John's scent. She took in a deep breath, enjoying the cozy, somehow compelling, fragrance she realized was quintessentially John. He gave her a funny look.

"Do I stink?"

"What? Oh! No! I'm sorry. You actually smell really gut. Like soap and...wood chips, I think." When he raised an eyebrow and looked down at her, she suddenly realized how close she was standing to him and jumped back. "I didn't mean to sniff you." She felt her face flush deep red and was mortified to have been caught sniffing her best friend's brother. "Let's see if they say anything about the missing manuscript."

John just smiled and went back to reading the old news story.

John bit his lips to keep from laughing out loud at Lizzie, knowing it would only embarrass her. She'd been sniffing him! He knew sniffing when he heard it. And it was sniffing he'd heard. He'd glanced down and caught her with her eyes closed, sniffing away. She hadn't looked offended, but he'd suddenly worried that his deodorant had worn off, which was why he'd asked whether he stank. He rolled his eyes at himself. *Smooth, John.*

Still, could have been worse. Wood chips and soap. He could understand that, due to his work and the fact that he'd showered before picking her up that morning.

But why had she been sniffing him? Did that mean she liked him? Or was she just being polite when she said he didn't stink? He frowned. The editor, returning from some errand up front, saw his frown.

"Something wrong? Are you finding anything interesting?"

"Oh, nothing is wrong. Ja, it's all interesting. But I haven't seen anything about a missing manuscript," John said, returning his attention to the old newspaper.

"Wait!" Lizzie cried, a finger going to a paragraph about halfway down the page. "Right here! Look! 'The deceased's literary agent and business manager, Mr. Ambrose Beckett, expressed his concern that nowhere in the murdered author's personal effects had he located the manuscript he had reportedly been working on. "He came here to write because he thought it would be peaceful. So if he was writing, where's the manuscript?" When questioned about the allegedly missing work of fiction, the Willow Creek police stated that when they searched the victim's room, they found nothing indicating a manuscript had been there. "I'm not convinced," Beckett said. "He was nearly finished with his next bestseller, and unless he'd already mailed it off to me which I doubt as he'd never let it out of his hands until a copy was made, then either someone took it, or it's still somewhere in that inn!"'"

Lizzie stopped reading and looked up at John and Phil. "There! That's why someone is breaking into my building! They think that manuscript is still in there!" She stood up from the stool. "Phil, would you please take photos of these pages too? And can you make us a copy?"

Phil nodded and took photos of the article, then flipped to the following week. "Nothing new the next week. Why don't you two look through here while I print these? I think that anything related to the murder will be on the front page, even weeks or months out."

They quickly looked through the rest of the year, and found one more article about the murder, but there was no new information. Clearly, the case had grown cold.

John took the heavy book and replaced it in its slot in the wall, and then he followed the editor and Lizzie back up to the front of the shop. Lizzie turned to Phil and held out her hand, which the editor shook. "Denki very much for helping us, Phil. This whole thing is so unexpected and unnerving."

"I imagine so." Phil reached over to a stack of newspapers on the counter and handed Lizzie one. "The story of your vandalism and break-in is in this week's edition. I doubt it'll help you, but it's good to have a record."

Lizzie held the newspaper and frowned. John figured she didn't like the idea of her troubles being reported in the Englisch news, and he couldn't blame her. But Phil was doing her job, and as she said, this gave them something of a record of what had happened so far.

Then he caught himself. It gave *Lizzie* a record, not *them*, as there wasn't a *them*. He was just a friend helping out where he could.

"And here is the story I did on the anniversary of the murder ten years ago. There's nothing new in it, but you might as well have a copy."

Lizzie added that edition to their collection and thanked Phil, and they left and walked to where the wagon was parked. Lizzie tucked the newspapers and photos into her bag and climbed up.

She turned to John, a determined gleam in her eyes. "I surely appreciate your help in this matter. You're gut at it."

He was surprised. "Does that mean you want me to keep coming around and helping you find clues and stuff?"

She nodded vigorously. "Ja. Because something fishy is going on, and I'm not going to stop until we figure it out!" She turned and focused on the road, lost in her thoughts.

John admired her determined spirit, and he believed she would accomplish her goal. And it would be fun to be along for the ride.

CHAPTER TWELVE

John thought hard about the way Lizzie made him feel as he drove her back to the bakery. He wasn't quite sure what to do about his feelings, new and unexpected as they were. He stole a glance at her and caught her looking at him. They both snapped their eyes back to the front. John rolled his, feeling ridiculous, as if he were eighteen and not twenty-eight.

That thought made him reflect on just how long he'd known Elizabeth Miller, and what their relationship had always been.

I remember when her knees were scabby from sliding into first base during baseball games at school. That made him chuckle a bit. She'd always gone for it, even as a child. *I remember when she wore her hair in braids falling out from her kapp. I don't know what to think about the fact that I've suddenly realized she's not a kid anymore.*

He snuck another glance at her. She was definitely not a kid anymore! She looked at him again, and he offered her a little smile. Her response to that was to frown. "John, what are you thinking about? Did I hear you laugh a minute ago? Were you laughing at me?"

"Ach, no! I was laughing at a thought I'd had, that's all."

"A thought?"

"Well, ja. To be honest, I was thinking about how long we've known each other, and remembering way back to our days at school. I was remembering how you've always gone for what you wanted. Just like you did when it came to getting your bakery."

She looked a bit surprised and turned her gaze to her hands, which she'd folded in her lap. "Oh, that's not what I thought you were laughing at."

He glanced at her again and found her staring pensively out at the field they were passing. "What did you think I was laughing at?"

"Well, at me. I thought you were thinking that you were sorry you'd gotten pulled into this whole thing, and laughing at me, or yourself. You know, ironically."

John felt his mouth drop open. "You thought I was laughing at you?"

She nodded, her face miserable, and he let go of the reins with his right hand and reached over to give her a little push on the shoulder, like he would have if she'd been Jane. "Hey, look at me."

She gave him a side-eyed look, and he smiled. "Lizzie, I would not laugh at you. Don't you know how much I admire you?"

Dumbstruck, she shook her head. "Um, nee."

He realized he was going to have to lay it out for her. "Lizzie, I've always liked you, ever since you were a young kid. You've been a gut friend to Jane, and to me too. And you've never been afraid to stand up to bullies, or to pitch in and do the hard work when it needed to be done. I chuckled because I realized that you've grown into a lovely, accomplished young woman and I hadn't even noticed. If I was laughing at anyone, it would be at myself, because I've been kind of blind."

She turned to face him fully. "Really?" she breathed. "You really think all those gut things about me?"

He nodded. Then he decided to go for it—for what he'd been thinking about for a few days. He swallowed. "In fact, Lizzie, I'd really love to get to know the adult you better as yourself, not as my little sister's best friend."

"Are you saying you want to date me?"

"Ja! I want to date you! What do you say?"

She looked upset and turned away.

This couldn't be good. This wasn't going as he'd imagined. "Did I say something wrong?"

"I told you I'm not ready to settle down yet, didn't I?"

He thought about it for a moment. Had she said that? "Um, maybe?"

She rolled her eyes. "I'm sure I mentioned it. I have a brand-new business I'm trying to get off the ground. And I can't do that at the same time as I'm trying to get a new relationship off the ground. You must see how impossible it would be!"

He blinked a couple of times. He didn't see that at all, really. "But you've got Jane and Eliza working with you, and I've been helping you figure out who's trying to run you out of business, right?"

She considered him for a moment before answering. "Well, ja, you have been very helpful, and I appreciate it. But that doesn't mean I want to date you!"

"Well, if you're not interested in me, just say so."

"Oh, John, that's not what I meant, and you know it."

His head was spinning. "So. . .you are interested in me?"

She actually rolled her eyes. "I'm not interested in anyone right now. Aren't you listening?"

He thought about pouting. But that would make him the one acting like a child. And he was the older one, so he should act like it. But in truth, he felt like pouting.

"Yes?"

"Yes? You are listening?"

"I'm listening. I just guess I hoped to hear something else. So, you're not interested in dating anyone right now? It's not just me?"

"No! John, you're my friend! If I were going to date anyone, I'd happily date you."

"Well that just makes it sound like you think all men are inter-changeable and it doesn't matter who you date."

She sighed. "That's not what I meant. I just meant I'm not ready to date anyone."

"But you're. . ."

She held up a hand. "If you're about to tell me I'm twenty-five, you'd better think again. Pointing out how long in the tooth I'm getting is not likely to make me feel more favorable toward you."

He sat back and buttoned his lips. He had almost said that. "Well, I'm even older."

"You know it's not the same. Men can wait longer. Amish women are supposed to marry young and start a family."

He started to argue, but she held up a hand. "Can we just agree that I like you fine, but I don't want to date anyone yet? Give me some time, John. I've got a lot on my plate. I'm under a lot of pressure. Plenty of people expect my business to fail, and someone is actively trying to make certain it does! I can't think about romance right now. Fashtay?"

He shrugged and nodded. "Yes, I understand. But, will you let me keep helping you to solve your case?"

"You really want to do that?"

He thought about it a moment. It was kind of fun, actually, and he got to hang out with Lizzie. Maybe if they continued to work together to figure out what was going on, she'd slowly come to feel comfortable enough around him to consider dating him. "Ja, I really do want to. So, can I?"

Lizzie looked at him for several heartbeats, and then she slowly nodded. "Ja, okay, I'll be happy to have your help. You're gut company, John Bontrager."

She climbed down from the wagon and started to turn away, and he called, "Lizzie, wait."

She turned back to look at him, and he worked up a cocky smile. "I just wanted to point out that if you do ever decide to date me, it wouldn't exactly be a new relationship. More a continuation and a maturing of a very old one. Just something for you to think about."

She looked surprised, and she nodded consideringly before turning and heading into her workplace.

He watched her disappear inside, feeling optimistic about helping her solve her mystery and optimistic about making her see him in a different light than that of "old friend."

He'd have to dig for patience so that someday instead of seeing him as just her best friend's brother—a relatively unimportant character in the story of her life—she would come to see him as the hero of her very own romance.

———————— ⚜ ————————

Lizzie closed the door of the bakery behind her, shutting out the guilt and worry over hurting John's feelings with the decided click of the door latch. She would think about all that later. It wasn't that she didn't have feelings for John. She was very much afraid she did! But how could she be a fraa—or even a girlfriend—and a business owner just starting out at the same time? You can't learn two new roles at once. "Ach, I need to talk to Mrs. Petersheim."

She shook her head and looked around. Several people were relaxing with coffee and pastries, reading books, visiting with friends, or using laptops. Just what she wanted to see. But she couldn't pause to gather her thoughts with all these people present, so she hurried toward the back, smiling and nodding at people who greeted her.

Behind the counter, Eliza was helping a customer, but there was currently no one else in line, so Lizzie didn't feel that she had to jump in and help.

"Good morning!" Eliza chirped. "Jane's in the back, and she has news!"

"Good, I'll head back there. I want to take a few minutes to call the Petersheims anyway."

Eliza nodded and turned back to the cappuccino machine she was using, so Lizzie pushed through into the kitchen. Jane was seated at the table, looking at some yellowed papers. When Lizzie had hung her bonnet and cape on a hook, she grabbed a cup of coffee from the ever-present carafe and joined her friend. "What do you have there, Jane?"

"Oh, I didn't hear you come in! This is just fascinating! Look!" She pushed the papers toward Lizzie, who gave them a quick look, not understanding at first what she was looking at. Then a word caught her eye, and she zeroed in on it, and suddenly she knew. It was part of a very old manuscript—possibly the famous missing manuscript by E. W. Fingle. Her mouth fell open, and she gaped at her friend.

"Jane! Where did you get this?"

Jane grinned at Lizzie, obviously very pleased with herself. "It was stuffed in a box upstairs! I was looking for some stationery so I could write to Carmen, my Mexican pen pal. I forgot to bring any, so I was checking all the drawers and cabinets in the living room and kitchen upstairs. Most of them are empty. So I went up into the attic to look around."

Lizzie shrugged. "We've been up there. There's some old furniture but not much else, right?"

Jane nodded. "So I thought. But I noticed a door set into the wall behind an old bookcase. I shoved the bookcase aside and pried the door open, and it was the eaves, and mostly just dust and spiderwebs. But toward the back in the dark, where they could easily have been missed, there were a couple boxes of personal belongings and this box of old correspondence. Most of it was old junk, but I thought this box looked interesting, so I brought it down where I could see it better." She pushed the box toward Lizzie, who flipped through a few things but didn't pull anything out.

"It has all sorts of old letters and other old papers in it!" Jane exclaimed.

"I'll bet the Petersheims never knew it was there," Lizzie mused. "What are you reading?"

Jane waved the yellowed papers excitedly at Lizzie. "This was in a letter dated 1914. Isn't that the year of the murder?"

Lizzie nodded. "May I see it?"

Jane pushed the box over to Lizzie and got up to pour herself a cup of coffee. "I'm dry from all the dust." She took a sip. "Is Eliza okay by herself? Maybe I'd better check while you look at the box. I'll be back in a bit." Jane took her coffee with her through the swinging door into the shop, leaving Lizzie alone with the letter, the pages of an old manuscript, and the box.

She found herself wishing John were there to share the moment. She didn't know what she was going to find in the box, but she suspected it would have a bearing on the case and hated for John to miss out. "Maybe I should wait until he comes by later to pick us up, and we can all look at it together."

She gazed longingly at the mysterious box. And then her eyes fell on the letter and manuscript pages already open and lying on the table.

"It can't hurt to look at these. Jane already has. I'll save the rest of the box until John gets here, though." She reverently picked up the old letter and opened it up. The writing was very small and neat. The paper was thin and light. "Probably to save money on postage," she murmured. She had to squint to make out the writing, which had faded to a light brown.

She read it through once, then again, and then she set the pages down and picked up the pages from the manuscript. There were only two pages, printed with precise type that Lizzie assumed must have been done on a typewriter.

She read through the manuscript pages and realized it was part of a story about a family getting their lives back into order following a tragedy. Brief though the pages were, she recognized good writing when she saw it. It pulled her right in, and she found herself curious about the rest of the story. If this was part of the missing manuscript, its loss was truly profound.

"But where's the rest?" She glanced at the box and moved a few things around, but she didn't see any other pages that looked like these. "Of course. He must have sent these pages to someone to read. Maybe to his agent? That would make sense." She examined the envelope, and it was from Mr. Fingle to another man, a Mr. Ambrose Beckett.

Lizzie stared at the name a moment, then sat up straight, her mouth falling open. "Ambrose Beckett is the name of Mr. Fingle's literary agent, the one who wanted the manuscript! John and I saw his name in the newspaper articles this morning!"

She hurried over to where she'd left her purse and pulled out the papers the editor had copied. She riffled through them and then cried, "Aha! I was right! He sent at least part of the manuscript to his agent, in this very letter!"

She sank back down onto the chair and stared at the old letter sitting on the table. She picked it up again and noted that it was postmarked 1914. So the timing was right too. "I can't believe it! Jane found a real treasure here."

She looked at the box again, wishing she could dig in right away, but she'd decided to wait for John, and anyway, she really needed to get to work.

Casting a last regretful look at the tempting box, she tucked the letter and pages back into the envelope and set them safely on top of the box. "But that doesn't mean I can't tell Jane and Eliza about this!"

Feeling better, she put on a work apron, then hurried up front to share the information she and John had found at the newspaper, and how it seemed to link with the letter Jane had found.

That evening, the friends all gathered at Eliza's apartment to eat a simple dinner and go through the contents of the box.

"Hurry and eat," Lizzie said. "As soon as we're finished, we can dig through the box. I can hardly wait."

"I can't believe you did wait!" Jane said.

Lizzie shrugged. "Well, I knew you'd all want to be in on it. Who knows what we may find? Maybe the whole manuscript is in there, inside various letters!"

"That would be something, wouldn't it?" Eliza sighed. "But I doubt it."

"I'm just hoping for a clue as to who would want to put you out of business," John said before finishing his second mug of soup. "I won't be comfortable until we figure this out and I know you are all safe in that building."

Everyone nodded in agreement, and talk turned to other things while they finished their meal.

As soon as supper was over and the dishes were all washed and dried, the four friends gathered around the kitchen table. "You're the one who found it, Jane," Lizzie said. "Why don't you choose the next thing to open?"

Jane's eyes lit up and she peered into the box, which was stuffed full of old letters, folded papers, and even a couple of small diaries or notebooks. "Wow, I don't know where to start."

"How did you choose the first letter?" John asked curiously.

Jane considered for a moment, then shrugged. "I was really looking for blank stationery, so I flipped through the contents of the box briefly. I saw there wasn't any, but then this letter caught my eye. I don't know why. It was open, with some old papers sort of peeking out, so that may have had something to do with it." Lizzie pulled a clean notebook toward her. "I'm going to keep track of what we find in here. So that first letter, Jane. Please remind us all who it is from, and who it's to."

"It's from a Mr. E. W. Fingle to a Mr. Ambrose Beckett. I gathered from the letter that he was Mr. Fingle's literary agent," Jane said. "I'd say Mr. Fingle was showing his first few pages to his agent, maybe looking for feedback."

Lizzie snapped her fingers. "That's right! We learned that at the newspaper this morning, remember, John? Mr. Beckett was Mr. Fingle's literary agent. Gut deducing, Jane!"

"All in a day's work!" Jane quipped.

"I read the manuscript pages," Lizzie told her friends. "They were really gut. I wished I had the rest so I could find out what happened. No wonder he was a bestselling author."

Lizzie took that letter and the manuscript pages and set them aside. "We got lucky once. Maybe there are more pages in there somewhere?"

John shook his head. "I doubt we'll find any more of the missing manuscript in there. If he was sending those off to his agent, why would there be more? Probably just a bunch of personal correspondence."

Lizzie grimaced. "We won't know until we look. Why don't we all choose something and read it, and we'll keep track of what we find? Otherwise it'll take us ages to get through all this."

"I suppose it's fine for us to be going through this stuff?" Eliza asked, looking around the table at her friends doubtfully. "It seems kind of nibby."

"Everything in that building belongs to Lizzie," John pointed out reasonably. "So if she says we can read this stuff, then we can, right?"

"That's true," Lizzie said. "I guess it all does belong to me, just like the furniture and other things the Petersheims left behind." She smacked herself on the forehead. "Ach! I forgot to call them again! What's wrong with me?"

"I'd say you were understandably distracted," Jane pointed out. "You can call after we go through this box. Maybe you'll find other things to ask them."

Lizzie nodded. "Fair enough. Okay, dig in everyone. Let's see what else we've got!"

It turned out that nearly all the remaining envelopes had been previously opened—not surprising, really. They each chose one at random and carefully removed the contents. Lizzie placed the notebook on the table, telling everyone to write down what they found. At first, everything was exciting. Eliza had a letter to a former owner of the inn, a Mrs. Agatha Bridgerton, from her sister, dated December 22, 1902, telling Agatha she'd be sorry to miss Christmas at the inn that year, but with a new baby in the family, she and her husband didn't want to risk travel. As Eliza skimmed it, she suddenly gave a little squeak.

"What?" Lizzie asked, and Eliza looked up excitedly.

"She tells her sister that she's especially sorry to miss meeting the famous author staying here! Could she be talking about the murdered Mr. Fingle?"

But Lizzie shook her head. "The date is wrong, Eliza. Look, 1902. The murder took place in 1914. Even if it was Mr. Fingle staying there, it was years earlier."

Eliza gave a dejected sigh. "Ach, you're right, Lizzie. Oh well."

John was digging through the box when he came upon a sealed envelope, dated April 15, 1914. "Look at this. It's sealed." He peered at the address, and Lizzie heard him catch his breath.

"What is it?" she asked, leaning forward eagerly.

He looked up at her, eyes wide. "I think it's a telegram, but it hasn't been opened! It's from Mr. Gregory Liptak to Mr. E. W. Fingle."

Jane gasped. "It's from the killer!"

"To the victim!" Eliza gulped.

"John! Mr. Rumpkin said there was a telegram! Remember?"

He nodded, eyes on the envelope in his sister's hand. "Ja, I remember."

Everyone leaned forward, their own letters forgotten, to see what the killer's telegram would reveal.

Lizzie found herself praying silently for something—anything!—that would help solve the mystery of who wanted her out of business, and out of her building.

CHAPTER THIRTEEN

"Open it!" Jane urged, setting aside her own letter, which contained several recipes and a lot of gossip from the sister of the innkeeper.

"Lizzie? Do you want me to open this?" John held the telegram loosely between his thumb and forefinger, as if it might be somehow dangerous.

And indeed, Lizzie realized, it was a message from a long-dead killer to his long-ago victim. She shivered a bit at the thought but quickly pulled herself together. No time for flights of fancy!

Lizzie nodded. "Sure! Be careful. We don't want to tear anything important."

Eliza jumped up. "Wait, I have a letter opener somewhere, so you won't have to tear it open." She rummaged through a couple of drawers until she found the letter opener. "Here it is!" She handed it to John, who carefully slit the envelope and set the tool aside before cautiously reaching inside and removing a crisply folded sheet of paper. He spread it on the table and smoothed it before picking it up.

He looked it over a little bit too long without saying anything, and his sister grew impatient. "John! What does it say?"

"Oh, sorry." He squinted at it a bit more. "Small type. Hard to see."

He reached into his shirt pocket and pulled out a pair of round readers, which he perched on his nose. Lizzie found herself staring stupidly at him, thinking how the glasses made him look very smart and even more appealing than usual.

John raised an eyebrow and looked at each of them before speaking. "Mr. Liptak seems to be threatening legal action against Mr. Fingle based on what he claims was an idea he had for a novel that he says Fingle stole and used to write a bestselling book. He demands that Fingle hand over half the proceeds from his novel, which he thinks is generous, since even though Fingle did the work, he claims the idea was his. Oh my." He looked up and met Lizzie's eyes, his expression serious. "There's a threat."

Lizzie could hardly contain herself. "John, what does it say?" She bounced in her seat, leaning forward to try and read it for herself, but John raised his eyebrows and pulled the telegram toward his chest.

"I'm getting there, be patient!"

"I'm trying, but the suspense is killing me!" Lizzie groaned.

"Come on, John!" Jane urged. "Don't keep us waiting."

"Fine." He returned his eyes to the telegram and found his place. "It says that if Fingle doesn't respond in the affirmative to Liptak's demands within two weeks by telegram, he will assume that means Fingle does not intend to share his ill-gained profits." John paused and looked up. "It really says that—ill-gained. Pretty dramatic."

"Go on, John!" Eliza said, and Lizzie and Jane nodded.

John looked back down at the page and ran his finger along the lines until he found where he'd left off. "All right, all right. Ill-gained profits. Here it is. Liptak goes on to say he will have no choice but to come to Willow Creek by train on the date of May 4, 1914, and exact another kind of payment. He urges Fingle not to take his threat lightly."

He looked up. "That's all."

Lizzie blinked. "Don't you think it's enough?"

John nodded. "But the telegram was never opened. So Fingle didn't know his danger. Liptak must have assumed Fingle was ignoring him, and he carried through with his threat."

"Without asking a single question first," Jane added.

They all sat silently staring at John, at a loss for words or understanding for a man who would kill another man, especially over such an intangible thing as a stolen idea.

Finally, Lizzie puffed a breath from between her lips and shook her head. "Wow. Just, wow. What would have happened if Fingle had opened this telegram? Would he have paid Liptak?"

"Or would he have fled the area, taking his unfinished manuscript with him?" Jane offered.

"He might have done nothing, and it could have turned out exactly the same way," Eliza said.

"Ja, Gott's will," John agreed, nodding his head.

"I wonder why he didn't open the envelope?" Jane mused aloud.

John shrugged. "Maybe he wasn't in when it arrived, and instead of giving it to him when he returned, the innkeeper misplaced it. He might never have had the chance to open it. It was stuffed into a box of correspondence and forgotten."

They all silently contemplated the tragic results of that possible ancient error.

Lizzie pursed her lips in thought, then met John's eyes. "I think we should take this telegram, and the manuscript pages we found with the other letter to the literary agent, to the historical society and show them to Mr. Rumpkin."

John nodded. "Gut idea. Maybe he'll have some insights to offer."

Jane was staring at the first piece of correspondence—the letter from Fingle to his agent, lying on the table by Lizzie's elbow. "I have a question," she said. Everyone looked at her. "Well, why would there be a letter from Mr. Fingle to his agent, that had obviously gone through the mail, in this box of correspondence received by people at the inn?"

Her question was met, at first, with blank stares.

"I mean, why would it be here? Shouldn't it be wherever it was mailed to, rather than where it was mailed from?"

Eliza blinked at her. "You're right. That doesn't make sense. If Mr. Fingle mailed it from the inn to his agent, shouldn't it have gone to the address on the envelope? How did it get here?"

Lizzie's eyebrows flew upward. "Jane, you're brilliant! Why didn't we think of that sooner?"

"Well, why didn't I?" Jane asked, a self-deprecating smile on her lips.

"I'm the one who found the letter, after all."

"You didn't open it, did you?" John asked. "Because if you did, then maybe we've made the wrong assumption. Maybe the letter just never got mailed."

Jane shook her head. "Nee. It was already open. And the stamp is canceled."

"But why would he write a letter to his agent, and then pay to send it, but not send it? That doesn't make sense," John said.

"Maybe he realized he needed to add something to the letter," Lizzie pointed out.

"Or remove something," Eliza said ominously. All eyes turned to her. "What?"

"Remove what? What do you mean?" Jane asked.

"Well, I don't know. Anything. Maybe he'd put money in and changed his mind. Who knows? But something made him change his mind, and it only makes sense that he needed to either put something in the envelope or take something out."

"I think if anything, he had to take something out," Lizzie mused.

"What makes you think so?" John asked.

"Well, he'd already paid for the postage, right?" Lizzie said. John nodded, and she continued. "So, if he added something, that might change the cost of the postage. He wouldn't have been able to use the same envelope. He would have wasted that money, and he'd have to start over with a new envelope. But if he took something out, it wouldn't matter. Who cares if the postage is too high? Not the post office."

Jane looked impressed. "Smart."

"I don't want to look prideful, but denki."

But Jane was shaking her head. "Nee, nee, sorry but you're forgetting—the envelope hadn't only been stamped, it had been post-marked. That means it was actually mailed. He didn't open it and take anything out. He couldn't have, because he'd already mailed it!"

"Huh, she's right," John said, sounding a bit surprised.

Jane smirked at her brother. "I often am, denki. So now what? If Fingle mailed the letter from here, how did it get back here?"

"Don't you see?" Lizzie said, sitting up suddenly with a gleam in her eye. "The letter must have reached its destination. And then the recipient of the letter, Mr. Beckett, brought it back here in person. Probably when he heard his client was dead, and wanted to look for that missing manuscript." She sat back, arms crossed, and eyed her friends to see what they thought.

"That makes gut sense," John said. "We already know from the newspaper article from 1914 that he showed up here after Fingle was killed. We just didn't have proof. I think Lizzie is right, and this letter constitutes even more proof."

Jane was frowning. "I have another question."

Everyone looked at her. "Although I don't use a typewriter, I'd have to guess it's a lot of work to type out several pages of a manuscript. And an entire manuscript would be a huge undertaking, right?"

Eliza nodded. "Ja. I do type. I learned how when I worked in the hardware store for my parents back home in Lancaster. They had forms that needed to be neatly filled out, and a typewriter did it better than writing by hand. I understand it's easier to do on a computer. You just write your letter or manuscript or whatever once, and then you can make corrections on the computer, and then print out as many copies as you like. But in 1914 there were no computers. So you'd have to type the whole thing out every time. Unless. . ."

"Unless what, Eliza?" Jane asked impatiently.

Eliza looked at her friend. "Unless you had carbon paper. You can use carbon paper to make more than one copy at a time. It really only works to make one copy. You put the two pieces of paper in, with the carbon paper between, and type away. If you make a mistake, you have to throw it away and start over, or correct it on both pages, by hand. I wonder if there was carbon paper in 1914? I wish we had access to a computer to find out."

"John has a computer at work," Lizzie said.

"That's right!" Jane exclaimed "John, will you look that up tonight, please? When was carbon paper in common use?"

"Sure, I can do that when I get home. But what was your question?"

"Oh! Right." Jane paused to think a moment. "So, if carbon paper existed in 1914, it's a moot question. I just wondered, if you had to type everything out each time you needed a copy, would Mr. Fingle have risked sending his only copy of those manuscript pages to his agent? I know I wouldn't! And I'd hate to type it all out more than once."

"Some people employ secretaries for that kind of thing," Lizzie suggested. "Maybe he had a secretary?"

"There isn't any mention of him traveling with anyone though," Jane said. "So maybe the carbon paper theory is the right one. If you could get it back then."

"Either way, those pages would be precious to the author," Eliza said.

"Which makes it even more important that we take this stuff over to the historical museum and see what Mr. Rumpkin thinks, John."

He nodded at Lizzie. "Ja, you're right." He tilted his head, staring off into the distance, then looked at her. "I think I can take an hour to do that tomorrow after lunch. Does that work for you?"

Lizzie glanced doubtfully at Eliza and Jane. "I don't know. My employees are going to think I hired them to do all the work while I run around having fun."

Jane and Eliza smiled. "Don't be silly, Lizzie," Jane said. "You and my bruder were the ones who first talked to Mr. Rumpkin, so you should be the ones to go talk with him. Besides, it's your building and your business. Who better to handle this? And John secretly loves this detective stuff, I can tell."

John looked at his rather perceptive younger sister with chagrin. Was he that transparent to her? While he had entered reluctantly at first into the "detective" business, recently he'd begun to enjoy it. It was fun finding clues and putting them together. In fact, he feared it could become rather addictive, and it definitely was not something his Amish brethren would approve of.

He frowned and made a small negative noise, and Lizzie looked at him in concern. "John? You don't have to do this if you don't want to. Honestly, I can do it on my own, or take one of the girls with me."

Eliza waved her hand and grinned. "Me! I'd love to go."

John shifted in his seat, uncomfortable with either choice. On the one hand, he could step away from this, tell Lizzie to let the police handle it, and get back to the business of furniture making. Not that there was any guarantee that if he quit, Lizzie would.

On the other hand, he'd just discovered feelings for Lizzie that he needed to explore. What better excuse to spend time with her than by helping her solve this mystery.

He realized all three women were watching him and waiting for an answer. He cleared his throat and sighed. "I'm already involved, so I might as well keep going."

When Eliza cheered, he frowned at her. "Look, I understand that we need to get to the bottom of this, but let's not make the mistake of thinking it's fun. This is serious business, and frankly, I expect Bishop Troyer to stop in any day and have a little talk with us all, reminding us that the Englisch police are the ones who should be seeking out clues, not us. So we'd better tread carefully, fashtay?" He looked each woman in the eye, seeing that they knew he was right.

Unless he was mistaken, in Lizzie's eyes, he also saw a tiny bit of defiance. He sighed again. Who could really blame her? If it was his business being threatened, or his property broken into, he would probably feel the very same way. Plus, he had no right to tell her what to do.

He cleared his throat. "So, what time can you go tomorrow, Lizzie?"

She frowned, then shrugged. "I guess when they open. I think that's at noon tomorrow."

"Okay, gut. Then I'll be here at noon. We can just walk over, ja?"

Lizzie nodded. "I'll bring the pages we found."

He stood. "Well, I'd better be getting home now. I'll have to get an early start tomorrow to make up for missing more work. My dat suggested this morning that maybe I'd rather be baking strudel than making furniture."

Jane winced sympathetically. "Oh, John, I'm sorry. You know he was just joking, right?"

John shrugged. "Ja, probably. But he's got a point."

"Well, I can't hire you to make strudels anyway. I just made a deal with a local woman to bring strudel in twice a week for a trial period. In fact, I believe she's bringing her first batches in tomorrow."

"Who's that?" Jane asked with interest.

"Linda Preece, from Sugarcreek. Do you know her?"

Eliza raised an eyebrow. "The dog groomer?"

Lizzie nodded absentmindedly as she gathered the papers she'd be taking to show Mr. Rumpkin the next day. "Ja, I guess she is a dog groomer. To me, she's a strudel baker."

"Well, she's a gut dog groomer," Eliza said. "Or so I've heard. But I guess she has a real passion for strudel too." Lizzie chuckled. "So she told me. I guess she'd tried selling her strudels to the Petersheims before, but they baked their own strudels. I'm perfectly happy to have someone else bake strudel so I can make French pastries. So it works out for both of us."

"Well, it does if we like her strudel," Jane pointed out reasonably.

"Guess we'll find out tomorrow." Lizzie nodded.

"I'd like to volunteer to test some strudel, just to give you ladies a man's opinion on the subject," John offered helpfully.

Lizzie laughed. "I'll keep that in mind! See you tomorrow, John."

"Wait!" Jane cried. "What about the rest of these envelopes?"

John and Lizzie looked at each other. John realized he'd forgotten all about them. "I guess we'll have to finish looking through them another time?"

Eliza waved her hand. "I don't mind looking at more tonight. I'm not tired."

Jane nodded. "Okay, fine, me too. There might be more you should take to the historical museum."

Lizzie sighed. "I'll get us some coffee and cookies, and we can all finish this job. John, you go on home. If we find anything significant, I'll tell you tomorrow."

"You're sure? I hate to abandon you."

"It'll be fine, John. Go home before Maem and Dat worry," Jane said, shooing him toward the door. "And look up that carbon paper. That's as important as going through these envelopes!"

"Fine, I'm going! I'll look that up as soon as I get home." He trotted down the stairs and grabbed his hat from the peg by the front door. He glanced back upstairs and found Lizzie standing at the top, gazing down at him. Her face was in shadows, so he couldn't make out her expression. But something about the way she stood, as if poised to act, spoke of—anxiety? Uncertainty? "Do you need something, Lizzie?"

She hesitated as if considering what to say. He thought he caught a soft sigh. "Nee. Just, be careful on the way home, John. And. . .I'll see you tomorrow."

He wondered if that was what she'd really wanted to say. "Will do," he answered. "And I'll lock this on my way out. But you know, there should really be a dead bolt on this door, for safety. I know we live in a small town, but we've already had one break-in!"

"That's a gut idea. I'll mention it to Eliza. She can get Reuben to install one, when he has a free evening. Well, gut nacht, John."

"Gut nacht, Lizzie. Sweet dreams."

He left, locking the doorknob carefully behind him. And he decided that Saturday afternoon he'd be back with a dead bolt. "Make that two. There's a back door too."

The next morning, Lizzie, Jane, and Eliza walked the three blocks to the bakery in the predawn darkness. It was chilly, and Lizzie found herself glad for the warm wool sweater she'd donned. It was one of her favorites, knitted for her by her grossmammi, who'd gone to heaven to be with Jesus several years before. It was a soft green, made from a lovely merino wool, with large, sturdy green buttons running up the front. She sighed in pleasure at its soft warmth.

"What are you sighing about?" Jane asked, trudging along beside her friends. Jane was not a morning person, despite having a job that required early mornings. Normally they tried to be in bed by eight thirty, but the night before they'd stayed up past ten reading the rest of the letters in the box.

They'd found little of interest, beyond a few recipes Lizzie wanted to try out in yet another letter from the innkeeper's sister.

"Oh, nothing really. I was just enjoying my sweater. It's so cozy." Eliza skipped a few steps to keep up with her longer-legged friends. "Hey, do you two mind slowing down just a bit?" she whined. "I'm afraid I'm going to trip on a sidewalk crack and fall on my face at this rate."

Lizzie and Jane immediately slowed down. "Sorry, Eliza," Jane said in a surly, early-morning voice. "I forgot you're so short."

"Me too, sorry," Lizzie added. "I'm anxious to get a start this morning since I'm leaving again with John to go to the historical museum at noon."

Eliza hurried along, clutching her black cape around her shoulders. "I understand, but I'm too tired"—she interrupted herself with a huge yawn—"to run. I need more kaffi."

"You need more kaffi?" Jane groused. "I didn't even get my first cup, Miss Bright-Eyed and Bushy-Tailed was in such a hurry this morning!"

Lizzie and Eliza exchanged looks but said nothing. Jane was always crabby in the morning, but this morning was worse than usual since she had lost a couple of hours of sleep. "Well, here we are anyway," Lizzie chirped. "You can have another cup of coffee right away, Eliza. And Jane, you can have the big mug, which will count as your first and second cups. That should help your morning grumps."

"I'm not grumpy," Jane muttered as they went inside. She headed straight back to the kitchen to start the coffee while Lizzie turned on the lights. As soon as Jane pushed through the swinging door and switched on the kitchen lights, she shrieked.

"What is it? What's wrong?" Lizzie hurried through the door, pushing past Jane, who seemed frozen in place. Eliza was right behind her. They stood blinking at the disarray of her normally well-organized kitchen.

"Oh no. . ." Lizzie breathed in dismay. "Not again."

"I'm calling 911," Eliza said, picking up the phone.

"Look!" Jane cried, pointing to the back door, which was standing open to the night air. She immediately drew closer to her friends, peering around suspiciously. "What if they're still here?" she whispered.

Eliza was speaking into the phone. "Someone broke into The Plain Beignet on Main Street. They made a mess, and the back door is standing wide open." She listened to the response from the police dispatcher, then looked around wildly. "We don't see anyone, but we can't be sure. It's a big place. They could be upstairs!"

She listened another moment, then nodded. "Ja, okay. We'll be out front." She hung up and grabbed Lizzie's and Jane's hands. "Come on! We have to go outside in case someone is still here!" The three women hurried back through the shop and stood huddled together on the sidewalk. They waited a moment and then heard police sirens in the distance.

"That was fast!" Jane gasped.

"Gut! I'm scared!" Eliza said, looking nervously around them at the deserted street. Suddenly, from inside the bakery building came a tremendous crash, and a loud curse. Then they heard someone running through the building, toward the back.

Jane grabbed both her friends by the arms, pulling them closer together. "Oh my goodness! There's someone in there! What if they run around this way? What will we do?"

Lizzie and Eliza were saved from answering by the arrival of two police cruisers, sirens screaming, lights flashing, in front of the building.

Officers Anderson and Jakes jumped out of the first car, and Sgt. Hernandez from the second.

"There's someone inside!" Lizzie cried. "They may have run out the back!"

"How long ago?" Sgt. Hernandez demanded, waving Officers Anderson and Jakes around to the back of the building. They took off running and disappeared around the corner.

"Just seconds," Eliza gasped, fighting for calm. "We heard a crash and someone yelled. I've never been so happy to see anyone as I was to see you all! Oh, I feel funny." She wobbled over to the bench beside the front door and sank down, laying her head in her lap.

"Oh, Eliza, it's okay, you're safe now," Lizzie said, sitting beside her friend and stroking her back. Lizzie reflected that Eliza had kept her head during the crisis, thinking to call the police and staying calm until the danger had passed. But now that they were safe, she fell apart.

After a few minutes, Officers Anderson and Jakes came out through the front door of the bakery. "We didn't find anyone, Sergeant," Anderson said, glancing at Eliza, who was sitting up but looking pretty rough. "We did a quick look around, but we need to do a more thorough search. Um, there's a real mess in there. Cabinets and drawers pulled open, contents strewn around." She grimaced, glancing at Lizzie. "Even a couple of holes bashed into walls here and there. It's as if they were searching for something."

Lizzie groaned. "That's probably what they were doing, Officer Anderson. Look, it's a long story, and I know we could all use a cup of coffee and maybe something sweet." She glanced at Jane, who nodded, and at Eliza, who gave a weak smile.

"I could use a Danish," she said. "I'm feeling a bit better."

"How about we go inside?" Lizzie said. "I'll make coffee, and then we'll tell you all about what we've learned in the last few days. I'd meant to update you today anyway. Looks like we'll be doing that sooner rather than later."

Ten minutes later, while Officers Jakes and Anderson were conducting a careful search of the building, including in closets and under beds, the three friends were seated at the table in the kitchen with Sgt. Hernandez, steaming mugs of coffee in front of them. Lizzie put a plate of yesterday's pastries on the table and took a seat with her own coffee. She looked around in dismay. "We won't be able to open today. There's not time to bake and clean up. I'll lose a whole day's revenues."

Jane looked around. "Actually, it's not as bad as it looks, Lizzie. Why don't Eliza and I start cleaning up and get the day's baking started, while you tell the sergeant what we've found so far?"

Lizzie looked hopefully at Sgt. Hernandez, who nodded. "Why not? I'd hate for you to lose business over this. Let me snap a few photos with my cell phone first, to make a record of this." He did so, then said they could get started.

"Great! Come on, Eliza, let's get to work," Jane said, jumping up and grabbing a broom. Eliza started picking up things that had been strewn around the room by the intruder while Lizzie filled the sergeant in on the letters they'd found, and their plan to take them to Mr. Rumpkin at the museum.

"Since all of this pertains to a hundred-year-old murder—and a solved one at that—we don't need to take it into evidence," Sgt. Hernandez said. "But if you find anything more recent, please don't wait to call us until the next time someone breaks in."

Lizzie nodded, waving her hand in the air to clear away some of the flour Jane's sweeping was kicking up.

"Can you think of any additional details about this morning?" Sgt. Hernandez pressed. Lizzie closed her eyes and thought hard. Something was bothering her. . .some detail her subconscious had picked up on, but try as she may, she couldn't pin it down.

"Nee, although there's something I can't put my finger on." She shrugged. "If I think of anything, I'll tell you."

Eliza had finished picking up broken dishes and scattered tools. "I'll get us some fresh supplies from the pantry. Hopefully it's not such a mess!"

As she opened the door to the pantry, a sudden, distinct sneeze issued from inside the small room where they kept their large containers of flour, sugar, and other baking supplies. Eliza froze, and Lizzie gasped.

"Someone's in there!" Jane squeaked, turning to hold the broom like some kind of weapon while Eliza was joined by Lizzie and Sgt. Hernandez in the open doorway.

They peered into the dimly lit interior, and Lizzie muttered, "What am I thinking?" and flipped the light switch, filling the space with light.

Huddled on a flour bag, trying his best to look very small, was the strange little man from the grand opening, the one with a French accent who had yelled at Lizzie. In one hand he clutched a beignet—in the other, Lizzie's recipe box.

He sneezed three times in fast succession, then used his sleeve to rub at his eyes and nose. He looked miserable.

"What on earth?" Lizzie murmured. "That's my grossmammi's recipe box!" She started to step forward, but Sgt. Hernandez gripped her arm to stop her.

"Just a minute, if you don't mind, Miss Miller?"

The little man peered from one to the other of them as they all stood in the doorway staring at him. He sighed in irritation. "Well, you caught me. Just as well. It's dusty in here!"

Lizzie's mouth fell open. Sgt. Hernandez pushed her gently behind him and took a step forward. "Are you armed, sir?"

"No, I'm not armed! I'm not an imbecile!"

The sergeant held out a hand, and the strange man looked at it, then at his own, occupied hands. He shrugged and stuffed the beignet into his mouth. His eyes rolled back in bliss. "Oomph, even a day old, it is delicious!" He took the sergeant's hand and struggled to his feet.

Stepping out of the pantry, he handed the recipe box to Lizzie, who pulled it into her chest to protect it. "What are you doing here?"

"May I have a cup of coffee while we discuss this?"

Jane snorted. "That takes some nerve! You've trashed our bakery, and now you want us to give you coffee? Maybe you'd like another pastry?"

"Actually, I wouldn't mind one..."

"Sit down, sir," Sgt. Hernandez ordered, guiding him to the table and standing over him when he'd seated himself. "Now, why don't you tell us what you're doing here?"

The little man looked around the kitchen, and suddenly his eyes grew huge and round behind his spectacles. "Oh my goodness! This place is a mess. You've got to believe me when I tell you I didn't do this!"

"Why would we believe that?" Eliza wondered, sitting down across the table and taking a sip of her cooling coffee. The little man eyed the cup longingly and licked his lips.

"Please, I'm very parched. I'll be able to explain if I have some coffee. And maybe one of those pastries?"

Lizzie huffed out a breath and took a seat. "Fine. Have some coffee and a pastry. And tell us what you're doing here. Aside from stealing my pastries and my recipes!" She looked at Sgt. Hernandez. "This is the man from the ribbon cutting! The one whose photo we gave you!"

The sergeant looked at the man with renewed interest. "Is that so? We'd have tracked you down eventually, but nobody we showed your photo to seemed to know who you were."

Lizzie skewered the man with a hard look. "Why did you trash my bakery? Why do you keep coming here? What are you looking for?"

The man looked panicked, and he shook his head desperately. "No! No, I swear I didn't do anything except taste one of your day-old beignets!"

She looked pointedly at her recipe box, which she had set on the table before her. The man had the grace to look a bit embarrassed. "And look at your recipes. But that's all! Honestly, I just wanted to see your recipe for beignets! The day of your grand opening, I had one, and it was so light, so fluffy, so *magnifique*, I had to see how you did it."

The more he spoke, the stronger his French accent grew. Lizzie shook her head. "You said terrible things! And you threw a brick through my window!"

He looked abashed. "No, no, that wasn't me. You have to believe me. *Oui*, I did say very rude things to you, and for that I apologize. But I did not throw a brick through your window. You must believe me!"

"Why should we believe you when we've found you here tonight, in Miss Miller's bakery?" Sgt. Hernandez asked, a very skeptical look on his face.

"Because I didn't do it!" He looked at Lizzie. "You put the fear into me, for my business! When I heard of your so-called Amish New Orleans–style French patisserie, I thought, how can this be? No Amish woman can bake authentic beignets, or croissants. But I thought I'd come here to check for myself. And then when I saw your pastries, tasted your beignet, they were perfection! I was afraid you would put me out of business!"

The man dropped his head into his hands and was quietly weeping. Lizzie sighed and pushed the plate of pastries toward him. "Eat something. You'll feel better."

Sgt. Hernandez took out a small notebook and a pen and looked at the strange man. "For the record, sir, please state your name."

The little man looked startled, as if he'd held to some shred of hope of anonymity. His face fell as he seemed to realize that wasn't an option. "My name is Benoit LaForest. I am a baker of fine French pastries!"

Lizzie's mouth dropped open. "You are? Where?"

Benoit's lips puckered as if he tasted something sour. "About an hour from here, in Ashland."

Lizzie blinked while she processed that. "But if your shop is so far away, why do you care about me opening up a patisserie here in Willow Creek?"

His eyes blazing, the tiny man leaned forward and slammed his fist on the table, causing the coffee mugs to jump. Spit flew from his mouth in his outrage. "There is only room for one specialty bakery selling French pastries in Ohio Amish Country! And since I was here first, then you must close your shop, or switch your wares to apple fritters and pumpkin donuts as suits your ethnic group and gender!"

"Excuse me? Did you just say I can't bake French pastries because I'm an Amish girl?" Lizzie, normally quite slow to anger, felt a small flame of indignation kindle in her belly. She had to take slow breaths to regain her temper before speaking again. "Because that would be ridiculous. So I must have misunderstood."

Benoit sat back and folded his arms, casting Lizzie a supercilious smirk. "No, I believe you got my message loud and clear. No little Amish girlie can bake proper éclairs, let alone beignets!"

Lizzie bit her lip, considering her answer. She didn't wish to be rude, but she also wasn't about to let this arrogant man walk into her bakery, steal her things, and insult her. She narrowed her eyes as she considered what to say.

Then, leaning toward the insulting man, she broke into a stream of fluent, New Orleans French, telling him exactly what she thought of his discriminatory attitude and, furthermore, suggesting that perhaps a man such as himself, obviously from France and not New Orleans, knew little of the baking style of the Delta. When she sat back, his mouth was hanging open in astonishment, his eyebrows riding high on his forehead.

Everyone was staring at her. Finally, Sgt. Hernandez asked, "What did you say to him?"

Lizzie smiled smugly. "I told him it was too late for him to dissemble. He's already told me how much he loved my beignet." She shrugged. "I also informed him I was trained in New Orleans by the best beignet artist in the city." She turned to Benoit, who was sitting in his seat, pouting, and gave him a small smile. "If you like, I'd be happy to share with you the proper preparation of French pastries, New Orleans style. I've no doubt you know more than I do about Parisian baking. But that's not what you're here to find out about, is it?"

He blinked at her owlishly. "I don't understand what you mean."

"Come now, Mr. LaForest. You don't think I'm naive enough to think you really care about my baking style? About my recipes? You're looking for the lost manuscript! Admit it!"

"Manuscript? What are you talking about? I'm here to taste your pastries and look at your recipes, as I said."

She frowned, wondering if she'd jumped to the wrong conclusion. "You're not looking for the lost manuscript of E. W. Fingle?"

"Uh, no. I've never heard of him. Her?"

Lizzie plopped into a seat, discouraged. "Him. So, you really do just want to find out what I know about baking?"

"As I said," LaForest said. "Not that I expect to actually learn anything from a wet-behind-the-ears child such as yourself, of course."

"Of course," Lizzie murmured.

"So, if not him, then who trashed the place?" Jane asked.

"Mr. LaForest, did you search the entire building and knock holes in the walls of some of the upstairs rooms?" Sgt. Hernandez asked.

Lizzie's head snapped up. "Holes in my walls upstairs? Oh no."

Mr. LaForest looked affronted at the suggestion. "*Mais, non!* Why would I do that? What I needed to find was all here in the kitchen. Why would I bother to go upstairs to the living quarters?"

The sergeant sat back. "Why indeed?" He looked at Lizzie, Jane, and Eliza. "Well, ladies, we may have solved the mystery of the man in the photo, but we are no closer to learning who broke into your apartment or threw a brick through your window, or trashed your kitchen and knocked holes in your walls tonight, I'm afraid." He looked at LaForest, who was eating another pastry with a thoughtful expression on his face, as if he were attempting to discern the various ingredients that had gone into its creation. "Do you want to press charges against Mr. LaForest here for breaking and entering?"

"Not to mention trying to steal your grandmother's recipe box," Eliza pointed out helpfully.

"And what, eating day-old pastries?" Lizzie asked impatiently. "No, Sergeant, I don't think so. As long as Mr. LaForest promises not to come here again uninvited, I won't press charges. It's not our way, you know."

"That's what I figured you'd say." He pinned the small man with a glare. "But I would like to know one thing, Mr. LaForest. While you were here, someone else obviously broke in. You must have heard them and hidden in the pantry. Did you get a look at them?"

Mr. LaForest shook his head. "Non! I was actually in the pantry, checking out the quality of the ingredients used here, when I heard the back door crash open."

At Lizzie's gasp of outrage, he shrugged. "Sorry. I thought maybe I could get you for skimping on the quality of your ingredients. But you use only the finest." He paused, and the sergeant urged him to continue.

"Well, I'd closed the pantry door when I went in so I could use my flashlight. When I heard the back door crash open, I hunkered down behind some boxes and covered myself with empty flour sacks. I heard the intruder searching the kitchen, throwing things around, and I was terrified they'd find me. But instead they left and went upstairs. I heard them stomping around up there, and I was about to sneak out myself when you all entered the kitchen, and I was trapped. As soon as you left out the front, they came running out through the kitchen again. And a minute or two later, the police came through. I wish I could be more helpful, but I saw nothing, and they didn't speak, so I can't even tell you if it was a man or a woman."

Hernandez snorted in disgust. "I'm going to go see what Anderson and Jakes have found upstairs, if you don't mind?" He got up and wandered out of the kitchen, carrying his coffee mug with him.

Jane stood up and put her hands on her hips. "Well, Eliza and I have this place pretty much back in order. Lizzie, John is going to be really upset when he gets here later this morning and finds out what happened. And the fancy new lock your dat put on the back door was circumvented simply by kicking in the door."

Lizzie sighed, knowing her friend was right. She wasn't looking forward to having to explain to John, who had suddenly become inexplicably protective of her, and rather bossy in the process.

"Ja, you're right, Jane. Maybe I need a steel door in the back."

"And maybe some of these new doorbells with cameras built in would be a good idea," Eliza suggested. When both Lizzie and Jane looked at her as if she'd lost her mind, she just shrugged. "Hey, you have to move with the times."

"We actually don't, though. That's pretty much the whole idea of our community—to be separate from all the rushing around, trying to keep up with the latest and greatest," Jane pointed out.

"I understand that," Eliza said. "But many of us use technology in our businesses, and in my opinion, with people breaking in here willy-nilly, it's only sensible to use technology to protect ourselves. We aren't being combative by doing it, so why wouldn't it be okay?"

Lizzie thought about it for a moment, then shrugged. "I'll ask Bishop Troyer what he thinks about it. He's forward thinking to a certain degree."

"But he's old!" Eliza complained. "He's probably stuck in his ways."

"Eliza King, his ways are our ways. Goodness, if your mudder finds out you're becoming so radical, she'll yank you right back to Lancaster. You'd best be careful."

"I don't think it's radical to use what's available to keep us safe. After all, you and Jane live here. I'm thinking about asking Reuben to put one of those doorbell cameras on the office door and back door of his building. After all, some people think doctor's offices have drugs, and break in. I wouldn't want that to happen with me living alone upstairs!"

Lizzie considered this. It was reasonable put that way. She decided to think and pray about it. "Okay, I see your point, and I'll think about it. Right now, we need to get ready to open for business. Let's get those ovens going and start the day's baking."

Mr. LaForest perked up at this. "Do you object to me sticking around to observe your technique? I'd be interested to see you work."

Lizzie stared at him. "You do have some nerve, don't you, Mr. LaForest?"

"Well. . ."

"Not an hour ago I found you crouched in my pantry, with my property in your hands, and now you want to, what, job shadow?"

He stood, jowls quivering in outrage. "Well, you don't need to be insulting! I only asked out of polite curiosity. I'd think out of professional courtesy you'd agree. Maybe I could give you some pointers!"

Jane gasped at his rudeness, and Lizzie thought she heard Eliza snort, but when she glanced at her, the younger woman was wearing a very innocent expression on her face. Lizzie turned back to Mr. LaForest and considered him.

"Oll recht, Mr. LaForest. You may stay and observe my work on one condition."

He frowned mightily. "Well? What is it, girlie?"

"First, do not call me girlie. Second, you must show me any variations you know on the New Orleans style when it comes to pastry baking."

He huffed. "You want to know my secrets? Impossible!"

She cocked her head and studied him for a moment. "I believe you came here to steal mine, didn't you? The least you can do is share yours, and I'll do the same. An exchange of information."

His eyes narrowed, and he stared at her for maybe half a minute. Then, just when Lizzie was sure he was going to refuse and storm out of her bakery, he relented. With a royal tilt of his chin, he acceded to her request. "Fine. I will watch you work, and if I see something we do differently, I will inform you. Good enough?"

Lizzie smiled sunnily at him. "Perfect! Jane, please get Mr. LaForest an apron. We wouldn't want him to get flour all over his natty suit."

At that moment, the back door opened, and John walked in, carrying a bag from the hardware store. He hung his hat on a peg, then turned and, seeing all the people in the kitchen, stopped short, eyes wide. He looked at the police officers, then looked at Lizzie, Jane, and Eliza, and then his eyes landed on Mr. LaForest. His mouth dropped open, and he pointed at the little man, crying, "You're the one from the picture on opening day! What are you doing here?"

Sgt. Hernandez looked at Lizzie. "I'll leave it to you to make the introductions and give him the explanation. We are out of here. Remember, call if anything—and I do mean anything—else happens. We'd rather come for a false alarm than not be here when you need us."

Lizzie nodded. "Denki, Sgt. Hernandez, Officer Anderson, Officer Jakes. Here, take some pastries for later!" She handed Jakes, who was closest, a large bag of day-old pastries, which he took with a huge grin.

"Thank you, Miss Miller! I hope the next time I see you it's because I'm here as a customer. Oh, and as soon as we have any news about the letter you received, we'll be in touch. Nothing yet." He waved and followed Anderson and Hernandez out the kitchen door.

John turned to his sister. "Well? Why is he here and not on the way to jail?"

Jane looked wildly at Lizzie and stammered, "He's going to observe our baking style."

John's eyes grew round. Spinning to face Lizzie, he bit out, "Have you lost your mind, allowing this dangerous man to be here, endangering you and your friends?" He stared at her for a heated moment. "I thought better of you. If you won't show him the door, I will!"

He stalked over to where Mr. LaForest sat at the table and reached for his arm, planning to help him up and out the door. But before he could touch him, Lizzie strode forward, fire in her eyes, and cried, "John Bontrager, don't you dare touch that man. He has my permission to be here in my business! And don't you dare tell me what to do!" She folded her arms and glared at John. Jane and Eliza looked at each other and headed toward the swinging door at the same time.

"I'll go lock up behind them," Jane said. "Come on, Eliza, you can help me get the display cases ready."

They hurried out, and Lizzie scowled at John. "You're early."

He stared at Mr. LaForest, who was still seated at the table, going through the recipe box with an occasional grunt or snort. John looked at the little man and then back at Lizzie. "I'd say I'm late to the party though. If you won't make him leave, do you care to tell me what that man is doing sitting comfortably at your table, eating your pastries and drinking your coffee, when the entire Willow Creek police department has been looking for him?"

At that, Mr. LaForest's head snapped up. "The entire department? Really? Huh, I didn't realize I was that important." He smiled a pleased, smug little smile and grabbed another beignet, took a big bite, groaned in pleasure, and then went back to the recipe box. Lizzie looked at John. "It's a long story."

John hesitated a moment and then, with a shrug, sat down across from LaForest. After a moment's hesitation, Lizzie heaved a disgusted sigh, poured him a mug of coffee, and pushed the plate of pastries toward him.

"This ought to be gut," John commented before tucking into an éclair. "Though I doubt it'll end with you coming to your senses and leaving the detective work to the police."

Lizzie glared. "Oh, it's gut, all right. Mr. LaForest is only the tip of the iceberg." And she filled him in while she started the baking.

When she finished talking, he set his coffee cup on the table and stared at her in disbelief. She stared back, her teeth clenched and her chin raised obstinately, waiting for him to lecture her.

Finally she couldn't stand it. "Well? If you have something to say, go ahead and say it. But remember, you're not my brother." She walked closer to him, her hands on her hips. "You're not my father." She leaned down until their noses were practically touching. "You're not my husband. And you're not even, nor are you likely to ever be, my boyfriend!" She threw her arms up in the air and spun around, hung her bakery apron on a hook and put on her everyday one, grabbed her bonnet and cloak, and started back through the kitchen. Before going through the swinging door, she turned and pointed at Mr. LaForest. "You! Don't touch anything, and don't take my recipe box anywhere." He shook his head no, looking a bit terrified.

She turned her eyes on John. "And you! If you can refrain from telling me what to do, you may accompany me. I'm leaving for the museum. Mr. Rumpkin is coming in early to talk to us." She pushed the swinging door open and sailed through.

John and Mr. LaForest exchanged looks, and John followed her.

Mr. LaForest went back to eating pastries.

CHAPTER FOURTEEN

John and Lizzie walked down the sidewalk, side by side, on the way to the historical museum. Lizzie carried a folder containing the telegram, the letter, and the manuscript pages they'd found. Her lips were pursed, and she kept her eyes pointed straight ahead, refusing to even look at John.

He grimaced. *You blew it, John. Maybe you should have thought twice before you started lecturing a grown woman about how she chose to conduct her own business. Maybe this will finally teach you to think before speaking.*

"I doubt it," he muttered under his breath.

"What was that?" Lizzie asked sharply, casting him a sideways glance before returning her eyes to the sidewalk.

"Nothing important," he said, looking at her to see if there was any sign of a softening in her attitude toward him. Nope.

He sighed again. "Look, Lizzie, I didn't mean anything. . . When I saw that man sitting at your kitchen table, I guess I sort of lost it for a minute."

She kept walking, eyes on the sidewalk. "Sort of?"

Well, at least she was talking to him. He saw that as progress. "Okay, maybe more than sort of. I shouldn't have overreacted."

"Overreacted?"

"Okay! I shouldn't have yelled. And maybe I shouldn't have been so, er, managing."

"Managing?"

"Fine! I shouldn't have told you what to do. I realize you're an adult with your own business, but I lost my head. I was worried for you. And for my sister and Eliza. Can you really blame me? I mean, the last I knew, the police were looking for him, and we all believed he threw a brick with a very nasty note tied to it through your window. He could have been very dangerous."

Just when John thought she wasn't going to respond, Lizzie stopped walking and turned to face him.

He'd been prepared for anger, but the disappointment in her eyes almost undid him. "Lizzie, I. . ."

She raised a hand. "Please let me speak, John."

He nodded reluctantly, hoping this wasn't going to be too painful.

She looked away, gazing across the street at nothing, really, then turned and looked at him. When she spoke, her voice was low. "John, I thought you knew me. I thought you respected me as a businesswoman and as an adult. I thought maybe you were even interested in me as a woman."

He opened his mouth to reply, but she shook her head once, firmly. "Nee, John. You said enough back at the bakery when you undermined my authority in front of my friends, your sister, and a stranger." Tears of anger filled her eyes, and as a man with a mother and several sisters, he knew these tears were the most dangerous kind.

"But today you demonstrated that you do not, in fact, even see me as an adult. You treated me like a child in front of my employees. My friends! You made it quite clear that you don't trust my judgment or my ability to make decisions. You even implied that I'd endangered your sister—my oldest friend—and Eliza." She drew a deep, ragged breath and shook her head. "I was starting to think maybe there might be something between us. But I can't contemplate tying myself to a man who disrespects and distrusts me. I'll work with you to solve this case, because you're already in so deep, but after that, I think it would be better if we didn't see each other, except at services and other public places where we just happen to run into each other as disinterested acquaintances."

She looked at him expectantly, as if waiting for him to agree. He swallowed hard, fighting back his emotional response to the thought that he'd blown it with her, maybe for good.

"John? Do you understand what I'm saying?"

He knew that now was not the time to try to change her mind. He realized with a sinking heart that he'd done worse than anger her today. He'd hurt her. And that was going to take hard, careful effort to reverse. So he did the only thing he could. He nodded. "Ja, I understand. All I can say is, I'm sorry. And I hear you."

She stared at him a moment more, then with another firm nod, turned and started on down the sidewalk toward the museum. After a few seconds, John fell into step beside her again. He didn't speak, but his mind was awhirl as he contemplated and rejected plan after plan for how to regain her trust and regard.

They reached the museum before he'd come up with anything remotely realistic or reasonable. She marched up the steps and opened the door. "Well, here we are. Here's hoping Mr. Rumpkin will have some fresh take on this stuff." She shook the folder at him, and John nodded. It was all he could do. She went inside, and he followed, heart hollow and mind racing.

"What do you have for me?" Mr. Rumpkin pulled a cross-stitched glasses case out of his pocket and withdrew a pair of black plastic-framed reading glasses, which he perched on the end of his long, thin nose. He held out his hand, and Lizzie handed him the folder containing the letter and the manuscript pages.

His eyebrows flew upward when he pulled the papers out and saw the manuscript pages. "Oh my goodness. . ."

He sank slowly onto a nearby chair, but when he met a ribbon saying Please Don't Sit Here he stood back up, muttering something under his breath. "Come," he said, heading into the kitchen, his eyes never leaving the manuscript pages. In the kitchen he sat down, laid the letters on the table, and continued reading through the manuscript pages until he finished. Lizzie and John stood nearby, waiting to see what he'd say.

When he finished, he went right back to the beginning and read through the pages again. That time, Lizzie glanced at John, and they both took seats at the table to await Mr. Rumpkin's verdict.

The elderly man finished reading the pages for the second time, and he laid them carefully on the table, then removed his reading glasses and closed his eyes while he polished the lenses with his shirt cuff. For a full minute he did this, obviously lost in thought.

Lizzie could hardly contain her curiosity. She leaned forward, as if she'd be able to hear his thoughts if she were just a bit closer.

She caught John giving her an amused look and frowned fiercely at him. He shrugged, sat back—one ankle crossed over his other knee, arms folded—and settled in to wait.

"Hmm. Very interesting. This looks authentic. But how can I be sure? Date the paper, of course. Check the ink. The handwriting. Do I have a sample of his handwriting? Beckett was the agent, wasn't he? Curious, curious." Rumpkin talked to himself as he examined the pages yet again. Finally, Lizzie couldn't take it anymore. She cleared her throat, and the elderly man looked at her in surprise, quite as if he'd forgotten she was even there.

"Oh! Sorry, got caught up in it! Well, well, you may have really discovered something important here, young woman! I do believe these pages may be part of the famous—or infamous, to be more to the point—lost manuscript of E. W. Fingle! Oh, this will set the literary world on its collective ear, to be sure!" He sat back, beaming with delight at the very idea.

"Mr. Rumpkin?" Lizzie ventured. "How do you think this relates to whoever is breaking into my building, and the other things that have happened?"

He blinked at her, his eyes huge behind the thick-framed glasses. "Other things?"

John looked at Lizzie, then said, "Such as someone throwing a brick through her window during her grand opening. A brick with a note telling her to close her business."

Mr. Rumpkin looked blankly at John for a moment, then slowly nodded. "Right, right, I'd forgotten that. Hmm. Well, I don't know. But I believe these pages are a clue! A clue to someone's motive."

"But, those pages have been languishing inside an envelope for over a hundred years, Mr. Rumpkin. And nobody has seen them or, for that fact, knows they exist, except for us three, and my friends Jane and Eliza."

He peered at her through his glasses. "Are you sure?"

She looked at John, who shrugged. "Pretty sure?" she said.

He sat back. "Okay then. Leave these with me for a few days, will you? I have some colleagues I wish to consult. Now, then, was there anything else?"

"What about the letter? And the telegram! I almost forgot the telegram!"

"Letter? Telegram?" He looked blankly down at the table, where the letter the manuscript pages had been in, from the author E. W. Fingle to his agent, Mr. Ambrose Beckett, sat beside the threatening telegram from Gregory Liptak to E. W. Fingle. "Well, what have we here? In my excitement over these manuscript pages, I didn't even notice these."

John nodded to Lizzie to explain, so she picked up the envelope from Fingle to Beckett first. "This is the envelope we found the manuscript pages in. It's from Mr. Fingle to his literary agent, Mr. Ambrose Beckett."

Mr. Rumpkin took the envelope and carefully withdrew the letter. "We technically shouldn't be touching any of these with our hands. But I assume you have all read all of these?"

Lizzie nodded, eyes wide, and glanced at John, who just shrugged. "We didn't realize there was any harm in it. We were very careful."

Rumpkin was reading the letter, so he just nodded absently. "Oil on our hands, not good for the old paper, you know. Yellows it. But what's done is done. The important thing is that you found these, and so amazingly well preserved! Where did you say they were?" He surfaced from reading the letter, peering at Lizzie through his thick lenses.

"My sister found a box full of old letters shoved under the eaves in the bakery building," John said.

Rumpkin looked up sharply. "You say a box full of old letters?" He looked around his kitchen, as if the box might suddenly manifest there. "Where are the rest?"

"We went through all of them last night," Lizzie said. "Most of them were from the innkeeper's sister to the innkeeper, a Mrs. Agatha Bridgerton. Mostly recipes, and family stuff about babies and weddings and such."

"What do you think about that letter, Mr. Rumpkin?" John asked, leaning forward in his seat.

"It's quite interesting. But something about it strikes me as. . .odd."

"Yes!" Lizzie cried, scooching her chair a bit closer to his. "It's that it was written to the agent in New York, and sealed and stamped, and opened, presumably by the addressee, but it was found in a box of letters received by people at the inn! Why would it be there? Wasn't it mailed? Or did the recipient bring it back with him at a later date and leave it there?"

"Good questions, young woman."

Lizzie and John looked at each other. "We were thinking that would explain it," John said. "If Mr. Beckett brought it with him after the murder, when he was searching for the rest of the manuscript, then accidentally left it behind when he left again."

"Do we know for certain that he didn't find the rest of the manuscript?" Lizzie asked.

Rumpkin nodded decisively. "Yes. The innkeeper, as you no doubt noticed from what you said about letters to her from her sister, was a prolific letter writer. We have several of her letters here in the museum's collection. If you don't want the ones you found, we'd be happy to add them as well." He cut the air with his hand. "But that's for another time. The point is, not only did she write and receive many letters, she also kept a diary very faithfully, writing in it nightly before bed. And she wrote very vividly of Mr. Beckett's arrival, his demands to examine everything left behind by Mr. Fingle, and his fury when he didn't discover the manuscript Fingle was working on in his possessions. He tore the room apart, then searched the inn. It was nowhere to be found, according to the innkeeper."

"May I see this diary?" Lizzie asked. "Maybe I'll see something you missed. I mean, as a woman."

Rumpkin considered her request for a few moments, then nodded and pushed to his feet. "I'll get it. Wait here a moment."

He walked slowly from the room, leaving John and Lizzie alone in an uneasy silence. Lizzie stared at a crack in the ceiling. John untied and retied his shoes. Lizzie picked at a hangnail. John examined his fingernails. Lizzie straightened her kapp. John hummed a few bars from a favorite hymn. Lizzie squirmed in her seat. Finally, John stood abruptly, startling Lizzie, who gasped a bit.

"Enough! This is narrish! We're acting like two kinner. Look, Elizabeth, the fact is, I like you. I like you a lot, fashtay? So when I saw you with a man I believed to be dangerous, I got a bit upset. I don't think that was any kind of insult to you or challenge to your ability to take care of yourself or make your own decisions. It was just the way I felt."

"Okay..."

"Please, let me finish." He glared at her, and she stared back, lips parted in surprise. He swallowed the sudden desire to see how they tasted, tearing his eyes away and focusing instead on her eyes, which were wide with surprise. He made a conscious effort to calm himself. "I am sorry for implying that you had put Jane and Eliza in danger. That was unfair. Look, Lizzie, what I'm trying to say is, please, don't say we can't still see each other socially after we figure out what's going on here. At least as friends. I don't have all that many gut friends, and I consider you one. I'd be very sorry if you pushed me out of your life entirely."

He sat back down next to her and took her hand. "I understand you aren't ready for a relationship right now. I understand you need time to figure out how to be a business owner and employer before you can take on any new role. But I'm patient. I have time. I really, really like you. I can wait for you. Will you let me?"

She sat quietly, just looking at him. He studied her face, the expressions crossing it as she considered his words. She bit her lip, and he drew in his breath. Here it comes, he thought. She's going to say no.

He threw up a quick prayer, not for God to intervene and give him what he wanted. John had never been a fan of such selfish prayers, which asked for his heart's desire without considering what someone else may want.

Rather, he prayed for a good outcome—for God to lead them both to whatever path would be best for them.

Please, Father, You know my heart better than I do. And You know Lizzie's. Help us to find a path that will lead us both to the lives You intend for us. Your will be done.

"I. . .I'm not sure what to say. I like you too. And if things were different, I do believe I'd be very interested in courting you. Er, in you courting me. Courting each other!" She threw her hands up in the air, and he smiled in response.

"Gotcha."

She smiled. "I just hesitate to take my focus off of my new business. It's such a delicate time. And it wouldn't be fair to you. I work long hours, and I get up so early that I go to bed really early. I'm not much fun, honestly."

He regarded her seriously for a moment before saying, "Maybe you should let me decide if I think you're fun."

She blinked. "Excuse me?"

He shook his head. "I just mean, I don't need you to entertain me. I just want to spend time with you. Even if it means I come by and help you out in the bakery from time to time, doing odd jobs you don't have time to tackle."

Her eyes had widened as he spoke, and he wondered if he'd gone too far. She opened her mouth to answer, but of course, that was when Mr. Rumpkin returned. John closed his eyes in frustration. Talk about bad timing! But there was nothing for it. Lizzie had already turned her attention to the elderly gentleman, who was holding an old leather-bound volume in his hands.

"Here it is. It took me a few minutes to locate it." He frowned. "Obviously our curation needs updating. Maybe I should consider getting one of those computers, and logging where everything is stored, and if we've loaned anything out. Like this journal, for example."

"Computers can be useful," John put in. "I used one last night to check a fact." He looked at Lizzie. "It turns out that carbon paper was widely available in 1914!"

"Really? Then that explains why Mr. Fingle was willing to send off pages of his manuscript. He'd made a copy!"

Mr. Rumpkin looked at them as if they'd lost their marbles. "Of course he did. Carbon paper has been around since the early 1800s, I believe."

"Since 1806, it turns out," John proudly proclaimed.

Lizzie smiled at him. "That's wonderful, John! So now we know." She turned to Mr. Rumpkin. "I don't know anything about computers either, Mr. Rumpkin. But do you have a logbook or something where I can sign this journal out for now?"

"Of course!" He smacked himself on the forehead. "I nearly forgot. I'll get it." He turned and bustled off, muttering something about getting old, and Lizzie turned her attention back to John.

"John, let me consider what you said. And, um, if you'd like to come by the bakery in the afternoons, there's always something to be done that we don't seem to get around to. I can't pay you much, mind."

He felt elated and sat up straight, beaming at her. "I don't want your money, Lizzie. I want your time."

She nodded. "Well, time is the only thing I have less of than money. So we'll see how it goes. You may find you don't have the patience to wait for me after all."

His grin dimmed down to a gentle smile of friendship. "Oh, I doubt that. But denki for the chance for us both to find out. I'll come by tomorrow afternoon, okay? I'll have to stay in the furniture shop today to make up for coming here."

She nodded, and he sat back, a surge of relief and hope filling up all the little hollow spaces inside of him. Mr. Rumpkin returned with a logbook, and Lizzie busied herself checking out the journal. John took a moment to check in with his Father in heaven. *Vader, I don't know if You had anything to do with Lizzie's change of heart, but if You did, denki!*

Now, please give me the wisdom to not mess this up. I'm afraid I might prove to be a difficult project for You. Amen.

"John?" He opened his eyes and found Lizzie and Mr. Rumpkin looking at him oddly. "We're finished here. Ready to go?"

"Oh ja! Sorry, I was just thinking." He stood and turned to the elderly curator. "Denki, Mr. Rumpkin. If we find anything else interesting, we'll bring it right over."

"See that you do. And you'd better not take too long. I'm not getting any younger!"

Lizzie glanced down at the table and saw the telegram sitting there, forgotten. She picked it up and handed it to Mr. Rumpkin. "I almost forgot! This telegram is the one the killer sent to the victim! It was never delivered to him, from what we can tell. It wasn't opened."

"Right!" John watched as Mr. Rumpkin took the envelope and carefully slipped the telegram out and examined it. "We think it was forgotten and misfiled. So Mr. Fingle never got Mr. Liptak's warning. We think Mr. Liptak probably assumed Fingle was being rude, and that was the last straw. He came here and killed him."

"Ahhh. This is another long-sought treasure as well! May I keep this for a few days, or weeks? I promise I'll be very careful."

"Ja, of course," Lizzie said. "Do you mind making a copy of it, and the letter and manuscript pages?"

"Right away." Mr. Rumpkin bustled out with the items and was back shortly with copies for Lizzie, who tucked them into the folder that had held the originals.

"Thank you, my dear. I need to have these officially authenticated. Could take a few weeks."

"No problem. We'll be in touch," Lizzie said.

She and John exited the museum, and he walked her back to the bakery, each lost in their own thoughts. At the door, he stopped and smiled at her. "I'll see you guys at closing time, ja?"

She nodded and gave him a shy smile he hadn't seen before. "Ja, see you then. I can hardly wait to dive into this journal! But it'll have to wait until tonight." Lizzie paused. "Do you have time for a cup of kaffi?"

He hesitated. "Just a quick one." She smiled, and he followed her inside, reflecting on how, although not much had really changed, he still felt oddly elated, as if he really had a chance with her.

Just goes to show, you never know what's around the next corner. And Gott does work in mysterious ways!

CHAPTER FIFTEEN

When Lizzie and John walked into the bakery, they were surprised to see Obadiah Stutzman, owner of Stutzman's Fine Amish Furniture, seated at a table near the window, sipping a mug of coffee and enjoying a pastry sampler.

John stopped in his tracks for a moment, then pasted a smile on his face and nodded at the man who bought more furniture from his family than any other individual business. This was not a man John wanted to alienate.

"*Guder mariye*, Obadiah. I trust you're well this morning?"

"Ja, ja, I'm fine. Guder mariye to you too, John." He peered at Lizzie and frowned. "And you must be the slip of a girl who bought this building right out from under my wife and me. Can't understand what the Petersheims were thinking. I thought we had a deal, and all of a sudden, they changed their minds and decided to sell to you."

Lizzie swallowed, unsure how to respond. As far as she knew, although the Stutzmans had indeed expressed an interest in purchasing the building, the Petersheims had never entered into any sort of agreement with their business neighbors from across the street. They'd approached her when they decided to retire, helping her work through the local small business incubator to get a start-up loan. That and the money she'd saved was just enough to purchase the building, and the Petersheims threw in all the bakery equipment, and a lot of furniture they didn't want to take with them to the *dawdi haus* behind their son's place in Shipshewana, Indiana, where they'd moved. When Lizzie had protested that it was too much, that surely they'd want money for the things, they'd just laughed. *"And what would we be needing with a deluxe professional mixer that makes enough dough to make twelve dozen donuts all at one time?"* they'd said. *"Nee, you keep it. Someday you'll help out some young person just getting started. What's that the Englisch say?"* Mrs. Petersheim had pursed her lips in concentration. *"Ach! Ja. Pay it forward, Lizzie."*

Lizzie had given them both teary hugs and promised to do that, someday.

So she looked at Mr. Stutzman, who seemed to her to be one of those perpetually dissatisfied people, and smiled regretfully. "I'm truly sorry for your disappointment, Mr. Stutzman. I had no knowledge of any discussions you had with the Petersheims, nor anything to do with their final decision."

He looked a bit uncomfortable. "Well, we didn't actually come to any agreements, if you want to be exact about it." He frowned darkly. "But I expected that we would, eventually. I wanted to expand my furniture business over here, and my children would have lived upstairs. And instead there's just you. What a waste of space."

John and Lizzie both must have looked shocked, because Obadiah burst out laughing. "Oh! Your faces. Priceless." He shook his head. "Not her, the fact that there's only one of her in this big place! That's what I meant, boy. I hope I'm not rude enough to call someone perfectly nice a waste of space. My mudder didn't raise me that way. Even if she did steal away a building that should have been mine. Now where will my sons live, I ask you? They're not farmers, and we don't have a farm anyway. No room in our home now that they're getting their families started. Ach! This place would have been perfect!"

He turned to Lizzie and quirked his lips to the side. "But, I came here to tell you I don't bear you any personal ill will, girl." He glared at John. "Got the idea maybe I was a suspect in what happened here with the brick."

"Where did you get that idea, Obadiah?" John asked, looking the older man straight in the eyes.

Obadiah frowned. "Well, both from your conversation with my boys and from the police showing up and asking me. Brick through the window! Break-ins! Intruders! I don't want the place that badly. I'm an honest businessman with a reputation I worked hard to create. I'm certainly not going to squander it away on shenanigans of that sort!" He stood but picked up his plate. Turning to look at John, he frowned again. "So, young John, will I be seeing the bookcases I ordered from you anytime soon? Or are you too busy playing detective to build furniture at the moment?"

John's mouth dropped open, and he snapped it shut. "I'm working on those every day, Obadiah. They will be ready at the time we agreed upon. I certainly appreciate your business, as you know. As does my vader."

Mr. Stutzman nodded. "Gut, gut. Well, I'll be off, then. I just wanted to clear up any misunderstandings you might have had about my fraa and me, or our sons, having anything to do with your recent misfortunes. Are we good?"

Lizzie nodded. "Ja, we are, Obadiah. Denki for coming over."

He nodded and turned for the door, taking another bite of his cream cheese Danish. "Now this is what I call baking. No need for all that fancy French stuff, if you ask me. Good old-fashioned Amish baking suits me just fine. Good day to you."

With that, he pushed through the door, and they watched him look both ways before crossing the street to disappear inside the front door of his business, plate of pastries and all.

John scratched his face, then turned to look at Lizzie. "Well, I didn't see that coming."

She shook her head. "Neither did I. So, do you believe him?"

She smiled at Eliza when she placed two steaming mugs of black coffee on the table, along with a plate containing several powder sugar–covered beignets. "Got to hurry, boss. Lunch rush soon," Eliza said, spinning around and heading back to the counter, where she was preparing plates of their specialty sandwiches.

Lizzie turned her attention back to John. "Where were we?"

"You asked whether I think Obadiah is telling us the truth. In a word, ja, I do. He's crotchety, but I believe he's honest. He's always fair in his dealings when he contracts furniture from my family, anyway."

"That's a gut way to learn his measure, I'd say," Lizzie said, picking up a beignet and biting delicately into it, dusting her chin and fingers and apron with powdered sugar. "If he's honest in his business dealings, don't you think he's probably going to be honest in other ways?"

John chose a beignet and ate it in two big bites, scattering powdered sugar all over himself and the table. Lizzie couldn't help laughing a little at him. "You have sugar. . ." She pointed at his hair. He brushed it off and took another beignet, biting in more carefully this time. "So, ja, I agree, he's probably telling the truth. He was disappointed about not getting the building, but he's moved on."

John was about to comment when the door crashed open, and fearing another attack of some sort, Lizzie let out a tiny scream and jumped up from the table, nearly upsetting it.

She looked up to see who had made such a dramatic entrance, and there stood her probationary strudel baker, Linda Preece.

"Good afternoon! I've brought the strudels! Got 'em right here." She patted a large box dangling from her other arm. "Twelve dozen, mixed varieties, just like you wanted, boss! Where do you want them?"

"I'll take them!" Eliza called, a welcoming smile on her face. "Good morning, Linda! I can hardly wait to try these. Come on, let's take them to the back."

"Who was that?" John asked, eyeing the swinging door to the kitchen.

"That was Linda Preece, our strudel baker—on a trial basis for now. I thought I'd give her a try."

He looked perplexed. "Preece, Preece. . .wait, isn't she a dog groomer?"

"Ja, a dog groomer and a strudel baker."

"Let's hope the two things happen in different buildings, or you may find dog hairs in your strudel." He pushed up from the table. "I need to go. Please, think about what I said earlier, okay?"

"I'll think about it, John. That's all I can say for now."

He smiled as he reached out and squeezed her shoulder. "I'll take it. See you this afternoon!"

Whistling, he turned and headed out the door. She watched him go for a moment, then turned as the kitchen door flew open and Linda came striding through. "Got two goldendoodles coming in an hour! Hope the owners listened to me this time and brushed them every day so I don't have to shave them all the way down. Let me know what you think about the strudel! See you later!"

Out she sailed, with Lizzie never getting a word in edgewise. Lizzie saw her climb into her bright orange convertible Volkswagen Bug and zoom away. She shook her head. She considered herself an energetic person, but Linda exhausted her.

Eliza came through the door more sedately. "Well, she's a lot, but wait until you try her strudel! Mamma mia! It's gut!"

Lizzie smiled at her younger friend. "Mamma mia? Where did you pick that up?"

Eliza giggled. "One of my older brothers worked in an Italian restaurant for a couple years in Lancaster. He got in the habit of saying it, and I liked it—so much energy!" Her eyes sparkled with humor, and Lizzie grinned in return.

"Okay, I want to taste these famous strudels. Let's go before we get swamped with customers."

They went back to the kitchen and found that Jane had placed a dozen strudels on presentation plates to go out front. Lizzie saw that she'd cut up several others of various types and set them on a sampler plate. "Hmm. They look moist. That's a gut sign." She selected a tidbit and bit in. Her eyes widened. "Ohhh," she breathed. "Apple. Appenditlich!"

Eliza nodded. "What did I tell you?"

Lizzie swallowed and grinned at Eliza. "Mamma mia, you were right!"

All three women burst into laughter, and Lizzie tasted another piece. "Mmm, apple-blue cheese! And the crust just melts in your mouth. The woman can bake!"

"And not a dog hair in sight!" Eliza laughed.

"We could sell these for lunch, along with the croissant sandwiches, don't you think?" Eliza asked, tasting a bite of a roasted veggie strudel.

"We could offer a strudel special. You get one savory strudel and one sweet, plus the drink of your choice."

"I think people would like that," Jane said.

"Well, they're not New Orleans–style French pastries," Eliza said. "But you did say you wanted to offer a selection of traditional Amish baked goods as well. I think these are a really gut addition to that."

"Exactly!" Lizzie grinned. "I'm running an Amish bakery in Amish country. I have to sell some Amish pastries, right? These definitely qualify. And I don't have to bake them."

"I'll go write on the blackboard that we have strudel!" Jane said, hurrying out front. "And that we're giving away free strudel today with every order between, say, eleven and one?"

Lizzie nodded. "Perfect. I'll get the usual stuff ready."

The three friends got busy, and soon everything was ready for the lunch rush. Lizzie had just hung up her dish towel after going over the counters when the front door opened and Lydia Coblentz came stumping in, followed closely by Bishop Troyer.

Lydia scanned the space, which was now populated by a scattered assortment of folks drinking coffee and enjoying baked goods while visiting or working.

Lydia greeted Lizzie and gave her a strong hug. "Well, how's the bakery business treating you? I hear you've had some additional challenges since your grand opening?"

Lizzie hugged her friend back, then pulled away. "Ja, it's true, unfortunately. Good afternoon, Bishop. Would the two of you like to have a seat? You're just in time to be the first to sample our new sweet and savory strudel selections!"

Bishop Abram Troyer's eyes lit up. "Strudels you say? I love those! My late wife, Amelia, baked outstanding apple strudels."

Lizzie led the pair to a comfortable table near the fireplace and saw them settled. "I'll get you both a cup of kaffi, ja? And a selection of strudels." She leaned down and added in a conspiratorial whisper, "On the house!"

"Now, now, child, how do you think you're going to make a go of your business if you keep giving everything away for free?" Bishop Troyer asked, stroking his long white beard with one hand. "I'll have your strudels, and I'll pay a fair price for them. Right, Lydia?"

Lydia patted him approvingly on his hand and nodded. "Well said, Abram." She turned to Lizzie. "The same for me, please. And you can serve up the latest news when you bring it!"

Lizzie chuckled. "Of course! Oh, here's Eliza now with your kaffi! Denki, Eliza."

"No problem," the cheery young woman said, placing steaming mugs of black kaffi in front of each of her elders. "Now, I believe you like yours sweet, don't you, Bishop?"

He smiled winsomely at her. "Well, now that you mention it. . ."

She reached into her apron pocket and pulled out a sugar bowl and a small pitcher of cream, which she set on the table.

"Now, not too much sugar, Abram," Lydia cautioned. "You know what *Dokder* Reuben told you."

He gave her a mock glare. "Woman, can't a man enjoy his kaffi the way he likes without being browbeaten and henpecked?"

"Nope, not when his gut friend is around to make sure he follows his dokder's orders he can't!" Lydia threw back her head and let loose a peal of laughter. "And here I am, like it or not!"

"Fine. I'll stick to one small teaspoon of sugar."

"Gut. And you'll be having a pastry, no doubt. It's not as if you're totally deprived," Lydia reminded him. He rolled his eyes, but nodded and stirred his meager portion of sugar into his coffee before adding a generous splash of cream.

Lydia stirred two heaping spoonfuls of sugar into her own coffee and grinned at Abram when he sputtered in indignation at her. "I'm not prediabetic," she said, smiling sweetly. "And my waistline isn't a size—"

He raised his hand to stop her from continuing. "Please! Don't say a number. Look, I'm enjoying my bitter coffee. I hope you enjoy yours too."

"Back in a minute with your food."

Lizzie fetched the plates of sweet and savory strudels and set them before her elder friends. "Here you go! I hope you like them!"

She went back to the counter and grabbed a mug of kaffi for herself. "Are you okay here, Eliza? I want to talk with Lydia and Abram for a few minutes."

"Of course. Go drink your coffee."

Lizzie nodded her thanks and returned to sit with Lydia and the bishop.

"These are delicious, Lizzie. They're sure to be a hit." Bishop Abram blotted his mouth with a napkin. "But that's not why we stopped by."

"It's not why you stopped by, you mean," Lydia said, frowning at the bishop, who, it seemed to Lizzie, squirmed in his seat.

"Now, Lydia, I have my duty."

Lydia sniffed. "As if Lizzie or the other girls would ever give you cause to worry."

"And there's John Bontrager too, don't forget."

Lizzie blinked. What was this about? She had a sinking feeling she knew, and it wasn't good. "Is there a problem, Bishop?"

He darted a quick glance at Lydia, then squared his shoulders. "I hope not, young woman. But I need to ask you some questions."

She nodded slowly. "For sure and certain. Ask away."

He leaned forward and spoke quietly. "This situation with your business. It's all very alarming, you must admit."

She nodded again. "Ja, it is. But I believe we have the situation under control. We're getting closer to figuring out who's behind the break-ins, and then we should know who wants to shut down my business!"

He sat back, eyes wide, and Lydia heaved a sigh and shook her head before taking a sip of her coffee. "So it's true, what I've heard!"

Lizzie leaned forward. "What have you heard?"

"And from whom, I might ask," Lydia added.

The bishop had the grace to look a bit uncomfortable. "Well, from Amelia Schwartz," he mumbled.

"Aha! As I thought. Are you going to credit a word she says?" Lydia slapped her palm down on the table, making both Lizzie and the bishop jump in their seats. "The woman is a menace! I thought she'd learned her lesson with her nasty gossip about other community members. But apparently not."

"Now, Lydia, even a broken clock is right twice a day," the bishop said. "Hmpf. We'll see about that."

"Well, she said that Lizzie, Jane, and Eliza, with the help of John Bontrager, have been behaving like amateur detectives, and attempting to do the work of the Englisch police!" He stared at Lizzie, then at Lydia.

Lydia looked at Lizzie, who was looking at her coffee mug. The corner of Lydia's mouth quirked up. "So, child, is the broken clock right?"

Lizzie wrinkled her nose and glanced at the bishop before nodding sheepishly at Lydia. "Ja, a little bit. But we aren't doing anything dangerous!"

The bishop threw up his hands. "Ach! It isn't about the danger, it's about getting involved in what shouldn't concern you. We need to stay separate! Let the police do their job!"

Lizzie pursed her lips while considering what to say. "I can understand that, and I agree that we need to let the police do their jobs. But there are a few things directly related to this building, and too old—historic, I mean—to relate to what's going on right now. Probably."

Bishop Troyer looked intrigued in spite of himself. "Really? Such as?"

Lizzie quickly explained about the old murder, the missing manuscript, and the box of letters they'd found, and how Mr. Rumpkin was helping them.

"Fascinating!" Lydia gushed. "I do love a mystery."

"Hmm." He eyed his empty plate. "I love these strudels. Especially the apple–blue cheese one. May I have one to go?"

"The whole strudel?" Lizzie asked, eyes sparkling.

He smiled sheepishly. "Well, I am a bachelor. Nobody is cooking for me, and I have to fend for myself." He tried to look hungry and deprived.

Lydia rolled her eyes. "You eat at my house two nights a week, and I know for a fact that other members of the community feed you at least twice a week as well. When does all this fending for yourself happen?"

"The other three nights, obviously," he said with a smirk. "So, that strudel to go?" He smiled charmingly at Lizzie, and she pushed to her feet. "I'll go get it for you, Bishop."

But he stayed her with a hand on her arm. "Lizzie."

She turned to look at him inquiringly. "Ja?"

He chewed the inside of his cheek for a moment, then gave a decisive nod. "I won't forbid you from pursuing answers in the matter of your business. But I caution you to be careful. Think things out before you act on them. Not only do I not want you being dragged too far into the Englisch world, but whoever is doing these things is potentially dangerous."

"I promise to be careful and if I ever think there is any danger, I'll call the police right away, like we did this morning."

She realized her mistake as the words left her mouth.

"This morning? What happened this morning? I hadn't heard of this?" The bishop's eyebrows drew together in a fierce line.

"I did say this morning, didn't I," Lizzie said weakly.

Lydia and Abram nodded. So Lizzie sat back down and told them about coming in and discovering the place in shambles, the intruder—intruders, as it turned out—still inside. Lydia gasped at least twice, and the bishop looked horrified.

"Please don't say this changes things," Lizzie begged. "The angry little man turned out to be a competing bakery owner from about an hour away. He meant no harm, just wanted to look at my beignet recipes."

"And the other one?" Every inch the authority figure now, the bishop pinned Lizzie with his stare. "What of him?"

Lizzie licked lips gone dry. "That one got away. And we don't know who he—or she—was. They ran out the back."

There were several moments of silence while Bishop Troyer digested this, and Lizzie feared he was going to change his mind and forbid her from looking into the matter with her friends.

The bishop opened his mouth, and Lydia laid a soft hand on his arm. He turned and looked at her. "Lydia, surely you don't condone..."

Lydia shook her head and patted Abram's arm. "Nee, nee, of course not. This is a bad situation, for sure and certain. But Abram, consider. Lizzie, Jane, and Eliza have to come here to work every morning. They are already taking the precaution of staying at Eliza's house. I understand better locks will be placed on the doors here and there?" She glanced at

Lizzie, who nodded vigorously.

"Oh ja, much better locks!"

"Gut, gut," Lydia continued. "Abram, I can't see what else the girls can do. And John is just being a gut bruder to Jane, and friend to Lizzie and Eliza." She glanced at Lizzie, who could have sworn she caught a twinkle of mischief in Lydia's eyes, but then the woman had turned her attention back on her friend, the bishop. "I think you were wise to allow them to look into the historical mystery. The police can take care of the current troubles."

"And if the two intersect, as seems rather likely?" Abram demanded.

Lydia shrugged philosophically. "Lizzie and the others have gut heads on their shoulders. They won't do anything narrish, right Lizzie?"

"Oh, absolutely, I promise." She looked imploringly at the bishop, who basically held her ability to stay in business in his hands. If he ordered her to stop looking into the old case, she would have to obey. But sooner or later, the person trying to put her out of business would succeed, if somebody didn't stop them.

Slowly, with obvious reluctance, he relented. "Very well. But you must be very careful! Promise me. And stay out of the Englisch police's business, ja?"

"I promise!" Lizzie decided it was time to make herself scarce. "I think Eliza needs me. The lunch rush is picking up. These are on the house. See you later!"

She hurried away, ignoring their protests that they wanted to pay for their meal. She waved at Eliza, indicating she'd be right back, and escaped into the kitchen.

Jane looked up from doing some dishes. "Well? Are we banned from pursuing our little mystery?"

Lizzie plopped into a chair. "Nee! Amazingly, we are not." She told Jane all about her conversation with the bishop and Lydia. Then she looked around. "Where did Mr. LaForest go?"

"Oh, he had to get to work. He said he'll be back another day."

"Huh. Okay. Oh! The bishop is taking an apple–blue cheese strudel to go."

Jane nodded. "Gotcha." She grabbed a couple of to-go boxes, put in the strudel, and added a few pastries into one of them. "To sweeten the deal. I'll bet he loves your new bread pudding." She winked at Lizzie, who grinned gratefully back, and disappeared through the swinging door.

Lizzie heaved a huge sigh of relief. "Vader," she prayed, "denki for letting the bishop see things from my perspective. Please, Vader, keep us safe, and help us figure out who wants us out of business, and how it all relates to what happened here so long ago. And I promise not to forget myself and do anything dangerous. Your will be done, Vader."

A glance at the clock told Lizzie the lunch rush would soon be in full swing. She stood up, dusted off her hands, and got busy.

CHAPTER SIXTEEN

John had picked the girls up after work as usual, and while he drove them the short distance to Eliza's apartment, Lizzie explained to all of them what Bishop Troyer had said.

"So, he's okay with us continuing to look into the historical aspect of the case, as long as we stay out of the way of the Englisch police?" John summarized.

Lizzie nodded. "Ja, although to be completely honest, John, I don't think the two parts of this case are actually separate. Do you?"

Jane shook her head vehemently. "Nee. I think we'll find out that one has very much to do with the other, when we get to the bottom of it."

"And maybe tonight we'll find something important in the inn-keeper's journal!" Eliza exclaimed as John pulled his horse and buggy into the parking area at Eliza's. They all piled out and went up the steps. Eliza dug in her small bag for the key to the new dead bolt John had installed. She opened it up, and John nodded in satisfaction. "That lock is gut and solid. Short of kicking the door in, which would make plenty of noise, nobody is getting in here uninvited."

"The old dead bolt was probably adequate," Jane pointed out.

John shrugged. "It was the kind that you could break the window, reach in, and turn. You need a key to open this one. It's in the drawer there in case of emergency."

"I suppose the second lock at the top of the steps was necessary too, though it slows me down, especially if I'm carrying anything," Eliza griped as she trudged up and unlocked the dead bolt John had installed, with Dokder Reuben's full approval.

"Well, ja, of course," John said as they all entered the apartment. "Because it will buy you time if you hear someone kick in the downstairs door."

Eliza shook her head. "And who is going to go to all that much trouble?"

"Remember, you live above a doctor's office. Some people think there are commercially valuable drugs in all doctors' offices. They might break in for those," John reminded her reasonably. "I can put a table on the landing at the top of the stairs, so if you're carrying anything you'll have somewhere to put it down while you unlock the door."

"Fine, if it makes you and my big bruder feel better, I can put up with it. And ja, a table is a gut idea, denki."

"Gut, because it does make us both feel better," John said, walking over to the back door and checking the lock. "This one bothers me a little. All anyone would need to do would be give it a kick, and they're in. I'd prefer a metal security door up here, but it seems a bit excessive, I have to admit."

"It would sort of ruin the homeyness of this room, John," Jane pointed out. He grunted and took a seat at the table.

"Fine, I suppose. It's better than it was, anyway. So, what's for dinner?"

A feline chirp sounded from the floor, and Lizzie laughed. "Little Mouse wants to know the same thing." She bent and picked up her cat, which snuggled its head affectionately beneath her chin and started purring loudly. "Oh, you missed me! I love you too, Little Mouse. I'll get you and your pal Secret dinner in just a minute."

John cleared his throat. "Ahem, don't forget your human friends who are hungry too."

He looked so pathetic Lizzie laughed again. "You're getting used to us feeding you every night, John. Don't your parents miss you at their table?"

"Oh ja," Jane said with a smirk for her brother while she filled the cats' water bowls with fresh water. "Maem misses him something wonderful, but he told her he's helping to keep me and all of the rest of you safe until this business is settled, so she gave in."

"I'm sure it's hard on her, only having half a dozen kinner at the table with the two of us gone," John said.

"Ja, very lonely!" Lizzie said. "My parents still want me to come home every night. It takes time to get used to change."

Eliza shrugged. "My maem is despairing of me finding a *mann* here, and has started saying I should return home to Lancaster, but I like it here. I have wonderful new friends, and I love my job. Plus, I enjoy having my own space here in my apartment. I told her I'd try harder to find a boyfriend."

"Really?" Lizzie asked, surprised because her younger friend had heretofore shown little interest in coupling up with anyone.

"Well, it's not hard to try harder, since I haven't been trying at all." Eliza chuckled. "At least now I'm looking at the local boys, sort of weighing my options for when I'm ready."

"If you spend too much time weighing, all the boys will marry someone else," Jane warned.

"Talk about the pot calling the kettle black!" Eliza hooted. "You're five or six years older than I am, and I don't see you looking around much at the boys."

Jane blushed and muttered something under her breath, and Lizzie hid a smile behind her hand.

"What was that?" John asked, a twinkle in his eye when he met Lizzie's across the room.

"Nothing," Jane said. "I'll start dinner. Let's have spaghetti. I put the meatballs from the freezer into the fridge this morning. They should be thawed by now."

"Yum!" Eliza cried. "My favorite! I'll make garlic bread."

John looked out the window at the nice vegetable garden at the back of the yard. "I'll go see if there are any tomatoes or cucumbers yet. We could have a salad with our meal." He picked up the key hanging on a hook not far from the door—out of sight and reach from anyone who broke a window and was looking for the key—and unlocked the door leading out to a tiny deck, just big enough for two small chairs and a minuscule table, where Eliza liked to sit and enjoy her coffee or a glass of lemonade. "I'll be right back!" He jogged down the steps and across the yard, where Lizzie saw him bending over the vegetable garden, searching for ripe fruits.

"Maybe I'll go help him," she murmured.

"Oh ja!" Jane grinned. "By all means, go help John find tomatoes and cucumbers. We'll be fine, right, Eliza?"

Eliza grinned at Jane. "Of course we will!"

"You two think you're being very clever," Lizzie said with a mock frown. "Stop it." When her friends gave her exaggerated looks of innocence, she laughed and went out the back door and down the steps. She crossed the green grass to the vegetable garden Reuben had inherited from the doctor who lived there before him, and maintained each year with Eliza's help.

"Having any luck?"

John turned and smiled at her. "There are several possibilities. I'm sussing it out."

She joined him in the tomato section. There were a dozen plants of various types, all with fruit in varying stages of readiness. "Wow, quite a selection. Romas, cherries, red tomatoes, and I believe yellow tomatoes. How do we choose?"

"I guess since we're making a salad, we should take Romas or cherry tomatoes, ja?"

She nodded. "A couple dozen. Let's mix it up."

So they each picked about a dozen assorted little tomatoes, and Lizzie placed them all carefully into the front pocket of her apron. Then they moved to the vining section of the garden, where Lizzie recognized pumpkins, watermelons, cantaloupes and squash all setting fruit, before she spotted the cucumbers. "Here we are!" She stooped down and moved leaves aside. "Ah! I was worried it was too early, but here's a perfect cucumber for our needs." She reached into her pocket and pulled out a small pocketknife she always had on hand, opened it, and carefully cut the cucumber from the vine.

"You're well prepared!" John smiled, reaching out to take the fruit, which was about eight inches long, dark green, and quite firm—just right!

"Ja, my little pocketknife often comes in handy."

He reached into his pocket, and pulled out a nearly identical knife, and she laughed. "Well, aren't we the pair?"

He looked at her intently with his Coke bottle–green eyes, and she felt her smile slide away. "Ja, aren't we just?" he murmured, not breaking eye contact, and somehow making it impossible for her to look away. She felt as if she were a captive to those eyes, which held so much more depth than she'd previously noticed. And looking at her as he was, his expression serious, she felt in danger of slipping into them and drowning in their depths. She couldn't think. Where had her brain gone? She really, really had to pull out of this moment, before it grew awkward. But she just couldn't seem to do it.

Then he broke the tension, tossing his knife up in the air and catching it before returning it to his pocket. "My dawdi gave me this knife when I turned nine. He taught me to whittle. Where did you get yours?"

Lizzie felt herself literally gasp for air—had she been holding her breath? She blinked and looked around quickly to reorient herself. Vegetable garden. Cucumber. Tomatoes. She felt her pocket. There they were. Right. "Um, my knife?" He nodded, a slow smile stealing over his lips as he realized she was befuddled by their little "moment," and she shook her head, impatient with herself. "I bought it a few years ago at Orme Hardware in Berlin. I liked the pretty blue color, and my dat said it's a gut brand that will last all my life if I take gut care of it. So, I do."

He nodded, then glanced at the house. "Well, the pasta is probably ready. We'd better go in."

"Right!" She spun and walked quickly back across the yard, up the steps, and into the kitchen, where Jane and Eliza were preparing the pasta and garlic bread.

Lizzie saw that the cats had finished eating and were taking their after-dinner baths. When Little Mouse saw her, she gave a contented-sounding little chirp, making Lizzie smile.

"We wondered if you two were ever coming back," Jane said.

"There's a bowl for your salad makings on the counter," Eliza said. Lizzie nodded and stepped over to the sink. She grabbed a strainer and poured the tomatoes from her pocket into it, then rinsed them. John washed the cucumber and then cut it into cubes, which he tossed into the bowl along with the tomatoes. Eliza had some chives, which she cut up and added to the salad. Lizzie got a bottle of vinegar from the fridge, and Eliza handed her one of olive oil. She tossed the salad with a little oil and vinegar and added the bowl to the table. As soon as everything was ready, they all sat to pray and then eat.

Lizzie didn't miss the amused look that passed between Jane and Eliza. But she was determined not to think about what had happened in the garden. At least not until she was alone.

After dinner, when the dishes were cleared away, they all gathered at the table again. "I made more lemonade, but I'll leave it on the counter so we don't risk getting it on all these documents, ja?" Eliza gestured to the pitcher and glasses on the counter, and they all nodded their understanding.

Jane brought a notebook and pen. Lizzie got the journal from her bag and set it upon the table in front of her. She took a deep breath. "I'm a little *naerfich*," she confessed. "I mean, I'm worried both that we won't find anything and that we will! Does that make any sense?"

"Ja, perfect sense," John said, his heart aching for her stress and knowing he couldn't fix it for her. Not easily or soon, anyway. "It's normal to be nervous when you have so much riding on all of this, I'd say."

Jane and Eliza nodded. Lizzie stared down at the book, and John wondered if she'd be able to open it.

She opened it. And she frowned. "Oh, sis yuscht!"

John, Jane, and Eliza leaned forward, eyes wide.

"What?" John asked.

Lizzie didn't answer right away. She scanned the first page, then looked up, a puzzled expression on her face. "I don't understand."

Her three friends looked at each other, then at her. John craned his neck, trying to get a good look at the pages, but the angle was wrong. Frustrated, he asked, "Lizzie, what's wrong? Can't you make out the writing?"

She looked up at him and frowned. "Ja, it's not that. It's just. . .look!"

She passed the journal to him, and he took it and turned it so he could see. At first, he didn't understand what he was looking at, and much as Lizzie had, he squinted at the pages, trying to make out the writing. When it dawned on him what he was reading, his mouth dropped open and he groaned. "Ach, no." He looked up at Lizzie. "I'm sorry, Lizzie. Maybe there will be something else we can find?"

Jane and Eliza exchanged alarmed looks. "What is it? What's wrong?" Jane asked, reaching for the book. John handed it to her, and she looked at it, Eliza crowding next to her to read it over her shoulder.

"But. . .this is nothing but recipes!" Eliza exclaimed. "I thought it was supposed to be a journal!"

Lizzie nodded. "Me too. That's what Mr. Rumpkin said it was, right, John?"

He nodded slowly. "Ja, he did. Jane, flip through. Maybe there are journal entries between the recipes."

Jane flipped carefully through the pages of the old journal, and suddenly she stopped, a small excited cry escaping her lips. "Oh! Wait, what's this?"

John's heart rate picked up. He waited for his sister to explain what she'd found that was more exciting than a hundred-year-old recipe for bread pudding to feed thirty people.

Jane read for a moment then looked up at her friends. "It's a diary entry all right, between two recipes. I think she disguised her diary as a recipe book to protect her privacy! This entry isn't very exciting. It's about some guests who caused a stir by stealing their towels and the candlesticks from their room. By the time the innkeeper noticed, they'd already boarded a train and were long gone. Between the stolen items and their food, and the wood to heat their room and bath, she was probably the poorer for their stay."

She looked up. "Not what we're looking for, but interesting anyway!"

Eliza was jotting down notes in the notebook. "I'll keep a list of what her entries are about here. What was the date on that entry, Jane?" Jane squinted at the top of the page. "It looks like August of 1912." She looked up. "That's two years before the murder, right?" Lizzie rubbed her hands together eagerly and scooched forward in her chair. "Now we're talking! Keep going, Jane. See if there are more entries, please."

Jane nodded, and John watched Lizzie's face light up with interest at the prospect of learning more about the mystery of the missing manuscript. She fairly glowed with enthusiasm, and he found it very attractive.

Jane spoke, drawing his attention from Lizzie. "Okay, a few recipes I actually want to take another look at, especially one for rhubarb pie, and here's another entry, marked September 1912. This time she's writing about replacing the toilet in the third-floor bathroom. Not very interesting to me, but she was pretty excited about it." She flipped through a few more pages. "More recipes, and here's an entry from October 1912. So, she seems to do an entry about once a month. Interesting, she must have left pages blank in between recipes when she created her recipe book-journal, intending to fill them in later!"

John drummed his fingers on the table. "That is interesting, Jane, and I'd like to hear more about it later, but do you think you could just flip forward to the year of the murder? It was in May of 1914, right?"

Lizzie nodded her agreement and leaned forward far enough that John worried she was going to crawl across the table. He stifled a smile, thinking it must be killing her not to be the one looking through the old book. But she was controlling her impatience fairly well.

Jane, meanwhile, had flipped through a number of pages. "December 1912. January, February, April 1913." She turned a larger number of pages all at once, slowing when she came across an entry. "Okay, getting closer. January 1914. Ah! She's excited because she has just received a request for a room by a well-known author named E. W. Fingle, who wants to spend at least a month, and possibly more, working on a new manuscript! He needs a quiet space where he won't be bothered, and asks if she can accommodate him! She of course answered yes, and he has booked a room on the third floor—she notes that she's happy there's a new toilet up there—and will arrive on April 1, 1914."

Jane looked up, her eyes wide. "This is him! This is it!"

Lizzie couldn't take it anymore and reached across the table. "Please, Jane, do you mind if I look for the next entries?"

Jane hesitated a moment, then handed the book over with a wry smile. "Of course! It's your building after all, and you got the journal. Thanks for letting me look through so much already!"

John smiled to himself at Lizzie's delight as she flipped through the book to the page Jane had marked with a strip of fabric. From there she paged through some recipes, then stopped to review a February 1914 entry. "Hmm. Nothing much here. It's snowy and cold. No guests. They've closed off the third floor to save heat for the winter. That's it."

She flipped through more pages, pausing at the March and then the April entries. "Ah! Here we go. I'll read it aloud. It's dated April 1, 1914."

All is in readiness for the arrival tonight of our esteemed guest, the famous author Mr. E. W. Fingle. I confess I hadn't read his work, but I took out his previous two books from the library and read them. They were a little dark for my taste. Murder mysteries! I have always preferred a nice romance with a predictable, happy ending. I've returned the books and will be able to discuss them if the occasion arises.

I do not expect our guest to be a very sociable man, however. I had another brief note from him confirming his expected arrival on tonight's train, and he is not, to all appearances, chatty. But never mind that. He's coming here to work, not to socialize. I shall endeavor to protect his privacy and give him room to work. But I confess, I've told a few of my friends about his coming, and everyone is fairly excited to have a famous personality visiting Willow Creek!

I shall write again soon, rather than waiting for my regular monthly post. After all, it isn't every day a well-known author arrives to stay!

Lizzie looked up. "That's it for that entry." She paged through the journal until she found the next entry. "Listen to this!"

Our guest arrived as expected last night, and is settled in his room on the third floor. He asked that no other guests be ensconced up there while he is in residence, and has compensated me for the two other rooms on that level for a month's time! I'm paid for empty rooms! I protested of course, but he insisted that it was worth it to him. So he is now the sole occupant of the third floor. We have a lovely couple from Denver staying in the second-floor suite, but I can rent out no other rooms while he is here. I'm not complaining!

But I must remark, if just in these pages no other eyes will ever see, that Mr. E. W. Fingle is not a pleasant man. He is difficult and demanding. He does not wish to take meals with the rest of us in the dining room, so I must carry his tray up to the third floor three times a day, and sometimes a fourth if he needs a snack in the afternoon! I am to place it on the table in the parlor, and am not to disturb him. To be honest, I may not see him above once a day, if that!

But again, I can't complain. He's paying for three rooms, and writers are known to be an eccentric lot, after all.

Eliza giggled at that, and Lizzie looked up. "He was an odd one, that Mr. Fingle."

John nodded. "Ja, and it seems he was a difficult customer. Difficult people sometimes make enemies. Perhaps that is what led to his murder."

"But we know who killed him and why," Jane protested. "It's not the mystery."

Lizzie pursed her lips. "But it all helps us to understand better what happened, and maybe why. If we find out why, then maybe that will lead us to understand more about Mr. Fingle and his killer, and maybe that will help us find the missing manuscript. I can't help thinking that if we found that, whoever is trying to put me out of business would give up and leave me alone."

John nodded slowly. While he knew he had to get up early, the girls had to get up even earlier. But he didn't think any of them wanted to leave with any of that journal left unread. He didn't know about the rest of them, but he was staying until they got through the whole thing.

"I agree, Lizzie. Let's go through the rest of the journal and see if there are any real clues to where that manuscript went."

"I'll get cookies," Eliza said, pushing to her feet. "We may be here a while!"

CHAPTER SEVENTEEN

Ten minutes later, everyone had taken a bathroom break, and Eliza had provided them with a fresh pitcher of lemonade. Lizzie sat down with a sigh, eager to get back to the journal and its possible clues to her situation.

Jane was looking around. "Where are our feline pals? I haven't seen them since dinner."

"Oh, they're both in the living room, sound asleep in the little beds I got them at the Amish Farm Market last week. They love them!" Eliza gushed. "And really, those beds look so soft and fluffy, I wish they came in my size!"

Jane grinned. "I know what you mean. The kitties do seem to find them comfy."

"I'm glad," Lizzie said. "I feel as if I've been neglecting Little Mouse lately, but things have been crazy! When this all calms down, I'm going to owe her some serious snuggles."

Jane nodded. "Ja, me too. But they have each other, which is gut."

Lizzie nodded, then turned to the next entry and scanned it. "It's just more news about the doings of Mr. Fingle and a couple little newsy items about Willow Creek, dated later in April 1914. Want to hear it, or shall I go on? We can come back to this sort of thing tomorrow, maybe?"

Everyone nodded, and she flipped forward. "Okay, here's one from a couple weeks later. Uh-oh, looks like Mrs. Bridgerton was getting tired of Mr. Fingle, famous author or not. Listen to this." She started reading.

Our third-floor guest grows tiresome. He tried to insist we cancel all bookings for guests through June, in case he decides to stay another month. He offered to pay for their rooms, but I told him no. He was not amused. He yelled and threw a coffee cup across the room at me! Amazingly, I caught it. Fortunately, it was empty, I am now serving Mr. Fingle in the second-best china. I will not risk my mother's service on that boor. I begin to wish, as does Mr. Bridgerton, that Mr. Fingle would finish his manuscript and depart. I do not know how much more of his ill-tempered tirades and demands we can stand.

John shook his head. "Wow, it sounds like he was a truly terrible man. I wonder if he did what his killer accused him of, and stole Mr. Liptak's idea for a book?"

"Well, maybe, but that doesn't make killing him acceptable," Jane pointed out.

"Of course not, but it sounds like he may have had plenty of people who didn't like him besides Mr. Liptak," John said.

Lizzie was thumbing through the journal and came to another entry. "Oh, there's just one more entry! And it's before the murder." She flipped through the final pages in the book, frowning. "Just recipes! Nothing about the murder! The last entry is just a few days before Mr. Fingle was killed." She closed the book and laid it upon the table. "There must be another journal!"

Jane frowned, and then said, "But there is! Remember? There was something that looked like a journal in that box! We didn't get to it, because at first glance, it looked like a recipe book!"

"Jane, you're brilliant!" Lizzie cried, hurrying around the table to hug her friend. "Where's the box?"

Jane's face fell. "It's at the bakery."

"Oh no," Lizzie said, disappointment evident in her voice, her face, and her posture. Then she darted a glance at the clock, and the door.

John, seeing where she was looking, stood up. "It's late. It'll keep until tomorrow."

Lizzie frowned at him, trying to decide whether it was worth arguing about. But another huge yawn from Eliza brought her to her senses.

"Ach, you're right, John. I'm sorry. I just really, really want to find out what happened to that manuscript! I sort of lost my head for a minute."

Jane grinned. "Well, I was right there with you! But much as I hate to admit it, my bruder is right. Let's go to bed. We'll look at it in the morning."

"But the baking. . ." Lizzie began.

"We'll get it all started, then we'll have time while the first batch is in the ovens," Eliza said, unsuccessfully attempting to suppress another yawn.

Lizzie gave in. She really was tired, anyway, and if her parents—or Bishop Troyer!—found out she was running out after old journals this late at night, she'd find herself back in her old childhood bedroom before the strings on her kapp stopped swinging.

John stood. "Well, good night then. I'll see you all tomorrow afternoon."

Lizzie smiled at him. "Denki so much for helping us, John. I think the fact that we have a man working with us relieves some of our parents' anxiety over the whole thing. And probably the bishop's too."

He shrugged. "I'm enjoying myself."

They exchanged smiles of understanding, and Lizzie felt her heart skip a beat or two as his green eyes twinkled into her blue ones.

Then Eliza yawned loudly and broke the moment. Lizzie laughed. "See you tomorrow, John! Gut night!"

"Gut night. I'll let myself out. I have that key you gave me until we're done with all this, remember, Eliza?"

Eliza nodded. "Ja, that's gut. You can give it to Reuben later. It's gut to have a spare."

John let himself out the door at the top of the stairs, and Lizzie listened to the snick of the lock engaging before hearing his feet tromping down the stairs. A moment later, she heard the front door close.

She turned to find her two friends smiling at her smugly.

"What?"

Jane shook a finger at her best friend. "Lizzie, it's very obvious that you and John like each other. And I couldn't be happier! I hope I'll be able to call you my sister before long!"

Eliza nodded happily. Lizzie gaped at them both, her mouth opening and closing like a landed fish.

"I told him I'm not ready for a relationship yet!" She blurted out.

Jane and Eliza stared at her.

Then Jane frowned. "Isn't my bruder gut enough for you?"

"Of course! Good grief! But I'm trying to get a business off the ground, not to mention the little issue of someone trying to put that business out of business, in case you forgot."

Jane looked sheepish. "Oh, right. Sorry."

"But if you like him, Lizzie, it'll all work out," Eliza said. "Just back-burner it and wait and see."

Lizzie sighed. "Ja, that's what I told him too."

Jane's eyebrows climbed toward her prayer kapp. "How did he like that?"

Lizzie shrugged. "He didn't, of course. But he understood, and he's respecting me enough to give me space. Which is why I'm still considering going out with him when this is all over. If he'd acted all resentful and childish, he wouldn't have a chance with me."

Jane and Eliza nodded. "Ja, that makes sense," Jane said.

"Okay, now that we know where that stands, let's go to bed. I'm exhausted!" Eliza finished the thought with another huge yawn, and all three women laughed.

"Tomorrow is another day," Lizzie quipped.

"It almost isn't!" Jane said, looking at the clock. "It's almost today!"

The three friends cleaned up quickly and headed to bed, Little Mouse and Secret rousing themselves from their cozy beds in the living room to follow their mistresses to their beds.

As Lizzie brushed her teeth and donned her nightgown, she thought about John and about how very much she did like him, even though it wasn't exactly convenient to be thinking about a special man at the moment. She picked up her Bible and sat holding it, thinking. Then she sent up a heartfelt prayer to her heavenly Father.

Vader, I'm pretty confused right now. I've worked really hard, as You know, to achieve my dream of having my own bakery. I don't feel as if this is the right time to think about romance and marriage. But I'm finding John Bontrager much more attractive than I ever noticed before. What does this mean? Does it mean You want me to get married now? To John? I'm still having a hard time picturing it. Or is it just a passing infatuation that I'll soon get over? Oh, please, Vader, help me to understand. And Your will be done, Vader.

She pulled up her cozy old quilt, a gift from her grandmother, and read her Bible for a few minutes before a huge yawn convinced her to switch off her battery lantern and turn in. Little Mouse moved from the foot of the bed to snuggle against the small of Lizzie's back, and Lizzie heaved a contented sigh as her eyes drifted closed.

She hoped tomorrow would bring some real answers, if they could find that second journal!

At six the following evening, John sauntered into The Plain Beignet. Jane brought him some coffee and a pastry.

"Denki, Jane. You're my favorite sister who is in this bakery right now."

"Wow, I'm honored. Go sit down and relax. We'll be a while yet, cleaning up."

He carried his bounty over to the sofa by the fireplace and sank gratefully into its soft cushions. It had been a long day, as his sore feet and a fresh blister on his hand could attest.

He set the mug on the table beside him, leaned his head back, and closed his eyes for a moment. The next thing he knew, someone gave his shoulder a shake. "John! Wake up. We're ready to go home, and here you are napping. Gut thing we knew you were here, or we might have turned out the lights and left you sleeping!" He opened his eyes and blinked a few times to bring Lizzie into focus.

"Sorry, I only meant to rest my eyes for a minute." He picked up his mug and drained it. It was now stone cold. Eliza bustled over, took the mug from him, and placed it in the little work sink behind the counter. "That will keep until morning," she said, walking toward the door. "Let's go. I can't wait to look through the second journal!"

John perked up at that. "So, you found it?"

Jane nodded. "Yep, right in the box where I thought it was." She reached into her bag and pulled out a book similar to the first—worn brown leather, embossed with *Recipes* on the front in faded gold script.

"And you checked? It's not just a recipe book?" John asked curiously as he followed his sister and the others out the door.

"Of course we did, bruder. We aren't rookies at this," Jane said, heading back to his buggy, which he'd brought instead of the wagon.

"Gotcha. Not rookies." John climbed into the driver's seat and headed to Eliza's. "But I thought you were going to look at it while you were baking this morning?"

Jane smiled at her brother. "We decided to wait for you, bruder dear."

"It was Lizzie's idea, actually," Eliza said with an innocent flutter of her eyelashes.

Lizzie nodded and offered him a shy smile. "It only seemed fair."

John smiled at her. "I appreciate it. I admit I was a little down at the idea of missing that."

Soon they were seated around Eliza's kitchen table, eating a pizza they'd picked up on the way and drinking Silly Sodas from Orme Hardware in Berlin. John was enjoying his bottle of Zombie Grape, which he'd barely scored right out from under Eliza's nose.

Dinner conversation centered around what they might find in the journal, once their hands were free of sauce and grease.

"I hope she had suspects, and listed them all out with why she thought they did it!" Eliza said around a mouthful of pizza.

"Did what? Stole the manuscript?" Jane asked.

Eliza nodded, tossing her crust into the box and taking a third piece.

"Ew, Eliza, don't put your crusts in the box!" Jane chastised her friend. "That's just gross."

Eliza snickered and picked up the crust, placing it neatly on her plate before taking another big bite of her third slice. "If you had a dog instead of a cat, I could feed him under the table!"

As if she'd conjured her up, Little Mouse chose that moment to enter the kitchen. She gave a small mew, as if acknowledging their presence, then made her way to her food bowl. When she found it empty, she sat down and sent what surely looked like a disapproving glance at Lizzie. A moment later, Secret joined them and, upon finding her bowl empty, gave a similar look to Jane.

"Oh! Sorry, Petite Souris! I'm afraid I've been neglecting you, you sweet girl." She hurried over and got the bag of kitty food from the pantry, poured a generous supply into the cat's bowl, and then poured some into Secret's. "And here's some for you, Secret."

"Sometimes I forget your cat has that French name," John remarked.

Lizzie glanced up from where she squatted by the cat, stroking her silky fur while she tucked into her dinner. She stood and picked up the cat's water dish, which she rinsed out and filled with clean water from the tap. "She doesn't seem to care, as long as her food doesn't run out." Lizzie returned to the table and continued eating. "Anyway, back to what Eliza was saying before. It would be useful if Mrs. Bridgerton, the innkeeper, had a list of suspects," Lizzie agreed, blotting her mouth after eating a second piece loaded with pineapple and onion. "I can't eat another bite. I'm stuffed!"

John eyed what was left. Two slices. He looked hopefully at Jane and Eliza. Eliza groaned and patted her stomach. "Oh, maybe I shouldn't have had the third piece. I'm done."

Jane grinned. "Me too, bruder. Looks like the last two slices are yours, if you have room."

"Believe me, I do." He picked up one of the slices and bit in while the women went and washed their hands and did their dishes. "You guys go ahead and get started. I'll sit here and listen, and keep eating."

Jane handed the journal to Lizzie. "You do the honors."

Lizzie smiled at her friend and opened the journal. "Recipe for fried chicken like Aunt Martha used to make," she said. "Hmm. Looks gut! Maybe I'll try this recipe."

Jane cleared her throat, and Lizzie looked up. "Oops! Sorry. It sucks you in. Okay, okay, moving on." She flipped through a few pages before coming to the first entry in the book. "It picks up right where the last one left off."

She scanned it and was about to comment when there was a loud knock on the front door downstairs. She looked up, alarmed. "Who could that be at this hour?"

Eliza jumped up and started for the door, but John stood and said, "Wait, Eliza, let me go first, if you don't mind."

"Really? Are we getting a little paranoid here, do you think? It's probably Reuben or Mary."

"Don't they have a key?" Jane asked.

Eliza looked blank for a moment. "Oh, right."

"It's probably nobody sinister," John said. "I just want to be sure."

Eliza stepped aside, and John felt a rush of relief that she wasn't going to argue. He unlocked the upstairs door and turned on the light on the steps before starting down. At the bottom, he could see Officers Jakes and Anderson standing on the porch. It was still daylight, and they waved when they saw him.

I wonder what they want? I hope nothing else bad has happened!

He opened the door, and Officer Jakes smiled. "Don't worry, nothing bad has happened. We just want to talk to you all. Actually, we didn't expect to find you here, but it's fine that you are. Are Eliza, Jane, and Elizabeth here?"

John nodded and stepped aside, allowing the officers to enter, before closing the door and engaging the dead bolt.

"I see you've upgraded the locks here. And no doubt at the bakery?" Officer Anderson observed, casting John an approving look.

"Well, yes, I did. The old locks were flimsy. But. . .have you been here before? I didn't realize."

"Yes, we stopped here one afternoon last week to update Miss Miller," Jakes said. "Although, we didn't really have much to update her on. Tonight, we may." He looked at John expectantly, and John realized he was keeping the officers downstairs.

At that moment, Eliza called from the top of the steps, "Goodness, John, invite the officers upstairs already. We're out of pizza, but we have plenty of cookies yet."

"Cookies?" Jakes asked with obvious interest.

John nodded. "Sorry, come on up. I know everyone will be eager to hear whatever you have to say."

"After you," Officer Anderson said, gesturing for John to go first. John nodded and jogged up the steps, followed by the two officers. In the kitchen, Lizzie was pouring fresh kaffi into two mugs, and Jane was setting a plate heaped with chocolate chip cookies on the table.

"Please sit, Officers. Welcome." Eliza gestured to the table. The officers sat. Jane, Lizzie, and Eliza stood around the table in various poses of eager anticipation.

Officer Anderson looked at them and laughed. "Um, Ron, something tells me these ladies are eager to hear our news."

Jakes looked up from his coffee, one hand stretched toward the plate of cookies, and froze at the sight of all three women staring eagerly at him. "Oh, right. I guess cookies can wait." But he cast a longing glance at the plate before reaching into his pocket and withdrawing an envelope, which he placed on the table before him.

Lizzie stared at the white, legal-size envelope with her name printed in block letters on the front. She swallowed nervously, then looked first at Officer Jakes, then at Officer Anderson. "That's the letter that came the other day. I'd nearly forgotten. . ."

"Did it reveal any clues?" Eliza asked brightly, as if they were discussing something from a book, John thought, rather than a scary, anonymous letter received by their friend.

Jakes grimaced. "Well, that depends on what you mean by clues, I suppose. There were fingerprints." At the delighted gasps from his audience, he held up his hands and shook his head. "There were fingerprints, but we didn't find any matches. So whoever it is has never been fingerprinted."

"Amish people rarely get fingerprinted," Lizzie said thoughtfully, almost to herself.

"True, but neither do a lot of Englisch people," Officer Anderson said. "So that doesn't prove the sender was Amish."

John frowned. He'd been hoping the envelope or its contents would provide easy answers. It wasn't to be, though. Besides, he really didn't want to discover the sender was Amish. Somehow that would be worse. He couldn't find the logic in that feeling, but there you had it. But the question still begged to be asked: "So, what was inside?"

"Go ahead and see for yourself," Jakes said. "Mind if I have a cookie? I'm really hungry. And they look amazing!"

"Help yourself," Jane urged, her focus on the envelope on the table.

John was reaching for the envelope, and his hand collided with another's. He looked up and found Lizzie also reaching for the envelope. And since it was addressed to her, he reluctantly withdrew his own hand and let her pick it up. She smiled gratefully at him and looked at the envelope as if it might contain particularly venomous spiders.

"Is it safe?" she whispered.

Jakes and Anderson nodded. "Or we wouldn't have let you have it," Anderson pointed out reasonably.

"Right, of course." Lizzie squeezed the ends of the envelope so she could peer inside. John wanted so badly to reach out and take it, both to safeguard her and because his curiosity was killing him.

"Go on and open it, Lizzie! I can't stand it!" Eliza cried.

"Sorry, sorry." Lizzie reached inside and pulled out a piece of paper. She opened it slowly and read the message, which was also printed in block letters in black ink.

"It's another threat!" she gasped, holding the page out to John so he could read it too.

He took it from her, and she sat down, shaken by the anger and hatred in the message. John felt shaky too, as he looked at what had upset Lizzie, who was no fraidy-cat by anyone's reckoning.

"This is your last warning," he read. "Close your business and leave the building before it is too late. I don't want to hurt anyone, but I WILL have what is rightfully mine. You have one week, and my patience will be at an end."

"One week? But. . .that must be about up by now!" Jane cried. "What's the postmark?"

John flipped the envelope over, but before he could answer, Officer Jakes spoke around a mouthful of cookies. "Six days ago."

"Oh dear, that's not gut," Lizzie said. "What should I do?"

John hated seeing her so helpless and frightened, when usually she was such a courageous woman. He closed his eyes a moment and spoke to Gott.

Vader, I'm very angry at whoever sent this letter to Lizzie. I am a peaceful man. But Vader, I feel violent right now. Please help us. Your will be done.

He opened his eyes and looked at Lizzie, and words came to his lips. "Lizzie, Gott will help us. He will keep you and the rest of us safe. And Officers Jakes and Anderson will find who is doing this and stop them. We need to stay strong and keep the faith. It will be all right."

She stared into his eyes, which were filled with assurance and faith, and she felt her own fear diminishing. "You're right, John," she whispered. She took a deep, calming breath and looked around the room at the others. Little Mouse jumped up onto the table and mewed to be picked up. "Naughty. You know you're not allowed up there." She picked up the small cat and held her close to her chest, stroking her and taking comfort from her purrs.

"She could tell you needed her," Jane said, placing a hand on Lizzie's shoulder. "She's a smart kitty!"

Eliza also stepped forward. "Lizzie, this will be over soon, I just know it. And everything is going to work out fine. Remember, Gott loves you and is watching over you."

Lizzie blinked back tears. "Denki, Eliza. That helps." She looked around at John, Eliza, and Jane, then at the two police officers.

"Well, we have a journal to read, and you two have a criminal to apprehend. What are we all waiting for?"

A brief silence was broken by Officer Jakes, who stood and looked at Officer Anderson. "Right. Let us know if anything else happens.

And. . .can we take cookies for the road? We need to keep our brains sharp, you know!"

Laughter broke the tension, and John saw everyone relax.

But he knew it was only temporary. He prayed that they would figure out who was out to get Lizzie before they did something else to harm her business—or her!

CHAPTER EIGHTEEN

The next morning Lizzie, Jane, and Eliza arrived at the bakery at four as usual. The streets were dark, and the streetlight outside the bakery building buzzed and flickered.

"We'd better let the city know that the bulb needs to be changed," Jane commented sleepily, stifling a yawn.

Lizzie nodded absently and was inserting the key into the newly installed dead bolt when Eliza suddenly gasped. "Look!"

Jane and Lizzie spun around, expecting some kind of assault, but all they saw was Eliza staring at their front window.

"What is it, Eliza?" Lizzie asked, leaving the key in the lock and moving over to see what her friend was looking at. When she did, she let out an involuntary cry. "Oh! Sis yuscht, what next?"

Jane stood staring at the window beside her friends, speechless.

In the flickering yellow light cast by the streetlight, they could see that someone had used red paint to place a message across the entire window.

Lizzie read the message aloud. "The Manuscript Belongs to me! Return it OR ELSE!"

"Ick, it looks like blood dripping down the glass," Eliza observed with a shudder.

"Someone thinks we've found the manuscript, obviously," Jane said.

Lizzie just stared at the message, anger growing inside her until she didn't see how she'd be able to contain it. She'd just had this window replaced! "Ach! I hope this stuff will wash off! I can't keep replacing windows because some fool has a bee in their bonnet about this building or some probably nonexistent old manuscript! This makes me so angry I could burst!"

Jane put an arm around Lizzie's shoulders and hugged her. "Look at the bright side, Lizzie."

Lizzie glanced sideways at her best friend. "There's a bright side?"

"Ja. In Ephesians it says not to let the sun go down on your anger. Well, the sun isn't even up yet, so you've got all day to calm down!"

Lizzie wasn't sure whether to laugh or cry. So she heaved a sigh and walked back over to unlock the door. "Let's go inside and call the police and tell them some crazy fool has vandalized my building. . .again! And then we have to find out how to get the paint off the window. Hopefully before our customers see it."

An hour later, Jakes and Anderson had finished taking their statements and photos of the window. Anderson had given Lizzie some suggestions on removing the paint, including scraping it off with a razor blade. Then they'd left, as their shift was nearing an end.

But Jakes had taken Lizzie aside before leaving and told her in no uncertain terms that he was getting a bit worried about the persistence of whoever was doing these things.

"This person strikes me as a bit of a wacko. Not insane but unbalanced, if you know what I mean. They are very focused on getting what they want—the missing manuscript."

"But it may not even exist!" Lizzie had protested.

Jakes had shrugged. "Doesn't matter. They think it does. And that makes them potentially dangerous. I want you to be very, very careful until we catch this guy, okay? I wish you didn't need to come here in the middle of the night, for one thing."

Lizzie had started to protest that she had to start her baking, and Officer Jakes had held up a hand to quiet her protests. "I know that. I just wish you didn't. I don't suppose you'd carry a weapon?"

She shook her head. "Nee. We are pacifists. We're supposed to turn the other cheek, not fight."

"Well, I'm afraid your persecutor isn't as peaceful-minded as you are. So, watch your backs, okay? And try not to be so predictable. Three young women walking to this bakery every morning from several blocks away? Not good, Lizzie. Too predictable. Change it up. Can you do the baking in the evening for a while?"

She started to say no, but then she thought about it. Could they do that? At least for a while? The baked goods would still be very fresh. "I'll think about it, Officer. Denki for coming."

He'd nodded and left with Anderson, who was starting to yawn.

"I heard what he said," Jane said. "Could we bake in the evenings and then maybe ride over in a buggy instead of walking? We could come around seven instead of four if we got most of the baking done in the evening."

Lizzie bit her lip. "It's not how it's generally done. But maybe it would be okay. But where are we getting a buggy? We don't have a stable, so where would a horse stay?"

"Actually, there is a stable," Eliza said. "The garage was converted when Reuben moved out. But I never got around to getting a horse and buggy. But we have a place to keep a horse if we can borrow one for a bit."

Jane considered for a moment, then said, "My parents have an extra buggy horse. She's kind of old, but we wouldn't be taking her far. Where would she stay during the day? We don't want a horse standing around on concrete all day."

"No need! There's a paddock near the bakery. It doesn't get much use, but I noticed it a few weeks ago," Lizzie said. "And I just thought of where we might borrow a buggy! This could work!"

"Right, I know the one you mean!" Eliza enthused. "We'll have to ask permission to use it. I'm not sure who owns it."

"Okay, we'll figure it out later. For now, let's get the baking started. It'll be time to open soon," Lizzie said, turning on lights and heading into the kitchen to look for something to get the paint off the window. "I'll work on the paint while you two start baking."

Several hours later, with the breakfast rush over and the lunch rush not yet begun, the three friends were relaxing in the kitchen over cups of coffee when the back door flew open, and John stomped in looking as if steam might start billowing from his ears at any moment.

Lizzie took another sip of coffee to fortify herself before observing to Jane, "I think John heard about the window."

Jane nodded. "Ja, looks that way."

Eliza snickered, and John's face turned red. "I'm glad you all think this is funny, because I, for one, do not. You've got a crazy person after you! And you sit here drinking coffee and laughing about it! You're all insane!" He threw his hands up in the air and stomped over to pour himself a mug of coffee.

The girls looked at each other, and Jane and Eliza gave little shrugs and nodded at Lizzie, letting her know they were leaving John to her.

With a sigh—she was sighing an awful lot lately, she thought—she stood and put some pastries on a plate, which she set on the table for John. "John, we don't think it's funny. But sometimes you laugh so you won't cry, fashtay?"

"Don't try handling me," he groused, sitting down and taking a pastry. "Or distracting me with your Danish!"

She shook her head, and Jane and Eliza slipped out to the front of the shop to get ready for the lunch crowd. "I wouldn't do that. I'm sure it wouldn't work, anyway."

He nodded as he chewed, two spots of color riding high on his cheeks and fire in his eyes. "I'm just keeping up my strength for this afternoon in the woodshop. I should be there right now, but when I heard what happened this morning from the delivery guy from FedEx—and why did I have to hear it from a delivery guy, anyway? I guess I'm not important enough for you to tell me yourself!—anyway, when I heard it from him, I told my dat I'd be back and came right over here." He took out his anger on another innocent pastry, demolishing it in three bites and washing it down with coffee. Then he put his hand on his stomach and groaned a little. "Oh, ach, maybe I shouldn't have eaten—however many I ate. I don't feel very well."

"Five."

"Pardon?"

She nodded. "You ate five pastries. It was impressive actually."

He threw up his hands. "Lizzie! That's not what's important here! Some maniac is after you, and you want to talk about pastries?" He groaned again.

"Not really. You said you weren't sure how many you ate, and I was just telling you."

"Never mind that! I came over here to tell you this has to end. Enough already! What are you waiting for—this person to become bold enough to confront you in person? Because that's probably next! Letters, and now painting on your window!"

"Well, ja, but what do you think I should do, John? I can't shut my business. Everything I have is tied up in this building and the equipment and supplies here. If I walk away, the bank will foreclose on me and I'll lose everything, including my home."

He pushed to his feet. "But you'll have your life, Lizzie! What good is all of this if something terrible happens to you, or Jane, or Eliza?"

She bit her lips and looked everywhere except at John. "I. . .I'm hopeful that nothing like that will happen, John. The police. . ."

"The police have gotten nowhere! There are no witnesses. There are no real clues. There's just a crazy person out there with you in his crosshairs, and I'm going crazy myself worrying about what could happen to you. Don't you understand? If something happened to you, I'd lose my mind!"

She stared at him. "Oh."

He looked at her with tortured eyes from across the kitchen. Then he crossed the room to her in three quick strides and took her hands. "Lizzie, you've grown very important to me." He stared into her eyes imploringly. "Do you understand what I'm saying?"

She stared back, pretty sure she understood but really wishing he'd spell it out for her in case she was wrong, and he was just trying to tell her she was an important friend to him, perhaps because of her long-standing friendship with his own sister.

"Um, I think so?" she stammered.

His eyes widened. "You think so?" He pulled her closer and opened his mouth to say something she was sure would be very important when the swinging door opened, and John jumped back as if she were a big copperhead snake he'd nearly stepped on. He ran a hand through his hair and swung back across the kitchen to sit down and finish his coffee in two big gulps. "Oh, I really shouldn't have done that," he groaned, standing up.

Jane stood just inside the kitchen door, staring at her brother with concerned eyes. "Are you oll recht, bruder?"

He grimaced and put his hands on his belly. "I will be in a few hours, but until then I'm going to have to suffer the natural consequences of my own sin."

Jane's eyes widened. "Sin?"

He nodded miserably. "Gluttony. I'll see you both later. We'll talk then." And out the door he went.

"But I need to ask you something!" Lizzie called. "Too late."

Lizzie and Jane stared at each other.

"Did I interrupt something important?" Jane finally asked in a small voice.

Lizzie thought about it for a moment, then shrugged. "Maybe? I'm not sure what he was trying to say. I guess he'll have to figure it out and tell me when he does. I do know one thing, though. He's going to push for us to shut down."

"Shut down! Nee! We can't do that! We'd lose everything!"

Lizzie nodded. "Ja. That's what I told him. If he hadn't eaten five pastries in quick succession, he wouldn't have gotten sick and maybe I'd have found out what he wanted to say. But he did! So I have to wait."

"Five pastries? What a glutton!" Jane moved to the table. "Well, the lunch rush has begun. Do we have enough chicken salad for the croissant sandwiches?"

Lizzie nodded. "Ja, I made up a big batch this morning. It's in the walk-in. I'll get it." She headed to the big walk-in refrigerator across the room to retrieve the jumbo bowl of cranberry-pecan chicken salad and thought about what John had almost said.

Was it something she wanted to hear?

"Oh, Vader!" she whispered so Jane wouldn't overhear. "Please guide me. I suspect John was going to say something important and personal and...I'm not sure I'm ready! What should I do, Vader? Not to make a bakery joke, but can I have my cake and eat it too? Please guide me in my decisions so that they are wisely made. I feel strongly about John. But I also want this business!" She picked up the bowl and turned toward the door, then paused as another thought hit her. "And please, please help the police to find whoever is committing these scary acts against us before someone gets hurt. And maybe help us to find that manuscript if the thing exists. Your will be done, Vader."

John suffered through the rest of the afternoon with an upset stomach. His father, Richard, and younger brother Samuel, who was sixteen and had been working with them in the woodshop for two years, teased him about it and said he had nobody to blame but himself.

But really, what was Lizzie thinking? He'd think that today's latest attack on her business would have finally gotten it through her thick head that someone wished her ill, and they weren't stopping until they got what they wanted.

But no, all she could think about was that dratted bakery. Didn't she know there were more important things than that bakery? Things like...well, things that were important to him.

He sat back on his heels, the brush he'd been using to stain a kitchen chair still in his hand as he realized how selfish he was being.

First, he hadn't told her how he felt about her. When had he had the chance? He'd only come to the realization himself within the last few days, and it seemed to him all he'd done lately was nag her about safety and suggest she might want to shut down for a bit.

But how could she? She had a mortgage payment due. She had other bills to pay related to the business, which was also her home.

Shutting down was not an option for Lizzie Miller, who was not a quitter.

So what was left?

"I have to help her solve this mystery, or I'll never have a chance with her," he muttered. "Because if she's forced out of business, she'll never be happy again, and she certainly won't be interested in the boy who didn't help her find a way to stay open." He frowned fiercely at the chair, not really seeing it. "But. . .what can I do?"

"Son, has that chair done something to offend you?" his father asked, snapping John out of his reverie. He realized he had just been squatting in front of the chair, stain dripping onto the floor, zoning out.

"Oh! Sorry, Dat! I was woolgathering." He dipped the brush into the stain and got back to work.

"About a certain schee young woman who owns a local bakery, by any chance?" his father asked with a twinkle in his eye.

John bit his lip and laid the brush down on a piece of cardboard. He turned to his father. Maybe he could help him think this through.

"Well, ja," he admitted. "Dat, the fact is, we're in a bit of a pickle and I could use your advice."

His father looked alarmed. "A pickle? What do you mean? Are you or Lizzie in some kind of trouble?"

He stood and held out his hands to stave off his father's flurry of questions. "Nee, nee, Dat. We're not in trouble. It's just that I really like her, and she's in this situation. And I think unless I can find a way to help her, she may lose her business, and then she'll be miserable and she'll never talk to me again."

Richard stared at his eldest child for a minute. "Son, I'm way behind. Start at the beginning and bring me up to speed. Then we'll see if I have any useful insights."

John nodded, then looked at Samuel, who was avidly listening. "Sam, do you mind finding something else to do for a while? I really just want to have a private word with Dat about this."

Samuel looked disappointed, but he was good-natured and smiled at his older bruder. "Sure, John. Dat, I'll go muck out the stalls a bit early."

Richard waved him off, and as soon as the shop door closed behind him, John started talking, and the floodgates of all he'd been keeping inside opened up. Before he knew it, he'd told his father everything, finishing with, "And so the police are no nearer figuring out who is doing these things, Dat, and I'm worried about all of their safety. And I'm worried about Lizzie losing the bakery, her life's dream. How can I help her?"

Richard sat back and crossed his arms. John knew from long experience this was his dat's "thinking" position. He sat back in his own chair and waited.

After mulling it all over carefully, Richard finally heaved a deep sigh. "Son, I'm troubled by all of this. Remember, your own sister is one of the young women in danger's way."

John nodded. "Ja, Dat. I never forget that. I'm equally worried for all three girls."

Richard regarded his oldest for a few more moments. "Well, that being said, I feel there is only one thing we as a family, and a community, can and must do."

"Ja, Dat? What do you think we should do?"

"It's obvious! We need to gather up all of our friends and family, and go over that bakery building with a fine-tooth comb until we can state for certain one way or the other whether that missing manuscript is there."

John's eyebrows flew up in surprise. He hadn't expected his dat to say that and was now a bit chagrined that he hadn't thought of it himself.

"Wow, that's a really gut idea, Dat!" He jumped up. "Come on, let's go!"

"Whoa, son, wait a minute. This isn't something we can do half baked. No pun intended."

"No?"

"No. We need to set a time that will work best for the most people and attack the problem in an organized manner. So, today is Thursday. They're calling for a lot of rain Saturday, so it seems to me that Saturday afternoon, perhaps just after the bakery closes around five, would be a gut time for us all to gather at Lizzie's building."

John tilted his head to the side as he thought about it. "Ja, that could work. All the businesses in the area close by then, and if it's raining, the farmers won't be working in their fields. Plus, we could offer pizza for dinner for everyone, so they don't have to worry about the evening meal that night."

Richard pointed at John. "See there, that's smart! You obviously take after me."

John chuckled. Then he impulsively hugged his father and headed for the door of the shop. "Denki, Dat. I'm going to go pick up the girls and tell them about the plan. We'll spread the news."

He left his father cleaning up for the day and hurried to his buggy, eager to share their plan with Lizzie, Jane, and Eliza.

He silently prayed as he steered Mike down the road toward Willow Creek.

Vader, I think my dat's plan is a gut one! We'll find out once and for all whether there is a manuscript hidden in that building. True, we won't know whether it really exists if we don't find it, but we'll know it's not there anyway, and hopefully whoever is after it will hear and give up. And if we do find it, we'll give it to the historical society! Win-win. Just please keep us all safe while we search, and help us to bring this matter to a safe and satisfactory conclusion, Vader. I need Lizzie, Jane, and Eliza to be safe. And I need Lizzie to feel free to pursue what is growing between us. If this isn't the right path, please let me know, Vader. And as always, Your will be done.

Feeling optimistic for the first time in days, John smiled to himself as he neared the bakery. At last, this situation would end. One way or another.

CHAPTER NINETEEN

That evening, everyone sat around Eliza's kitchen talking about the plan. Little Mouse was curled up in Lizzie's lap, purring loudly, her eyes squeezed shut in contentment. Lizzie absentmindedly stroked her as she discussed the plan with her friends.

John looked around the table. "So can you think of anyone else we should invite?"

"I think we've pretty much asked the entire district," Lizzie said. "Plus a few other people we knew would be interested, like Mr. Rumpkin from the museum. I can't think of anyone else."

Jane snapped her fingers. "We should invite Officer Jakes and Officer Anderson! They'd definitely be interested."

"Gut thinking," John said. "Who wants to call them?"

Eliza stood up and stretched. "I recently got a cell phone, so I can do it."

They all stared at her. "What? I'm not baptized yet. I can have a phone if I want. And Reuben thought it was a gut idea, with all the scary things that have been happening around here."

"I have to admit, I feel better knowing you have it," John said.

"Me too," Lizzie said. "I'm just surprised you were able to keep it a secret from us! When did you get it?"

"It wasn't a secret," Eliza said, blushing a bit. "I only got it yesterday, and I was sort of learning how to work it before I said anything. I guess I wasn't sure how you'd all react."

Jane chuckled. "We're not exactly the strictest group of friends you could have, though."

"Yeah." Lizzie smiled. "Here I am, a baptized Amish woman with my own business. And no husband!"

"That makes two of us, except for the owning a business part," Jane reminded her.

"You could both marry as soon as you like," Eliza said. "There are plenty of young men interested in you. I see them watching you at church."

"Who's watching them at church?" John blurted out. Then when all three women looked at him in surprise, he blushed. He looked from one woman to the next, and he cleared his throat. "Could we please change the subject? If we've called everyone we can think of, then let's call it a night. We know what we're going to do, right? And I'm tired."

Jane nodded. "Ja. We've divided up the building and each group of people will be assigned a section."

"The size of the groups will depend on how many people show up," Lizzie added. Then she smacked herself on the forehead. "Ach! I nearly forgot to tell you all, I finally called the Petersheims today!"

"You did?" John said. "That's great! What did they say?"

"Well, I spoke with Mr. Petersheim, and he confirmed that the Stutzmans did want the building, and that Mr. Stutzman had gotten a little salty when they said they were selling it to me, but he didn't think they were angry enough to become violent."

"But what about the murder? And the missing manuscript? And the box of letters?" Eliza asked. "Did he know anything about any of that?"

"He knew about the murder and the missing manuscript. He said his family even spent a little time looking for it back when the articles about the anniversary ran in the newspaper! But they didn't find anything, so they lost interest."

"And did they know anything about the box of letters and the journals?" Jane asked eagerly.

Lizzie shook her head. "Mr. Petersheim didn't. He said he couldn't remember ever noticing that door to the eaves. He said he'd ask his wife, but she was out when I called. And when I told him about the search we're having Saturday, he said it sounded like fun, and he wished us all luck and asked me to tell him if we found anything."

"Well, I suppose it would have been too easy if they'd said they had found the manuscript and still had it!" John laughed.

They all agreed. "I hope they come Saturday," Lizzie said. "It's pretty far, but you never know! Mr. Petersheim said he'd tell his wife about it. I guess we'll see!"

They went over the rest of the plans until they couldn't think of anything else to do.

"Our youth group volunteered to supply the pizza and pop," Eliza piped up. "Which I thought was very nice."

They all nodded. "Sounds like it's all covered," Lizzie said. "Eliza, why don't you call the officers so we can be sure they have no objection. Then John can head home and we can all get to bed on time for a change."

They listened as Eliza spoke with Officer Anderson, who apparently thought the idea a good one. She smiled as she hung up and dropped her phone into her apron pocket. "Officer Anderson said she and Officer Jakes will stop by and make sure there's no trouble Saturday evening. She thought it was a smart plan!"

"So we're all set! I'm excited. Maybe we'll finally be able to sleep in our own place soon, Jane!" Lizzie exclaimed.

Eliza frowned. "But I'll miss you. I've gotten used to having company here, and I'm afraid I'll be lonely when you go."

"You could get a cat," Lizzie suggested, scratching Little Mouse between her gray ears.

"Maybe," Eliza said, looking at the snoozing animal in her friend's lap. "She's certainly no problem. And it would give me company."

"You could get a roommate," John suggested.

"But who?" Eliza asked.

"What about my sister, Susan?" Jane suggested. "You two have gotten to be pretty good friends, haven't you?"

Eliza perked up. "That could work. Do you think she's ready to move out of your parents' house, though?"

Jane shrugged. "You'll never know unless you ask. You're both about the same age, and she works within walking distance, at the Amish farmers' market. Remember? She opened her little tea-and-coffee nook. She might like the idea of living closer, and then my parents wouldn't have to bring her into town every morning."

"I like her booth. She recently started selling secondhand Christian romance books too. So you can go in there, find a new book, and relax over a cup of coffee. It's really pleasant. Sort of like your bakery, Lizzie, but on a much smaller scale, and without the baked goods."

"She actually asked me recently if we could make scones for her a couple mornings a week," Lizzie said. "I said I thought that would be fine. What do you think?"

"Why not? We already make them for ourselves. We'd just need to make a few dozen more, right?" Jane asked reasonably.

"You're not worried about the competition?" Eliza asked with a small frown.

"Nope," Lizzie grinned. "Because she's going to have little cards printed up saying where the delicious baked goods came from, and where people can go to try even more lovely treats, including New Orleans–style French pastries!"

John smiled at Lizzie and clapped. "Great idea! Sounds like a plan. And I can tell you Susan is easy to live with. I think this could really be gut for both of you."

Eliza smiled. "It sounds like it. I'll ask her! What have I got to lose? And I really do love her booth. Lots of people go there, Amish and Englisch. Just a couple weeks ago I saw Mr. Rumpkin from the Historical Museum meeting there with his board. Did you know Mrs. Stutzman from the furniture store is on it because of her knowledge of furniture?"

"No, I didn't!" Lizzie said, surprised by the information. "How unusual."

"Ja, I know. But there they were, chatting about historical things. I didn't really listen. I was actually talking to Susan while she made my coffee. But I thought it was interesting."

Lizzie frowned. So Mrs. Stutzman knew Mr. Rumpkin. She supposed that wasn't so strange. It was a small town, and they were both interested in historic furniture.

John interrupted her thoughts. "Well, if everything is settled, I'm going home to bed. Something tells me tomorrow is going to be a very long day." John pushed to his feet and smiled at Lizzie. "Walk me to the door, Lizzie?"

"Ja, in fact I have something to ask you anyway."

Jane and Eliza exchanged looks and smiles, and Lizzie rolled her eyes as she followed John out of the kitchen. He smiled back at her and unlocked the top door, holding out a hand to her before starting down. She stared at his outstretched hand for a moment, then tentatively reached out and let their fingers brush together before clasping his warm hand in hers and allowing their fingers to intertwine. He smiled at her and then turned and led the way down the stairs and outside, waiting for her to pass through the door before reaching around her and closing it quietly behind them.

He reached out and took her other hand, and they stood smiling at each other on the front porch.

"Well, maybe soon we'll find the manuscript and have an end to all this business," he said.

Lizzie swallowed and tried not to show how affected she was just holding hands with him. She knew that she liked him but wasn't quite ready to throw caution to the wind and commit to a relationship.

"Ja, maybe we will," she allowed. "I would like to move back into my own place. That was a gut idea about Susan becoming Eliza's roommate. I wonder if she'll be interested?"

"If I know my little sister—and I do—she'll be interested. She'll jump at the chance."

Lizzie nodded, then raised her eyes to meet his again. "This is nice," she murmured, looking at their joined hands.

He smiled. "Ja, it is, isn't it? I'd like to kiss you, Lizzie." When she moved to pull away, he tightened his grip on her hands. "Nee, don't run away. I won't kiss you tonight. I just want to be honest with you, and I need you to know I'd very much like to do so. I. . .just wanted you to know."

Lizzie released the panic that had washed through her when he said he wanted to kiss her, and it was replaced by a calm sense of. . .hope? Hope that maybe what was growing between them was real, and that they could let it develop slowly to give them both—all right, to give herself—time to adjust to the idea of being part of a couple with the concerns of a couple, rather than an individual worried only about her own problems.

So she smiled slowly at him, to let him know that was all right, and that maybe eventually she'd want him to kiss her too.

"Did you say you had something to ask me?" he prompted.

"Oh! Ja. The officers suggested that maybe we should bake in the evenings for a while to break up the predictability of our daily routines. Then we wouldn't need to go in until around seven in the morning. But we'd be staying later, and we'd need to drive home rather than walk. I wondered if maybe you'd lend us your buggy for a short time, since you also have the wagon?"

"What would you do for a horse? Surely not your pony, Goldie. . ."

"Nee, nee, she's too small, and she just had a foal. Jane said your folks have an older mare we could probably use."

He thought about it a moment, then nodded. "Ja, it would work. But Lizzie, I like coming to get you all each evening. It's something I actually look forward to. If you borrow a horse and buggy, I won't have that excuse to see you each evening." He gave her the saddest look, and Lizzie suddenly couldn't help giggling.

"Ach, John! Fine. If you don't mind coming and going all the time, then who am I to say no? We'll just leave things the way they've been, except we'll be staying later in the evening. And happily it will be daylight when we walk over in the morning, so no worries there!"

He grinned at her and squeezed both of her hands. "Excellent. Denki, Lizzie. Well, much as I'd like to stay and talk with you, I need to go home and sleep. I'll see you tomorrow afternoon. Good night."

"Good night, John. Sweet dreams."

With another smile, he waved at her and jumped down the steps and ran to his buggy.

"My, he's full of energy, isn't he? It must be love!" Eliza's voice from behind her made Lizzie spin around in surprise to find her two friends standing just behind her. She hadn't even heard the door opening!

"Sorry!" Jane said, looking embarrassed. "Eliza said she heard the outside door close, and she opened the top door and started down. So I followed." She shrugged. "I hope that's okay?"

Lizzie looked at Eliza in disbelief. "You heard the sound of the door closing from upstairs, through another closed, solid wood door?" She folded her arms and waited.

Eliza looked chagrined, and she gave her older friend a winsome smile. "Okay, maybe the top door wasn't exactly all the way closed."

Lizzie raised an eyebrow. "Maybe?"

Eliza looked at the ceiling and sighed. "Okay, definitely. But I wasn't looking and I couldn't hear what you guys were saying out on the porch. I promise! I just wanted to come down when he left."

Jane looked embarrassed but she nodded. "It's true. I was up there gesturing for her to close the door, and I couldn't hear you either. Or see you. Not that I was looking! Oh, ach, anyway!"

Lizzie suddenly found the whole thing funny, and she started laughing. Soon all three of them were laughing, and Lizzie felt the weight of her worries falling from her shoulders. She wiped tears from her cheeks and said, "You girls are gut for me. But let's go to bed. I'm beat."

They all went upstairs, and Eliza locked the upstairs door behind them. They straightened the kitchen together, and Lizzie gathered Little Mouse into her arms before turning down the hallway toward her bedroom. At her door, she paused and looked down the hall at the other two women about to enter their own rooms. Jane was holding Secret, and Eliza had a steaming cup of tea and a book.

"Just one more thing. . ."

They paused, hands on doorknobs, and regarded her curiously.

She smiled. "If I ever catch either of you spying on me like that, I'll put spiders in your beds. You won't know when." At their gasps, she smiled and closed her bedroom door behind her, locking it for good measure. You never knew.

CHAPTER TWENTY

It was about half an hour after closing on Saturday. The bakery was crowded with people who wanted to participate in what they were calling a treasure hunt, even though the so-called treasure was a hundred-year-old sheaf of papers that may not even exist. The din inside the shop was deafening.

"I can't believe how many people showed up for this!" Lizzie shouted into Jane's ear as they stood by the fireplace waiting to begin. Eliza was seated at a nearby table, stacks of lined notebooks in front of her that she'd purchased on her lunch break earlier, along with a cup of pens.

"Good idea about the notebooks," Jane said. When Lizzie shook her head and pointed at her ear, Jane leaned in and repeated herself loudly, and Lizzie nodded emphatically.

"Ja! People can write down exactly where they looked in their spaces. And we have each space covered by two groups, so every place will be thoroughly searched."

Jane nodded. Then she looked around. "Ach! Here come Officers Anderson and Jakes! And John!" she fairly shouted, and Lizzie turned to see where she was looking.

"Gut! Then we can get started."

Lizzie stood up and raised her hands above her head. She waited for people to quiet down, and then she smiled at everyone. She was a bit surprised to see more people than they had asked to come gathered in her shop. Her own family and friends were there, along with other

Amish members of their church community including Bishop Troyer and Lydia Coblentz. She smiled at them, then noticed the Petersheims sitting at a table nearby, grinning at her. She grinned back and waved. They'd arrived the night before and had stopped in to say hello and check out the changes Lizzie had made in the bakery, promising to come back later to take part in the big search.

Then to her surprise the door opened again, and in walked the Stutzman family—mother, father and both sons. They weren't from her church district, but she supposed as her neighbors across the street, they had an interest, and she smiled welcomingly. They didn't smile back, but she shrugged that off. Baby steps. And there was Mr. Rumpkin from the museum, sitting with some people she didn't know but suspected were members of the local historical society. She saw John's buddy Noah Lapp, with a few other young, unmarried Amish men, talking with a group of unmarried Amish women off to one side of the room. Among them were Zeke Yoder and Evelyn Troyer, who looked over and waved cheerily at her. It was as if they were hosting a church social, Lizzie thought, and she suppressed a giggle at the thought.

Perhaps the most surprising faces she saw belonged to the editor of the *Willow Creek Examiner*, Philomena Jones, and the reporter from *The Budget*, Mike Young, who were seated at a table with a woman she thought was the Holmes County Chamber of Commerce Director, and Anita Frederickson of Willow Creek Main Street.

And all by himself in a corner was the odd Mr. LaForest, who nodded sheepishly at her when she smiled tentatively at him. *Time to get started.*

"Good evening, everyone!" Lizzie said loudly. "I confess I didn't expect so much interest in our little venture tonight!"

Laughter rippled through the assembly, and Lizzie relaxed a bit. Most of these people were friends, and really, she had nothing to lose. She opened her mouth to say more, when the door opened, and the tall man with the mustache, Mr. Valentine, she recalled, slipped inside. He nodded to her, then took himself off to stand against a wall to listen to her. She frowned. What was he doing here? She hadn't seen him since the day she and John spotted him in the park across from the bakery.

What could it mean? Jane cleared her throat, and Lizzie pulled herself back into the present.

"We are here tonight because, as many of you have doubtless heard, we have been having some trouble here at The Plain Beignet. There's been vandalism and a couple of break-ins. We are working under the assumption that whoever is behind this is after a very old, probably unfinished, book manuscript which rumor places somewhere inside this building."

She explained about the old murder and waited for the gasps of dismay and surprise to die down before going on. "So, the possibility does exist that Mr. Fingle's manuscript is hidden somewhere in this building. So tonight we'll search thoroughly." At the upswing of excited voices, Lizzie again raised her hands. "That does not mean you can bash holes in my walls! The building was thoroughly renovated recently, back to the studs down here, although not upstairs. So I guess it's possible that someone hid the thing in the wall and plastered over it. But if we are going on the theory that the author hid it quickly on the day he was murdered, then that doesn't wash."

Everyone again started talking, and Lizzie looked at John, who raised his eyebrows and shook his head. Lizzie again lifted her hands for quiet, and once it was gained, she spoke. "But you can knock on wood and walls and floors looking for secret compartments. You can look into closets and behind furniture. Some of it is original to the building dating back to when it was an inn, am I right, Mr. Rumpkin?"

The tiny man stood and cleared his throat. "Thank you, Miss Miller. I'm Mr. Rumpkin, curator of the historical museum, and I can tell you that yes, much of the furniture has been here for more than a hundred years. I don't know about secret passages or the like, but I suppose anything is possible in a building this old. Please treat everything with respect. And if you have any questions about a piece of old furniture, come find me."

Bishop Troyer raised his hand and waited to be recognized. Nervous about her bishop being in on such an unusual undertaking, Lizzie nodded at him to speak. He stood. "Gut evening. I am Abram Troyer, bishop of this Amish church district. I just want to remind you that in addition to being a historically significant building, this is a home, and a place of business. These young women work and live here. Please keep that in mind when searching for this manuscript. Denki. Now, let us bow our heads in prayer."

Bishop Troyer led the group in a short prayer, and then he nodded again at Lizzie to proceed.

Lizzie felt a surge of warmth toward the bishop wash through her. How considerate of him to remind the excited group that this wasn't some kind of entertainment venue, but a home and business. And then to ask Gott for guidance and protection. She blinked back tears and looked around the room.

"Okay! Denki to Bishop Troyer, Mr. Rumpkin, and everyone here. Now, here's how we're going to do this."

She explained that each group would be given an assigned area, from the basement up through the third floor, to be searched. Each would have a person acting as a recorder, writing down everything they did and observed in their area. Each group was assigned two areas, so everywhere would be searched twice. When she was finished, she looked around. "Are there any questions?"

She answered a few, and then when there were no more, she looked at John, who was going to be in charge of the search. He stepped forward and invited the groups to send a representative to the table to collect their assigned areas and notebooks and pens. A line formed, and Lizzie reckoned there must be twenty groups ranging between two and five people each. She was astonished.

It seemed to Lizzie that one minute the room was teeming with people, and the next, everyone was dispersing to their search areas. Soon there were only a handful of people in the room besides herself, Eliza, and Jane. John had taken himself off to wander the building, moving from area to area supervising the searchers to make certain nobody did anything they shouldn't. Officer Jakes and Anderson had gone off on similar errands.

Eliza sat next to Lizzie and handed her a cup of coffee. "Well, it's begun! Now we wait."

Jane frowned toward the stairway. "Did you see that tall man with the mustache slip in just before we started?" she asked.

"Yes," Lizzie said. "It was that Mr. Valentine; the one who asked me about finding any old documents the day I opened." She looked around. "Where did he go?"

Jane shrugged. "Off with a group, I guess. When he said he was curious about old documents, do you suppose he meant old manuscripts?"

Lizzie puffed air from her cheeks. "Ja, that seems possible. I should tell the police about him being here tonight."

Jane nodded. "Ja, that's a gut idea."

"I really want to be in on this," Eliza said. "Do you mind if I go join Reuben and Mary's father, Joe? I think they're up on the third floor. I'll keep an eye out for the man with the mustache, and if I see him, I'll tell the officers, or John."

"Sure, go have fun! Be careful!" Lizzie said, smiling as Eliza hurried to the stairs and disappeared up them. Lizzie turned to Jane.

"So, it's just us two who are not searching. And really, at least I should be the first one to look. But we've assigned every conceivable place to the others! So now we have nowhere to look."

"Well, we can go join any of the groups if you think we should."

Lizzie tipped her head to the side, considering while she toyed with one of the strings of her prayer kapp. "Maybe I'll just sit here and enjoy my coffee for a bit, and see what happens. I suppose someone should be here in case any of the searchers need anything."

"I agree. Besides, I'm tired. Last night I finally got a full night's rest, but it didn't make up for the weeks before it. I think I'll enjoy sitting here waiting for the searchers to report in."

Lizzie chuckled, and she and Jane sat back to enjoy their coffee and wait.

Soon the group searching the café space arrived over by the fireplace, which was not burning because it would need to be searched.

"Excuse me, Lizzie, Jane, but we need to look up this chimney. Do you mind letting us in there?" Lizzie stood from her seat, as did Jane, and they moved away behind the counter while the group made a thorough search of the chimney, looking up inside it with flashlights and even checking it for loose bricks. They found nothing, but their spirits remained high as they headed off to their second assigned area, down in the basement.

"That basement is not my favorite place," Jane commented as they left. "Too many spiders."

Lizzie nodded. "Ja. And centipedes. There's really nothing down there except some old canned goods left over from who knows how long ago. I really should clear them out. But whenever I think of doing it, I think it would be a shame to waste those old jars, and I should really clean them out, but I just don't want to open them so I end up doing nothing."

Jane chuckled. "I understand. Yuck. Oh, here comes someone. Maybe they found something!"

A group of people clattered down the steps, excitement shining in their eyes.

"Did you find something?" Lizzie called as they hurried over to the table.

"Maybe! We aren't sure. Look!" Frank Gerber, the Mennonite man who owned the local saddlery shop, and his wife, Megan, hurried up to the table. Frank was clutching an old cloth bag. "This was up high on a closet shelf on the third floor! We didn't open it."

"We thought you'd want to be in on that," Megan added breathlessly. "Give it to her, Frank, so we can see what's inside!"

Several other people had arrived in the room, and now they all gathered around the table where Lizzie and Jane sat, waiting excitedly to see what was in the bag the Gerbers had discovered.

Jane looked at Lizzie, wide-eyed. "Well? Aren't you going to open it?"

Lizzie licked her lips and pulled the old bag toward her. It smelled musty and was covered with a thick layer of dust. "Goodness, I'm afraid it'll fall apart in my hands. It's pretty fragile looking," Lizzie said, carefully pulling the drawstring ribbons, one of which broke off in her hand. She pried at the opening of the bag, finally pulling the two sides gently apart, and opened the bag. She almost expected a host of moths to come flying out, but nothing of the sort happened. She peered inside and frowned in puzzlement. "What's this?"

"What is it?" John, who had just arrived downstairs after helping Lydia and the bishop down, stepped closer so he could see.

"I don't know," Lizzie said. "I'm almost afraid to put my hand in the bag." She laughed self-consciously.

Megan Gerber laughed with her. "I totally understand. But it did feel as if something chunky was inside. Not really like paper, actually."

Word had spread that something had been found, and it looked to Lizzie as if everyone had returned to the room to watch her pull out whatever the Gerbers had found. She saw the Petersheims standing toward the back of the crowd, and she held up the bag so they could see.

"Does this look familiar?" She asked. They shook their heads.

"Nee!" Mrs. Petersheim called. "I hear it was shoved way back on a high shelf. I never saw it!"

Lizzie nodded. Deciding there was nothing to do but get it over with, she bit her lip, reached inside, and pulled out an old hairbrush. It was very tarnished, but she thought it might be silver, with boar bristles. "There's something else."

She reached in and pulled out another tarnished item, this time a mirror, the glass somewhat blackened but still usable. She put her hand back inside and found a silver comb.

"Why, it's an antique dresser set!" Mr. Rumpkin exclaimed. "I'll bet if you cleaned it up you'd have a nice souvenir of some former occupant of your building! May I see it?"

Lizzie handed the items over, privately thinking that she couldn't imagine using such filthy items in her hair. But Mr. Rumpkin seemed pleased, so she was glad something interesting had been found.

Even if it wasn't the missing manuscript.

"Did anyone else find anything?" John asked those assembled. There were general murmurs of no, although one of Lizzie's brothers claimed to have discovered bats roosting in the attic.

"I just left them alone. There was nothing else in there. We checked the floorboards and all the corners."

"I'm glad you didn't bring down any bats." Lizzie laughed.

"I'm glad I didn't see them when I was searching the eaves!" Jane shuddered.

Most of the groups still had to search their second areas, so everyone dispersed again, including John and Eliza, leaving Lizzie and Jane sitting with Mr. Rumpkin, Lydia, and Bishop Troyer.

Lydia stumped over to the table and sat next to Lizzie. "I found something, but it isn't a manuscript so I didn't say anything." She reached into her apron pocket and pulled out a small china doll, which she handed to Lizzie.

Lizzie turned the small doll over in her hands, marveling at its delicacy. It was wearing a pretty, though faded, red calico dress. Shiny black hair and the suggestion of facial features, including blue eyes and red lips, had been carefully applied with paint. Her hands and feet were china, the hands encased in painted gloves and the feet in painted black boots. Her body was stuffed cotton. Lizzie held it carefully. "I can't believe something like this survived unbroken all these years. Where did you find it, Lydia?"

Lydia looked smug. "It was in the very back of one of those little cabinets that line the wall under the windows in a room on the third floor. I had to get down and peer inside. Fortunately Abram has a flashlight, or I would have missed her. Isn't she pretty? I wonder how many years she's been tucked back there, waiting to be discovered."

"Now, Lydia, don't go getting all fanciful on us. It's a doll, not a person. It hasn't been waiting at all," Abram said.

"Well of course I know that, Abram," Lydia told her old friend. "Goodness, you're so literal. Lizzie, can an old woman get a cup of coffee?"

Jane stood. "If I see an old woman, I'll get her some coffee. Would you like a cup while we wait for her to turn up, Lydia?"

Lydia laughed and lightly slapped Jane on the wrist. "Oh, you! Yes, please, with plenty of cream and sugar. And I wouldn't say no to a pastry if you have one handy."

"Coming right up," Jane said.

"What are you going to do with this doll?" Lizzie asked.

"Well, it's your doll, since it was found in your building," Lydia replied.

"Hmm. I'll think about it. Of course, it has a face painted on, so it doesn't really belong in an Amish establishment. And I can't give it to one of the Amish children."

"You could give it to the man from the museum, I suppose," Lydia pointed out before blowing on her coffee.

"I could," Lizzie said. "I'll think about it."

They chatted as the groups gradually finished their search and reported back. The Petersheims looked at the little doll, and once again said they'd never seen it before.

"But it's a big place, and there was a lot of stuff here when we got here. I can see missing a couple little things, even though we did live here a long time!" Mrs. Petersheim said.

Finally the last group was finished, and nothing else of interest had been found.

The groups that had searched the basement acknowledged the old canning jars, which were labeled peaches and plums and Chow Chow. But nobody had wanted to risk picking one up and possibly breaking glass jars filled with rotten old fruit. So the jars remained where they had remained for untold years.

By then the pizza had arrived, and everyone consoled themselves with plenty of tasty pizza and soda. The mood was festive.

After the food was eaten, people started coming up to Lizzie and thanking her for such a fun evening, then taking their leave. Soon there was nobody left except Lizzie, Jane, and Eliza; Eliza's brother, Dr. Reuben, and his wife, Mary; Lydia and Abram; the girls' friend Ruth and her husband Jonas; Mr. Rumpkin and Mr. LaForest; and the two police officers. Lizzie realized in all the excitement, she'd forgotten to tell John or the officers about the man with the odd holiday name. Was it Easter? Christmas? She shook her head in frustration. Looking around, she didn't see him. He must have satisfied his curiosity and left.

The Petersheims had told Lizzie the place looked great, and it was fun to visit now that they were happily settled in at their new home. They'd be staying for a few days before heading back to Indiana, and Lizzie asked Mrs. Petersheim if they could have lunch one day, as she had some things to ask about running the business. Mrs. Petersheim had happily agreed, and Lizzie looked forward to asking the older woman about balancing a business and a family in the big old building.

The Stutzmans had grumpily thanked Lizzie for letting them take part in the search, though they said they didn't see what all the fuss was about some old manuscript and they still thought they'd have made better use of the place than she ever would.

Lizzie had waited until the door closed behind them before making eye contact with John, and then she'd had trouble stifling a strong urge to giggle.

Lizzie's and Jane's parents had been among the last to leave.

"Well, Elizabeth," her mother had said, not looking happy. "I'd really hoped we'd find something that would end all this nonsense. Your father and I can hardly sleep at night we're so worried about you girls. Won't you consider closing the bakery just for a few weeks and moving home until the police figure it all out?"

Lizzie had genuinely hated to have to deny her mother's request, as she knew it came from a place of love, but she knew if she walked away now it was unlikely she'd be back. She'd hugged her mother and kissed her on the cheek, and begged her to understand. Reluctantly, Agnes and Henry Miller, along with Lizzie's brother and sisters, had departed, accompanied by the Bontrager family.

"Well," Lizzie said with a yawn, "at least I know every square inch of this place has been searched. There's no way that manuscript, if it exists, is hidden here. There's simply nowhere left that wasn't poked and prodded by several dozen people. And if we're lucky, that'll be all it takes to make whoever wants to get in here quit."

"For all we know, they were here tonight, searching alongside half the population of Willow Creek!" Ruth Hershberger suggested as she tucked an errant strand of shiny red hair back beneath her kapp.

"Oh my, that's an alarming thought," Lydia said, shuddering a bit. Abram patted her on the arm, and she smiled at her old friend.

Officer Jakes looked at Officer Anderson, who said, "Actually, we were watching for exactly that, Mrs. Coblentz. We hoped they'd be here and that they'd give themselves away."

"Really?" Mary King asked. "That's kind of thrilling in a twisted way.

Too bad they didn't get on board with that."

"I'm just so disappointed," Mr. Rumpkin murmured. "I was so sure we'd find it! It has to be here!"

"I thought you'd find a good clue in the recipe journals," Mr. LaForest pointed out in his heavy French accent. "I even read through both of them thoroughly, and there's nothing except recipes and entries about mundane daily activities."

"They did make very interesting reading though," Jane said. "There are a number of recipes I want to try myself. And I loved reading about the innkeeper Mrs. Bridgerton's daily routines. She really got into details about how she did some things, which I think will be of interest to Mr. Rumpkin."

She glanced at Lizzie. "What did you like best?"

Lizzie pondered that for a moment. "Well, I remember reading an entry about putting up canned goods and thinking that it could be the same jars that are still sitting down there in the basement now. That made me feel a connection with her. I suppose because there's still something physical here that she may have touched with her hands, besides the journal, I mean."

"That struck me too," Jane said. "I guess that's part of why we haven't thrown away those old jars, despite the fact that they're probably full of spoiled fruit and vegetables now, and would be really disgusting to open."

Lizzie sighed. "It does seem a shame to throw away those old glass canning jars. The lids wouldn't be any good, but the jars could be boiled and reused."

Jane nodded. "I understand, waste not want not, but maybe in this case, you could just toss them out. I've seen them, and they look like they could be a hundred years old."

"Yuck," Eliza said, and everyone chuckled and nodded.

Lizzie pondered how there could be fruits and veggies in her basement that had grown in the garden out back over a hundred years ago. It boggled the mind.

But then a sudden thought hit her, and she sat up straight, an arrested look on her face.

"What is it, Lizzie?" John asked, drawing everyone else's attention to Lizzie.

She blinked and then whispered, "A hundred years old."

"What?" Eliza asked. "The old canning jars?"

Lizzie turned to her friend and nodded. "Exactly, Eliza. The old canning jars are probably around a hundred years old. That means they've been sitting there, in that spot, undisturbed..."

"Since the time of the murder!" John exclaimed, jumping to his feet.

A look of understanding had dawned on both Jane's and Eliza's faces, and both of them were standing as well. "How many of them are down there?" Jane asked.

"I'm not sure," Lizzie said. "A couple dozen at least. I've never really given them a thorough look, because I always see them and think, yuck."

"Well, I think it's time we took a look, then, don't you?" John asked, an eager light in his eyes. He held out a hand to Lizzie, who took it and followed him down into the old basement.

Most of the group trailed after them, with the exception of Mary, Lydia, the bishop, and Mr. Rumpkin.

"I'm sure glad this place has electricity," Ruth said as she brushed a cobweb out of her way as she followed the group through the old basement. It was chilly and musty down there, with the stone walls and floors allowing the damp to seep in. The basement was under the entire footprint of the house, and the canning room was three or four rooms back.

"It's gut you have a cat," Officer Anderson said with an uneasy look into the dark corners of the room they were crossing. "Because I guarantee you'll have mice down here." She shuddered, and Lizzie and John exchanged amused smiles.

Finally they reached the room where Lizzie had noticed the old jars of preserved food. The light bulb in there was burned out, unfortunately, but a couple of their group had flashlights, which they switched on. They approached the shelves holding the jars.

"Careful," Jonas warned. "If the jars are a hundred years old, so are the shelves."

"Gut point," John said.

Reuben was holding a powerful flashlight, which he trained on the jars. Most of them were labeled with the name of a fruit or vegetable, and you could sort of see into them, although the contents were uniformly dark and unappetizing after all this time.

"They just look like jars of old fruit," Reuben said. Jonas nodded, and Lizzie tended to agree. But she wasn't ready to give up yet.

"I want to take a better look. It's possible that one of them isn't really full of preserves," she said.

John gave her a sideways smile. "You're hoping one of them is full of a missing manuscript, neatly curled up and placed here for safety by a murder victim a little over a hundred years ago, ja?"

She smiled at him. "I know it seems ridiculous. But humor me, okay?"

"Of course. Okay, let's go about this scientifically. We'll remove the jars and take them all upstairs. Then we'll open them all up and see for ourselves."

"This is not going to smell good, is it?" Officer Jakes muttered.

"Probably not," John confirmed. "Everyone grab a couple. And whatever you do, don't drop any!"

They carefully carried them up to the kitchen, where they were placed into the big double sink. Everyone stood staring at them.

"What now?" Mary, who had come into the kitchen along with the others who had remained upstairs, asked.

Lizzie bit her lip. "Now, we open them. We have no choice."

"I was afraid you were going to say that," Mary said.

Lizzie got a silicone gripper from a drawer and offered it to John. "Would you like to do the honors?"

He smiled at her. "No. But I will." He stared at the jars for a moment, then chose one at random. He put a little elbow grease into it and turned it with the gripper, and with an audible pop the lid gave way.

"It was still sealed!" Jane squealed. "It's probably still safe to eat!"

"Imagine, after all these years!" Eliza gasped.

John, meanwhile, looked at Lizzie. "Do you have a big strainer or colander?"

She hurried to get the biggest colander she had from its hook on the wall and brought it to John, who placed it in the other sink and upended the can of fruit into it. It fell out with a sucking sound, and a jar full of ancient peaches glistened in the bottom of the colander.

Everyone leaned in to look at them.

"Peaches," Lydia observed. "Just old peaches. And Jane's right, they're probably still good. Not that I'd risk it."

Lizzie shuddered. "Yuck. Okay, just set the empty jar into the sink and try another one."

John nodded and opened another. That one didn't pop, and the contents were unrecognizable black glop, plopping into the colander. "Oh, those don't smell good," John said, turning his face away. He put the empty jar down next to the first and repeated the process.

This went on for some time, the collection of unopened jars dwindling and the colander filling up with fruit, veggies, and even a little meat, in various stages of decay. It was not pleasant. Eventually there were only three jars left. John reached for one, but Lizzie put a hand on his arm.

"Wait, John, look at that one in the middle. It looks different from the other jars. I didn't notice before, because it blended in. But. . .has it been painted?"

John put down the jar he was holding and picked up the one Lizzie had indicated instead. He held it up to the light, and everyone gasped. It had been painted a dark brown that had caused it to blend in with the jars of fruits and veggies. He hefted it. "It feels different, as if there's no liquid inside."

Lizzie felt excited. "Oh, John, this could be it!"

"Only one way to find out," Bishop Troyer said.

Everyone nodded, and John unscrewed the lid on the jar. He set it aside and looked inside. "Well, I'll be," he murmured.

"What? What?" the others all clamored to see.

"Hold on, I'll see if I can get it out." He reached inside with two fingers, carefully, and withdrew a thick roll of paper. Everyone gasped.

He held the paper and turned to look at Lizzie, who had gone quite pale.

"Is it. . . ?" she asked, her voice shaking.

"Why don't you open it and tell me?" he asked softly, handing the roll of paper over to her. She stared at it for a moment, then looked at Mr. Rumpkin, who nodded.

"Go ahead. I know we probably shouldn't touch it, but it won't hurt this once. After all, it's been protected in a dark, airless container. It should be fine."

Lizzie took a deep breath and accepted the roll from John. She turned to the table, and Jane hurried over and cleared off some dishes. Eliza placed a clean cloth on the table, and Lizzie laid the roll of paper down on the cloth. Then she carefully placed her hands at the top and bottom, and gently smoothed it out until it lay flat.

Everyone craned their necks to get a look. And then everyone gasped.

For on the first page of paper, clearly printed in bold black letters, were the words "*Back to Their Roots*, a novel by E. W. Fingle."

"Oh my goodness!" Lizzie whispered. "It's really real!"

They all began talking at once, until all conversation stopped when the air was rent by a long cry coming from the direction of the swinging door into the front of the shop. "Noooooooooooooooo! It's not fair! It's mine! Give it to me! Give it to me!" And to everyone's utter astonishment, in rushed Mrs. Stutzman, a crazed look in her eye. She made a beeline straight for Lizzie, who feared she was about to be run right over by the older woman.

But before that could happen, Officer Anderson leaped forward and caught Mrs. Stutzman around the waist, while Officer Jakes grabbed her hands and pulled them around behind her back and cuffed them there. He then pushed her down into a kitchen chair, where she sat, sobbing incoherently, still saying something unintelligible about how the manuscript was hers by rights.

The swinging door crashed open again, and Mr. Stutzman hurried inside, looking wildly around until he spotted his sobbing wife. "Wilma! What are you doing?"

When she babbled something about the manuscript, he stepped back, a look of dismay on his face. "Ach! I thought you'd left this crazy obsession behind!" He hurried over to her but was stopped by Officer Jakes.

"Sir, I need you to step away from the suspect and remain calm."

"Suspect? That's my wife! What's she suspected of? Why is she handcuffed? Wilma?" He looked around the kitchen at all the shocked faces of his neighbors. "Would someone please tell me what's going on?" Mrs. Stutzman sniffled and coughed and slowly got herself under control. Then she opened her eyes and looked pathetically up at her obviously bewildered husband. "Obadiah. They found it! They found my great-great-great"—she paused for breath before finishing—"great-grandfather's missing manuscript!"

Then her eyes rolled right up in their sockets, and she fainted.

Officer Jakes caught the unconscious woman before she fell. Mr. Stutzman, looking a bit dizzy himself, staggered over to a chair and plopped down, moaning about his wife's obsession and covering his face with his hands.

The swinging door crashed open again, and Tucker Stutzman slid inside as if he'd hit the door at a run. He looked around the room, took in his unconscious maem and his weeping dat, and let out a loud cry, followed by an unrepeatable word in Pennsylvania Dutch.

Everyone stared at him in amazement, but Lizzie slowly rose to her feet and pointed at him with a shaking hand. "It was you! You're the one who broke into my building twice!"

John stood next to her as she faced Tucker, who was glaring at her, fists clenched at his sides. "You can't prove it!"

"Maybe not, but I know!" She leaned toward him. "You just gave yourself away when you swore! It was the same thing you yelled the day you were running out of the bakery when you heard the police coming. Now I know what bothered me about the whole thing. You cursed in Deitsch! I guess I was so shaken up at the time that I didn't realize it. But now I remember. You used the same swear word that day, Tucker. The day you trashed my building!"

A loud moan from behind her made Lizzie spin around in time to see Mrs. Stutzman's eyes roll up as she passed out again. This time,

Officer Jakes wasn't fast enough, and she rolled off the chair onto the kitchen floor.

Lizzie turned shocked eyes to John and whispered, "What else can happen tonight?"

She was answered by a second loud moan, as Mr. Stutzman passed out and fell off his chair, hitting the floor with a thud.

The swinging door crashed open again, and Tucker's younger bruder, Isaiah, rushed inside, looked around, and then pinned Tucker with a glare. "Tucker! What's happening? Why are our parents lying on the kitchen floor?"

Tucker closed his eyes and said that Deitsch word again.

CHAPTER TWENTY-ONE

An hour later, nearly everyone had gone home, leaving only John, Jane, Eliza, Lizzie, Lydia, and Bishop Troyer in the kitchen of Lizzie's bakery. It was getting late, but nobody seemed ready to leave yet. They were full of energy, and everyone still wanted to hash out the events of the evening.

Eliza had brewed a big pot of hot chocolate despite the warm night, saying it always comforted her, and she might as well make enough for everybody while she was at it.

Lizzie blew on her cocoa, wanting it to cool so she could slurp out the tiny marshmallows. She shook her head in wonder. "I still can't believe it was Mrs. Stutzman all this time! And I had no idea she had an Englisch three-times great-grandfather."

"Let alone an Englisch three-times great-grandfather who was a famous author!" Jane added, grabbing a peanut butter cookie from a plate on the table.

"Let alone an Englisch three-times great-grandfather who was murdered right here in this building!" Eliza added with a gleeful shudder.

"It does stretch the imagination, but I'll tell you now that I've always thought Wilma Stutzman was a bit odd. This explains it. She had secrets!" Lydia sat back with a smug look on her face and carefully perused the cookie selection before choosing a gingersnap.

"Now, Lydia, you've never mentioned that to me," Abram said. "Are you sure you aren't just remembering her that way now that you know she's capable of violence?"

Lydia turned and frowned sternly at her old friend. "Now, Abram, I'll have none of that! My mind is as sharp as it ever was, and I've always thought Wilma was a few nuts short of a full pouch. A few clowns short of a circus. A few crayons short of a box. A few hens short of a coop..."

Abram snorted and muttered, "Well, I'm beginning to think maybe you're a few sandwiches short of a picnic, the way you're going on about that poor woman."

Lydia's mouth dropped open, but before she could say anything, John interrupted. "I've been delivering furniture to the Stutzmans for years, and I never saw anything odd about her. She hid it well."

"And all this time, she's been dying to get in here to thoroughly search the place, hoping to find the missing manuscript!" Lizzie marveled.

"She even convinced her husband to try and buy the building, telling him that they could expand their business here and their kinner could live upstairs!" Eliza said, eyes wide. "That's dedication to a cause."

"But he knew about her obsession with the old manuscript. You heard him earlier, telling her he thought that she'd let it go," John said.

"Guess not," Eliza said. "You'd think he'd have figured out that was the real reason she wanted the building!"

"Maybe he knew, but he hoped she really was over it and just wanted a good real estate investment," Jane suggested.

"They've had the store across the street for decades," John said. "Plenty of time for her to figure out a way to have a good look around if she really wanted to!"

"Mrs. Petersheim told me when I called to tell her about this that Mrs. Stutzman waxed hot and cold over the years toward her, and that several times she caught her in areas of the building where she shouldn't have been. Once, she was digging through the drawers of the linen closet upstairs! She just thought the woman was very odd but never suspected she could be obsessively dangerous!"

"Yet she convinced her husband that she'd gotten over it, so she must have been able to act reasonable most of the time," Jane pointed out.

"Well, she looked anything but reasonable tonight," Lizzie said.

"She must be quite an actress to convince people who know her well that she wanted the building for the business and for her kids to live in. Her husband had to suspect!"

"He wanted her to be okay, so he convinced himself she was."

"Yep," Eliza said. "And all along, she was hiding a single-minded determination about getting a chance to search this place."

"Yet when she finally got the chance, she still couldn't find the manuscript," John said, smiling at Lizzie with a glowing admiration that made her cheeks flush red. "It took Lizzie putting it all together for us to find it!"

Jane snorted. "Well, Lizzie and all the rest of us. If I recall, it was a group effort, both the thinking and the searching."

Lizzie grinned at her best friend. "Jane's right, John. Be fair."

He shrugged. "Well, all that matters is that we found the manuscript, and it's out of the building! That was smart of you, Lizzie, sending it with Mr. Rumpkin to lock up in his attorney's safe until ownership can be determined."

"I sure didn't want it in here for another night! It's caused enough trouble!"

Jane munched another cookie. "I still can't believe Mrs. Stutzman threw a brick through your window! And sent her son Tucker to break in, not once, but twice!"

"So, Tucker is the one Little Mouse attacked and knocked down the stairs?" Lydia asked.

John nodded. "Ja, and I believe he's going to be in more trouble than his mudder when this is all sorted out. After all, Wilma asked him to break the law, but he chose to do so. He could have said no. You know, I wondered where he'd gotten that scratch and sprained wrist, but it never, not in a million years, would have occurred to me that he did it breaking in here! And he's baptized. What was he hoping to gain from all this? He's really made a mess of his life."

Abram nodded sagely. "You're absolutely correct, John. I'll be driving over to Berlin to have a chat with the Stutzmans' bishop tomorrow. He needs to know what's happened here, and he'll want to be able to counsel the family in their time of need."

"Even if they did bring their time of need upon themselves through really poor decision-making," Lydia pointed out.

"Even though they did," Abram agreed.

"Okay, so to be sure I have this straight, let's go over it all one more time," Lizzie said. "The day of my grand opening, it was Mr. LaForest who accosted me in the bakery, and he later turned out to be harmless."

"Ja," Jane said. "He just wanted a peek at your recipe book!"

"Of all the foolish things! He could have just asked!" Lydia said.

"Right," Lizzie confirmed. "And that night, it was Tucker who broke in, at his mother's request, and then fell down the stairs when Little Mouse attacked him!"

"She's such a gut cat!" Lydia said. "I'm going to bring her a treat tomorrow. After all, she's my grand-kitty, and it's my right to spoil her!"

"Then after that, we found the box of letters and the journal, which Wilma somehow heard about, causing her to panic and escalate her campaign to frighten me out of my own building!" Lizzie said, outraged.

"I wonder how she found out about that?" John asked, reaching for the pot of cocoa to refresh his mug, then looking around the table. "Do we have any more little marshmallows?"

Eliza handed him the bag of mini marshmallows. "I think we'll discover that Mr. Rumpkin may have inadvertently told her. Lizzie, remember I told you she's on the historical museum board, because of her expertise in furniture?"

Lizzie nodded, and Eliza continued. "I've seen them at your sister Susan's booth at the Amish farm market. About a week ago I overheard Mrs. Stutzman and Mr. Rumpkin discussing the piece John was volunteering to restore, and I heard Mrs. Stutzman say she knew John did good work, and then Mr. Rumpkin started to tell her something about another project John was working on with his friends from the bakery across the street from her. But then they got up and walked away, and I couldn't hear any more. I meant to tell you, but it slipped my mind."

"Interesting. You may be right," John said, a speculative look in his eye. "But I don't think Mr. Rumpkin is in cahoots with her, do you?"

She shook her head, sending her kapp strings swinging. "Oh, no. I think he was an innocent bystander. She just grabbed the information and ran with it."

"Ja, the next thing she did was send me that threatening letter," Lizzie said. "It really frightened me, although I tried not to let on."

John reached over and patted her hand, smiling into her eyes. "I wouldn't have let anything bad happen to you, Lizzie. You didn't need to worry."

"Between John, your gut friends, and Gott, you were well looked after, Elizabeth," Abram said.

"What happened next?" Lydia asked, pulling some knitting from her large bag.

"Next was the second break-in, the one where Tucker was searching the building and knocking holes in my walls! And that was the day we met Mr. LaForest."

John's lips quirked. "Ja, and I got angry because I thought he might be dangerous."

"When he's actually rather sweet," Eliza said. "Grumpy but sweet."

"After that, Wilma either painted the window, or had Tucker do it," Lizzie said. "And then we decided to invite everyone in for a search tonight, and we ended up flushing out the villain! Yay, us!"

"Yay, us!" everyone cheered, lifting their cups of cocoa.

Lydia finished her cocoa then put the cup down with a click. "Come on, Abram, and drive me home. This old woman needs her rest." She pushed to her feet, grabbed the cane she carried more than used, and looked with approval at the young people gathered around the kitchen table. "Well done, all of you! You worked together and trusted in Gott, and look what happened! You solved the mystery!"

Abram gave them a mock frown. "Don't let this go to your heads, though. From now on, this sort of thing is for the Englisch police to solve, fashtay?"

They all nodded and said they understood. Abram and Lydia turned to go, but before she left the room, Lydia turned and grinned at them all and gave them a big wink before preceding Abram through the door. The bishop followed, and John thought he heard the older man mumble something about trying his patience, but he couldn't be certain.

"I think we'd be safe staying here tonight, but all our things are at your place, Eliza," Lizzie said.

"Ja, and I'd rather you waited just a few more days, to be sure this is really settled, if you don't mind too much?" John asked tentatively. "I realize you're adults and can do as you like, but I'd feel much better, and I'm sure Maem and Dat. . ."

Jane held up her hands to stop his flood of words. "John, peace. I think we're all fine with that." She looked at her friends, who nodded their agreement. "Gut. Then let's go home. I'm bushed."

They headed back to Eliza's, where Jane and Eliza said good night and went upstairs while John and Lizzie lingered on the porch.

"Want to sit a minute and talk?" Lizzie invited, and John smiled at her.

"Ja, I would like that."

So they sat looking out into the night, listening to katydids and watching fireflies light up in the darkness.

After a while, John cleared his throat.

Lizzie glanced over at him. "Do you need water?"

"Nee, denki. So I'm just going to come right out and ask you. Are you still uninterested in pursuing a relationship with me? If so, I can wait. But I need to know whether there is any hope. You're too kind to let me suffer. If you're not interested in me, please just be honest and say so." He clasped his hands, bit his lip, and waited for her verdict.

Lizzie looked at John and thought about how he'd crept his way into her heart, despite all the roadblocks she'd erected to keep him out. She frowned. When had that happened? She'd been sure she didn't want a relationship. She was too busy building her business!

And John was so familiar, almost like an older bruder. But her feelings toward him were not sisterly at all.

Look at him, he's actually afraid of what I'm going to say!

She needed to put him out of his misery. She opened her mouth to tell him how much she liked him and that she thought maybe they could explore a relationship and think about a future together, when a sudden sound caused them both to glance sharply into the yard.

"John, what was that?" Lizzie peered into the darkness, trying to see what had caused the odd sound.

"I'm not sure, but probably just an animal."

"Afraid not, young man," a British voice said as a tall, shadowy figure stepped out from behind a large oak tree in the front yard. He stepped into the moonlight, and Lizzie gasped as she noticed a gun in his hand. It was pointed at her and John.

Then she realized she recognized him!

"Mr. Valentine?" she gasped as his name came back to her. "I saw you at the bakery earlier tonight! Why are you pointing a gun at us? What do you want?"

John stepped in front of Lizzie, staring at the man, who was a good fifteen feet away. Too far to tackle, but close enough that John, a hunter since childhood, knew he was unlikely to miss if he fired his weapon.

"Yes, Lizzie, we meet again. But tonight my business is urgent, and so I'm afraid I don't have time for chitchat. I have a plane to catch soon. So give me the manuscript, and I'll be on my way."

She blinked at him and stepped out from behind John, who reached back and caught her arm. "Lizzie! Stay put!"

She spared John a look and found his expression to be very fierce. "I'll stay here, John, but I want to be able to see Mr. Valentine, which I can't do from behind you. Mr. Valentine, I won't pretend not to know what you're talking about. We found the old missing manuscript earlier this evening at the bakery. Which you obviously know."

"Of course I know! I waited outside the bakery to see what would happen when you were all alone, after the crowd left. I didn't trust your act, you see. 'Oh, too bad, it's not here! Thanks for helping! Now leave us alone!' Ha! Do you think I'm stupid? So I know you found it. Rather brilliant of you to think of the canning jars. No one else did, not even me."

Lizzie glanced at John, then back at the angry man with the gun.

"What I don't understand is your interest in it. Why do you want it? Is it that valuable?"

"Of course it's valuable, you silly girl! A missing manuscript by the famous author, E. W. Fingle? It's probably worth millions! But that's not my only interest. You see, I have a legitimate claim on the document, so I'm here to take what's mine by family right."

Lizzie glanced at John, who hadn't taken his eyes off Valentine. Then she returned her gaze to the man holding the gun. A man she was about to make angry.

She cleared her throat and said, "I'm sorry, Mr. Valentine," but before she could tell him that the manuscript wasn't there, John interrupted.

"What's your connection with the manuscript?"

"Did I forget to mention that? Well, I'm the great-great-grandson of Mr. Gregory Liptak. Perhaps you've heard of him?"

"The man who murdered the author," Lizzie breathed.

"My ancestor was also a great author!" Valentine took an audible breath, as if to calm himself. "Fingle stole his greatest idea and wrote what should have been my ancestor's bestselling novel. Can you blame my great-grandfather for what he did?"

Lizzie and John exchanged uneasy glances, and Valentine asked again. "Well? Can you?"

"We're pacifists, so it's hard for us to relate," Lizzie tentatively offered.

"Bah! People are people! Imagine if someone greatly harmed a member of your family. I doubt you'd be so peaceful then!"

"We believe in turning the other cheek, and in things happening according to Gott's will," John said calmly. "Of course, it would not be easy under the circumstances you name."

Lizzie nodded her agreement, and Valentine seemed satisfied. "Well, I think if I threatened to harm this lady, you would soon forget your pacifism." He chuckled. John stepped back in front of Lizzie, and Valentine laughed aloud. "Ha! You see? I'm right. But don't worry, I don't intend to harm anyone. I just want the manuscript. Where is it?"

Lizzie searched her mind for an answer that wouldn't infuriate the man, who was clearly desperate, and therefore dangerous. John slid his hand down her arm and twined his fingers with hers. He gave her hand a squeeze and drew her back behind him again. "Mr. Valentine," he said, and Lizzie knew he was going to tell the truth, and that he was standing in harm's way to protect her.

"Tell me where it is! Is it inside?"

"The fact is, Mr. Valentine, the manuscript isn't here. We gave it to the curator of the historical museum, who was taking it to his attorney's office to place in his safe while ownership is being determined."

"What? No! You stupid fools!" Furious, Valentine took a step toward John and Lizzie.

Lizzie didn't know what was happening. She saw Mr. Valentine approaching, gun held before him, fury reflected in his moonlit eyes. She felt John turn and push her toward the ground, heard him yell at her to get down, and then she heard a terrible, unearthly shriek followed by a loud bang.

Then everything seemed to stand still for a long moment, before voices started yelling.

"Lizzie! Are you oll recht?" She looked up and saw John's panicked expression. "Were you hit by the bullet?"

She took stock and realized she was unharmed, just a bit shaken up. "Nee, John, I'm fine, please get off me!" For he had her pinned to the ground with his weight.

"Oh, I'm sorry, hold on." He leaped nimbly to his feet and reached a hand down to help her up.

She stood and brushed off her skirt, then looked at him. "Are you all right?"

He nodded. "Ja, I'm fine. Thank Gott for protecting us both!"

She heard shouting and looked over to where Mr. Valentine was lying on the ground, face down, with Officer Jakes handcuffing him. Officer Anderson was putting her weapon into her holster and looking down to make sure Valentine didn't pull any shenanigans. Then Jakes stood up and heaved Valentine to his feet, hands cuffed behind his back. In the moonlight, Lizzie could see several long, bloody scratches across his face. What on earth?

Jakes and Anderson, breathing hard, looked at Lizzie and John. "Are you both okay? We heard his weapon discharge!" Anderson said, coming toward them.

"Ja, denki, we're fine," John said. "But what happened? How did you know to come?"

"And what happened to his face?" Lizzie asked, pointing at Valentine, who was standing next to Officer Jakes, tears mingling with blood on his cheeks. "I thought I heard a yowl or a screech. . .did something attack him?"

Anderson chuckled. "Yes, and that something is sitting right over there, looking very pleased with herself." She pointed to a patch of moonlight several yards away, and Lizzie saw a small form sitting there, carefully cleaning its paws.

Her mouth dropped open. "Little Mouse!" She hurried over to the cat and picked her up, cuddling her to her chest. "Did you rescue us? But. . .how?" She turned back to Anderson. "She's an inside cat. I don't know how she got out."

"That would be me," a voice said from the porch behind them. Lizzie turned and saw Eliza and Jane standing on the porch. "Is it oll recht for us to come out now?"

Anderson nodded. "Yes, and I want to hear how you knew to call us."

"You called the police?" John asked, sounding astonished. "But how did you realize we needed help?"

"I looked out the window, and I saw that man standing there, moonlight reflecting off what I was pretty sure was a gun. So I ran downstairs and grabbed my cell phone and called 911," Eliza said. "Then I hurried back up and cracked the window a bit, so I could hear what was being said. And right before I saw the officers creeping toward you, Little Mouse jumped up onto the windowsill and darted out! She jumped off the roof and right onto that man! She was the one who screeched something wonderful. And she knocked him down. Then the police grabbed him. It was very exciting!"

Jane rolled her eyes. "Ja, a bit too exciting if you ask me."

Two more police cars sped up the driveway and came to a halt, doors flying open and officers jumping out.

"We've got it all under control, Sergeant," Jakes told Sgt. Hernandez when he hurried up.

"I can see that. Good job, Jakes, Anderson. Was anyone hurt? I had a report of gunfire."

"Nobody was hurt, except for a pretty good cat scratch on the perpetrator," Anderson said. "I think he may need stitches. And antibiotics."

"Serves him right," Lizzie murmured, stroking Little Mouse.

"So that cat is the hero of the hour!" Officer Jakes said, and explained to the other officers what had happened.

"We'll need you to make a statement," Hernandez told Lizzie and John. "But it can wait for morning. We'll take him downtown and book him. I suppose this has something to do with that missing manuscript and the hundred-year-old murder?"

"Good guess. It sure does," Lizzie said.

"I'll look forward to hearing all about it in the morning. Please come in by nine. Jakes, Anderson, get him downtown, and don't forget to read him his rights."

He turned back to Lizzie and her friends. "Tomorrow we'll need to see if we can find the bullet he fired from his weapon."

"It was an accident! I didn't mean to shoot!" Valentine yelled as he was led off to one of the police cruisers.

"People get hurt all the time by accidental discharges, Mr. Valentine. You came here with a loaded weapon to commit a crime. You're lucky nobody got hurt, except you," Jakes said as he guided Valentine into the back seat of the cruiser. "See you in the morning," he called to Lizzie, John, and the others.

"I'll ride back with him if you go get our cruiser, Anderson," Jakes said, climbing into the passenger seat of the car driven by another officer. Anderson nodded, tossed a final wave at the four young Amish friends, and hurried off into the darkness.

Hernandez stepped forward. "Are you sure nobody got hurt? Sometimes it takes time to realize when your adrenaline is up."

Everyone looked at each other and then back at him. "Nope, we are all fine!" John said.

Hernandez nodded, then turned to the remaining police officer. "Let's get back to the station. I'm looking forward to hearing this guy's story, and I don't take kindly to people bringing deadly weapons into my town. Good night, all."

The officers drove away, and John, Lizzie, Jane, and Eliza stared at each other, while Little Mouse purred securely in Lizzie's arms.

"Well, I did not see that coming," Eliza finally said. The dam burst on all their pent-up tension, and they started laughing, and maybe crying a little bit too, and couldn't stop for several minutes. Finally they wiped the tears of mirth and relief from their eyes.

"Come on, let's go inside," Jane said. "I'll make tea."

They all agreed that was a fine idea and headed inside to calm down and rehash the events of the evening.

As they climbed the stairs to Eliza's apartment, Lizzie glanced back at John, who was following behind her. "Well, at least now we know it really is over, and we are completely safe, ja?"

He reached out and caught her hand. "Ja, thank Gott! But Lizzie, you and I have unfinished business to discuss tomorrow, ja?"

She smiled back at him. "Oh ja, John. You can count on it, right after you talk to my dat."

He grinned at her and nodded, then followed her the rest of the way up the stairs where he could keep an eye on her. He didn't plan to take his eyes off her now, or for the rest of their lives.

EPILOGUE

Several weeks later Lizzie and John walked into the lobby of the Willow Creek Historical Museum to talk to Mr. Rumpkin about what was going on with the manuscript.

"Ah! Two of my favorite amateur sleuths! Come back to the kitchen. I have tea and shortbread." He bustled off, and Lizzie and John grinned and followed. They took seats at the kitchen table while Mr. Rumpkin readied the tea.

He poured them each tea in delicate china cups and saucers, and put out matching creamer and sugar bowl. The shortbread biscuits were displayed on a lovely hand-painted plate.

"Ach, this is very nice, Mr. Rumpkin!" Lizzie gushed. "You didn't need to go to such trouble for John and me, though."

He shrugged and smiled sheepishly. "I love this tea service and don't get near enough excuses to get it out and use it. So humor me if you don't mind."

They doctored their tea and took their first sips, John's cup looking rather dainty in his large hands.

"So, is there any news about the manuscript?" John asked after a few minutes of polite conversation.

Mr. Rumpkin nodded vigorously. "Oh my, yes! It seems that, as ill-advised as both parties were in their attempts to obtain it, they both actually do have a legitimate claim! Mrs. Stutzman's may be the stronger, as she is the proven, direct descendant of the author. But if one believes

Mr. Valentine's claims, it's arguable that perhaps he is due some compensation. Normally that wouldn't be the Stutzmans' problem, but with the appearance of a valuable lost manuscript, which is already drawing a lot of attention, let me tell you, Valentine may have an argument. But since you can't profit from a felony, he may be out of luck, unless he can turn up an heir. All this will take years to sort out. Meanwhile, it's safely locked away."

John and Lizzie exchanged relieved glances. "That's gut news," John said, returning his attention to their host. "Now, let me tell you about that chest I'm working on for you."

A short while later, John and Lizzie were walking side by side back to the bakery. Although they didn't touch, they glanced at one another often, smiling into each other's eyes.

"So, I've enjoyed these last few weeks, officially dating you," John said, glancing at Lizzie, who smiled back at him and nodded.

"Oh ja, me too. I'm froh to be your girlfriend, John. And the best part—well, maybe the second-best part—is that Jane is happy about it too! She told me."

He gave her a curious look. "Were you worried that she wouldn't be?"

She shrugged. "Maybe. A little. But now I can relax on that point. And it's so gut that Jane and I are living above the bakery again, with our little cats!"

"And our sister, Susan, moved in with Eliza. How are they getting along, do you know?"

"Eliza says it's an excellent arrangement. And guess what?"

He looked at her and smiled. "What?"

"They're thinking about getting a cat! Or maybe two!"

He laughed. "Of course they are! Eliza probably misses your two!"

"Ja, I think so. Ach, we're here already."

He grabbed her hand and pulled her a little ways down the street to a bench situated beneath a large old maple tree. He sat and tugged her down beside him.

"John! I need to get back to work! It's not fair to the others."

"I know, but I need to talk to you about something important first."

Lizzie held her breath, wondering what it could be. John didn't keep her waiting.

"When I first noticed you in a new way a few months ago, I resisted my attraction to you," he said.

She nodded. "I know what you mean about noticing me in a new way. That happened to me too. Suddenly the John Bontrager I'd known all my life as my best friend's bruder became someone new. Someone almost. . .strange to me." She gave him a beseeching look. "Do you understand what I mean?"

He nodded. "Ja! Exactly, because it was the same for me. I almost felt guilty, as if I were attracted to someone inappropriate—as if you were my sister!"

She nodded vigorously. "Me too! It was really weird at first."

"But then I knocked myself in the head and said, 'John, this woman is not your sister! Stop being narrish!'"

"Aw, you're not foolish, John. It was a big change for us both. But I'll tell you something. I sure don't think of you as my bruder now. Not. At. All."

He smiled down at her and reached out a gentle finger to tuck a stray strand of hair back under her kapp. "Nor do I see you in a sisterly light, my lieb."

She gasped. "You. . .you love me?"

His face grew serious, and his eyes tender. "Oh yes, totally." He searched her eyes. "Do you. . .could you. . .feel the same for me?"

She looked into his eyes and saw the truth. Her own filled with tears. "I love you too! I don't know when my feelings for you changed, but I know they'll never go back to the way they used to be."

He leaned in and brushed a soft kiss over her lips, and her eyes fluttered closed. It was heavenly!

"Would you marry me, Lizzie? I spoke to your folks, and they gave their blessing."

She caught her breath as joy filled her heart. It was what she wanted more than anything!

Well, more than almost anything, and even that was pretty much a tie. Could she have both? "John, I really, really want to say yes. But I need to know: Would you expect me to give up my business? Because I just don't think I could stand that. I want you, but I want my dream too. Can you understand?"

"Of course! I admit, back in the beginning, when I first realized I was developing feelings for you, I wasn't sure I wanted to make my home above a bakery instead of on a farm. But now I know that my home is where you are. And since I'd much rather you didn't have to walk to work at four in the morning, I think it makes the most sense that we live above your bakery."

Lizzie's heart leaped for joy! "Oh, John, you've made me so happy! I talked to Mrs. Petersheim while she and her mann were visiting. I asked her how she had managed to have a business and raise a family here, quite happily, for so many years. And do you know what she said?"

He shook his head, and she smiled into his eyes. "She said all it took was love. So my answer is yes. Yes! Yes, I'd love to marry you, and I'd love for you to move into the bakery with me!" Then a thought struck her.

"Oh! Is it okay if Jane still lives there? There's plenty of room. She could even have a whole floor to herself. That way we could have some privacy." She blushed.

"Ja, that sounds just right, Lizzie. So, do you want a long engagement, or a short one?"

She thought a moment. "Well, if we get married this fall, we only have a few months to prepare."

He nodded. "True. But if we wait until next fall, we have to wait for over a year."

They looked at each other, eyes wide, and at the same time they both blurted out, "A short one!"

They laughed and hugged and shared another brief kiss—after all, they were engaged!

Then John stood and held out a hand for Lizzie, who took it and stood, then smoothed out her skirts. She smiled up at him and said, "I know traditionally this is supposed to be a secret."

He raised an eyebrow and waited for her to continue. "But?"

She heaved a sigh. "But Jane and Eliza are like family!"

"Jane *is* family to me. She's my little sister!"

"Right!" She pointed at him. "So we have to tell her! And then we really should tell Eliza too, because she'll guess anyway, don't you agree?"

He nodded. "Ja, so Jane and Eliza. And, of course, my parents and yours. And our other siblings."

She nodded. "Ja, and really, we need to tell Lydia and Bishop Troyer—of course the bishop, as he's going to instruct us to prepare us for marriage!"

"Of course," he murmured, a gleam of amusement lighting his eyes.

She didn't notice, as she was deep in thought. "And John, if we tell Lydia, we need to tell Ruth and Jonah. They live together, and they're practically family. Oh! And Mary and Reuben too, of course."

John began laughing, and Lizzie glared up at him. "What's so funny?"

"Well, is there anyone left in the district we aren't going to tell ahead of time?"

Lizzie gave him a sheepish grin. "Oh, sure, lots of people. But if we're getting married in just a few months, I guess it doesn't make that much difference, does it?"

He laughed again and kissed the tip of her nose. "Nope, I guess it doesn't. Come on, Lizzie mine. We both need to get back to work. And you can tell the girls without me, I don't mind."

"You're sure? Because I can wait if you'd rather." Lizzie stood with her hands clasped, dying to run inside and tell her friends, but she waited for John's decision.

"I'm sure. Go. It's killing you that you aren't already in there telling them everything. I'll see you tonight."

He turned and walked to his buggy, untied Mike, and was soon headed down the road. She watched him go until he turned the corner.

"You too, John." She blew a kiss after him, then turned and hurried inside the bakery to tell her friends the wonderful news.

Lizzie's New Orleans–Style Beignets

Beignets are simply luscious squares of fried dough coated in powdered sugar. They are similar to powdered donuts, but when eaten fresh and hot, they're an experience not to miss! Lizzie perfected her recipe in New Orleans. Here's her recipe for you to try out. I've included a couple of tips Lizzie passed along from her mentors in the Big Easy.

INGREDIENTS TO MAKE HALF A DOZEN MEDIUM-LARGE BEIGNETS:

½ teaspoon active dry yeast
1 pinch sugar
2 teaspoons butter or vegetable shortening
1 tablespoon sugar
3 tablespoons whole milk
1 egg white
1¼ cups flour
1 pinch salt
Powdered sugar

You'll need a deep fryer with a thermometer. This is not for the faint of heart!

Stir 2 tablespoons warm water, ½ teaspoon active dry yeast, and a pinch of sugar together in bowl. Allow to sit for 5 minutes until it begins to foam.

In different bowl, combine 2 teaspoons butter or shortening, 1 tablespoon sugar, 3 tablespoons whole milk, and 1 egg white. Whisk it all together until well mixed.

Be careful with this next part! Slowly add 3 tablespoons boiling water to second bowl containing butter or shortening mixture. When temperature of this is between 110 and 115 degrees, carefully stir into first bowl containing yeast mixture.

Now that the contents of the two bowls are combined, add 1¼ cups flour and a pinch of salt. Mix the dough (but not too long) and then cover it with plastic wrap and place it in the fridge overnight. Why?

Lizzie says the secret to the best beignets is to allow the dough to rest overnight in the fridge, to allow for a slow development of the yeast, making a very fluffy beignet.

The next day, heat your deep fryer oil to 360 degrees.

Place your risen dough on a well-floured surface and roll it out into an 8x4-inch rectangle. Here's a trick: Instead of using a knife, use a pizza cutter to cut the rolled dough into squares!

When the oil is ready, drop in a couple pieces of dough and fry for a minute or two; flip them carefully with a slotted deep-fry spatula, and fry for another minute.

Scoop them out with the spatula and put them on a wire rack to allow oil to drip off. Then toss them with powdered sugar. You can sprinkle it on or just toss them into a bowl of powdered sugar to really coat them. Do it while they're still piping hot!

Repeat with the rest of the dough squares, making sure the oil temp stays around 360 degrees.

And voilà! You've made beignets!

Tips:

Don't overmix the dough, or you could end up with tough beignets.

Make sure everything is well floured to keep dough from sticking to table, rolling pin, etc. You might even butter your hands to keep it from sticking.

To look like a pro when eating your treat, remember not to inhale when taking a bite, or you'll end up with a nose full of powdered sugar. All that coughing will ruin the experience.

Some people recommend using shortening rather than butter, saying it yields a fluffier beignet. Try both and see for yourself.

Linda's Peach Strudel:
It's Doggone Good!

INGREDIENTS:

6 to 8 fresh peaches, peeled and sliced (You can use canned in a pinch,
    or even peach pie filling!)
1 teaspoon cinnamon
1½ cups sugar
1 cup flour, sifted
1 teaspoon baking powder
1 pinch salt
1 large egg
Optional: 1 can cake frosting

Grease medium baking dish and layer in fruit.

    Sprinkle cinnamon and ½ cup of sugar over peaches. (Note, if using cherries or berries, substitute a bit of sugar for the cinnamon. But if using apples, use the cinnamon!)

    In bowl, mix sifted flour, remaining sugar, baking powder, and salt. Add egg and mix it together with fork until it is crumbly, like streusel or crumble topping.

    Scoop this mixture over fruit and pat it down gently, covering all fruit mixture. Bake at 350 degrees for about an hour, or until top is golden brown. It will smell amazing! (Lizzie jokes that this is the universal temperature and time for so many things!)

TIPS:

Linda says you can swap in different fruits depending on what is available. And again, if no fresh fruit is close at hand, go ahead and use canned fruit, or even pie filling!

Do you fancy a sweet, sugary topping? After your strudels come out of the oven, spread a little vanilla cake frosting on them, right out of a can from the store. You can go to the trouble of making a glaze, but Linda is a busy dog groomer and doesn't have time for that! Feeling adventurous? Try different icing flavors for toppings! Or try putting the icing on before you bake the strudels! Mix and match your fruit and icing flavors. Have fun!

Anne Blackburne lives and works in Southeast Ohio as a newspaper editor and writer. She is the mother of five grown children, has one wonderful grandchild, and has a spoiled poodle named Millie. For fun, when she isn't working on Amish romance or sweet mysteries, Anne directs and acts in community theater productions and writes and directs original plays. She also enjoys reading, kayaking, swimming, searching for beach glass, and just sitting with a cup of coffee looking at large bodies of water. Her idea of the perfect vacation is cruising and seeing amazing new places with people she loves.